PRAISE FOR NICOLE MARY KELBY'S

The Pink Suit

"*The Pink Suit* is tailor[...]by's narrative rises to stylish heights when s[...] fashion and, of course, that eponymous outfit." [...]rol Memmott, *Washington Post*

"Beautifully written and engrossing, *The Pink Suit* gives us an extraordinary alternative reality, transforming JFK and Jackie's romance into the unforgettable love story of a seamstress and a butcher. Kate and Patrick are wonderful creations, and the evocation of the early 1960s is moving and convincing. Kelby spins a compelling tale of one of the most iconic garments ever sewn, and makes it entirely her own." —Claire Kendal, author of *The Book of You*

"Inspired by the true story behind Jackie Kennedy's iconic outfit, Kelby has stitched a compelling tale of politics, fashion, and history." —*People*

"A subtly heartbreaking, completely believable tale inspired by the Irish immigrant dressmaker who made Jacqueline Kennedy's Chanel knockoff." —Joyce Sáenz Harris, *Dallas Morning News*

"*The Pink Suit* is a rare work, fascinating and beautifully crafted. Nicole Mary Kelby's sensuous prose is as opulent as the couture she describes." —Jennifer Chiaverini, author of the *New York Times* bestseller *Mrs. Lincoln's Dressmaker*

"Luxuriate in shades of pink, in descriptions of haute couture so exquisite and precise that you can feel elegant just by reading the words. Nicole Mary Kelby has stitched together from scraps of facts a compelling novel, a lovable heroine, and a living neighborhood in its last few moments of innocence. From its startling opening to its poignant ending, *The Pink Suit* shows us that behind events of global significance, there are unknown individuals worthy of our interest." —Susan Vreeland, author of *Clara and Mr. Tiffany* and *Luncheon of the Boating Party*

"A remarkable novel.... Nicole Mary Kelby has a talent for blending history and fiction—seamlessly."
—Christina Appleyard, *Daily Mail* (UK)

"While the novel is filled with politics, history, and lots of insider views of designer fashion, Kate remains grounded.... It's a look at an ordinary woman and how she played a small role in an extraordinary time." —Celeste Williams, *Fort Worth Star-Telegram*

"A novel that's just about the pink suit worn by Jackie Kennedy that day in Dallas? Yes—and it's terrific."—Tina Jordan, *Entertainment Weekly*

"*The Pink Suit* is a wonderfully absorbing and richly textured novel, strikingly rendered with a keen eye for the details of art and fashion and an equally acute ear for the workings of the human heart. Kelby captures perfectly the yearnings, disappointments, and aspirations of an unforgettable heroine against the backdrop of a national tragedy."
—Anne D. LeClaire, author of *Entering Normal* and *The Lavender Hour*

"The suit of the title is the iconic rose-hued, Chanel-style ensemble that Jacqueline Kennedy wore on the day in 1963 that her husband died in Dallas, but this is not yet another fictional version of that assassination. Instead it focuses on Kate, a young Irish immigrant working as a seamstress at a chic New York boutique, where she helps to craft the suit. She never meets its owner, but their lives intertwine. Kelby's sharp eye for the details and implications of fashion and her sensuous prose complement the story."

— Colette Bancroft, *Tampa Bay Times*

"One of history's most tragic and iconic outfits has long had its own strange and compelling story. Now, at last, that story has been told—and beautifully."   —Jeffrey Kluger, author of *Lost Moon: The Perilous Journey of Apollo 13*

"A delectable romantic novel with brains and a heart."

— Maggie Gee, author of *The White Family*

"*The Pink Suit,* built around the Garment District backstory of that now-famous outfit, is sure to catapult the writer's career straight from prêt-à-porter to haute couture....Kate gets an insider's glimpse into the rarefied world of high-society matrons and wealthy socialites so often cloaked in mystery to outsiders. So do we....The Minnesota author herself seems poised to reach rosy new career heights with the publication of this carefully tailored novel."

— Andrea Hoag, *Minneapolis Star Tribune*

"A luxurious narrative....This is a novel that book clubs will relish."

— Elisabeth Atwood, *BookPage*

"Getting a behind-the-scenes glimpse inside the fashion industry of the 1960s was a treat. But the real charm of the book is the protagonist herself, portrayed as a strong, independent, and courageous woman who defies conventional expectations."

—Historical Novel Society

"If you like a fully engrossing read this is a must-have novel. It is beautifully written and utterly fascinating. Ostensibly this is the story behind the famous pink suit worn by Jackie Kennedy on the day President Kennedy was assassinated in Dallas in 1963 and the Irish seamstress Kate who played a pivotal role in its creation. In fact it is so much more; it's a story about passion, fashion, Irish immigration to the States, the American Dream, and like the suit itself, it is full of subtle nuances. I was so engrossed by the story that I completely forgot about the ultimate fate of the pink suit. This is an utterly fabulous book and one that I cannot recommend highly enough."   —Anne Marie Scanlon, *Sunday Independent* (Ireland)

"This is a fascinating novel about politics, fashion, and history."

—*Irish Country Magazine*

"Here reality and fiction intertwine, held together by the power of a single, fascinating narrative thread."   —*Harper's Bazaar* (UK)

THE PINK SUIT

THE

Pink Suit

A NOVEL

NICOLE MARY KELBY

BACK BAY BOOKS
LITTLE, BROWN AND COMPANY
NEW YORK BOSTON LONDON

Copyright © 2014 by Nicole Mary Kelby
Reading group guide copyright © 2015 by Nicole Mary Kelby and Little, Brown and Company

Back Bay Books / Little, Brown and Company
Hachette Book Group
1290 Avenue of the Americas, New York, NY 10104
littlebrown.com

Originally published in hardcover by Little, Brown and Company, April 2014
First Back Bay paperback edition, April 2015

Back Bay Books is an imprint of Little, Brown and Company. The Back Bay Books name and logo are trademarks of Hachette Book Group, Inc.

The publisher is not responsible for websites (or their content) that are not owned by the publisher.

The Hachette Speakers Bureau provides a wide range of authors for speaking events. To find out more, go to hachettespeakersbureau.com or call (866) 376-6591.

Portions of this book appeared in the *Virginia Quarterly Review.*

ISBN 978-0-316-23565-5 (hc) / 978-0-316-23567-9 (pb)
Library of Congress Control Number: 2014931142

10 9 8 7 6 5 4 3 2 1

RRD-C

Printed in the United States of America

For those of us who fell under her spell

THE PINK SUIT

"What a strange power there is in clothing."
—Isaac Bashevis Singer

November 1963

*T*here was that odd thing where he seemed to tilt to one side as if to whisper something to her, as lovers often do. Her head turned, the perfect hat still in place, and she, out of instinct, leaned in as if for a kiss.

His face softened.

It took a moment for her to understand.

It was then that something—gray, dark—tumbled down the back of the limo. She pushed him away and followed after it. Held it in her hands as if it were a broken wing.

The film shows this: the agent jumped onto the 1961 Lincoln and pulled her back into the seat. Unseen are the thirty-six long-stem red roses tumbling to the floor and the agent pushing her on top of her husband and then covering them both with his own body.

Heartbeat upon heartbeat. Then silence.

"Oh, no," she whispered.

It was not a wing at all.

In the chaos of the moment, the agent focused on the suit. He knew she was crushed beneath his weight. He couldn't help that. He knew her face was pressed into her husband's. He couldn't think about that. But he could focus on the pink beneath his body.

She was so quiet. He expected her to scream, but she didn't.

Beautiful suit, he would later write in his memoirs.

Most who can recall that day in Dallas think of the film's grainy black-and-white footage. Those who were there remember the suit.

That morning, an entire ballroom awaited her arrival. The President joked about her being late, but she wasn't late at all. The advance man knew that the Wife was to make an entrance that would not be easily forgotten. The band played "The Eyes of Texas Are Upon You."

When she finally walked into the ballroom, every head turned to watch her take the stage. The applause was thunderous. Even her husband took to his feet, laughing. "Nobody wonders what Lyndon and I wear."

The suit was his favorite. She wore it often. "You look ravishing in it," he told her. Asked her to wear it that day.

She was "lovely in a pink suit," an advance man would later tell the reporters. Even Lyndon smiled at the sight of her.

When it was all over, in the underground parking garage of the hospital, Lady Bird would glance over her shoulder for one last look at the President. His limo was sideways, as if abandoned. The doors were flung open. The agents were desperate to get him inside: some hovered over the dark-blue Lincoln, pleading with the Wife, who lay across her husband's body, refusing to move. Some stood with their backs to it all, their guns drawn.

There were no doctors or nurses; there was really no need.

In the midst of it all, Lady Bird remembered seeing "a bundle of pink, just like a drift of blossoms, lying across the backseat." It was that immaculate woman, in that beautiful suit, covering her husband's body.

Aboard Air Force One, ninety-nine minutes after it all began, LBJ stood with his hand on the Bible. The widow stood next to him, still in the pink suit. The photographer posed her so that only a small stain on her sleeve could be clearly seen. Lady Bird tried to persuade her to change; the maid laid out a white dress.

"Very kind of you," the Wife said, but would only wash her face, which she later regretted. "Let them see what they have done."

The photos ran in black and white; nothing could be seen.

At five a.m. on November 23, twenty hours after the Wife met her husband in the ballroom—and after his body had been delivered to the Bethesda Naval Hospital for the autopsy—she returned to their private quarters for the last time. Twenty hours. One thousand, one hundred and eighteen miles. Wife to widow.

Finally, she removed the suit.

While she was in her bath, it was taken away. Some say that the maid put it in a brown paper bag, which may have been hidden in the Map Room. Some say it was given to the Secret Service. At that moment, the suit was unimportant.

Random bits of detritus made it through the chaos of that day—a typed copy of the itinerary, a stained breakfast program, partial lists of who had tickets to the event, and photographs of the motorcade in front of the Hotel Texas. But the pink suit went missing.

The National Archives in Washington, D.C., houses the Constitution, the Bill of Rights, and also what's left of that day in Dallas. There's the white lace-up back brace—the President's back had become so painful that he couldn't have sat in the car without it. There's also his tie, nicked by the bullet, and the shirt that was cut off by the medical team. In a cave somewhere, in an undisclosed location in Kansas, the Archives have also stored the entire contents of Parkland Hospital's trauma room 1, where he was pronounced dead at one p.m., Central Standard Time.

They also have the pink suit.

It's never been cleaned.

No one at the Archives seems to know exactly how it got there. It's currently stored in a climate-controlled vault in area 6W3, although no one can recall it arriving. It may have been mailed, although the package had no postmark. It had been wrapped in plain brown paper. There was no return address. A single-digit postal code was written on the address label, and yet the United States had adopted five-digit zip codes on July 1, 1963. Inside, the suit, the blouse, the handbag, the shoes, and even the stockings were bundled together, along with an unsigned note on the letter-head stationery of her mother. *Worn Nov. 22, 1963.* That was all it said.

How the mother came to have the suit is still a matter of specu-lation, but in an audio recording stored in the presidential library, she reveals that she'd kept it in the attic of her Georgetown home. She had Alzheimer's when she gave the interview. She doesn't say how she got it, or why it was kept there, or for how long. But she did say that she'd given strict instructions to the maid not to have it cleaned. It was the "last link." And so she put it in her attic, next to her daughter's famous wedding dress.

Who sent it to the National Archives instead of the presidential library, and why, is still unknown. When it was finally discovered, the suit was not in a brown bag but in the original box from the dressmaker Chez Ninon.

CHAPTER ONE

"[The presidency] was like a film and I had the opportunity to dress the female star."

—Oleg Cassini

September 1961

In the newspaper, next to the photo of the First Lady in Palm Beach, there was a story about the Greyhound bus that had been firebombed on Mother's Day. The Attorney General, whom everyone in Inwood just called Bobby, had finished his investigation and now blamed "extremists on both sides." It was such a shame that the story was next to the photo of the Wife, who was looking so very happy after spending the weekend poolside with her in-laws and children and an assorted tangle of dogs. It just made it all seem sadder. Kate hated to read that this sort of thing was still going on, especially on Mother's Day. If Patrick Harris's mother, *God rest her soul,* hadn't sponsored her at Chez Ninon, Kate had no idea what she would have done. A magnificent seamstress Peg Harris was. Her son, the butcher, could truss a lovely roast, too.

Kate gave the man at the newsstand a dime for two newspapers because she liked the photo of the First Lady so very much, and then put her subway token into the turnstile. While she waited for the A train, she said a prayer for all those people who had been on the Greyhound bus, and their mothers, and her own mother, who had died young, and Patrick Harris's mother, Peg, who had recently passed, and Mother Church, just to put a good word in. All the way downtown, from Inwood to Columbus Circle, Kate could not stop staring at the photo of that dress. It was quite flattering. The Wife was leaving Florida on Air Force One—smiling, fit, and tan. She was wearing a white scarf and gloves. The neckline of her dress ran right below her collarbone, right where it should be.

Kate had lost track of how many times that neckline had needed adjusting so that it would hit just so. It had been worth it, though. The cut of the dress was remarkable. It hid every flaw—and there were many. Kate thought of the First Lady as "Slight Spinal Sway." Patrick Harris, the butcher, told her that kind of thinking was an occupational hazard. "I always think of people by what they buy. Mrs. Leary is 'Pork Loin Joint with Rind.' "

Kate, fine boned and pink skinned, always wondered what part of the pig Patrick thought of her as but certainly understood the sentiment—entire families were known to her only by what they wore: fathers and sons in matching suits with the cut of Savile Row, or mothers and daughters with their identical rabbit-trimmed bathrobes. Unless they were extremely famous, appearing in newspapers or magazines, Kate had no idea what they looked like. Chez Ninon had strict rules about mixing. Kate never left the back room. Maeve did the fitting. Kate just followed the marks. She knew everyone's tucks and pleats but not their faces.

Still. She knew them. More important, she knew who they thought themselves to be. It was Kate's job to know. As soon as those people were out of diapers, there was a constant need for various wardrobes for skiing, horseback riding, private school, and spring holiday in Paris—along with Having Lunch with Mummy at the Four Seasons dresses and Meeting Other Children in Central Park Harris tweeds.

Stitch by stitch, hour by hour, Kate imagined every formal dinner, every exotic holiday, and every debutante ball as if she lived them herself. It was the only way to get the clothes right. She needed to understand how long a cape could be without being too long and thereby unfashionable, or what type of lining a Belgian-lace suit needed so it would stay cool and yet not wrinkle in the Caribbean sun. Kate was just thirty-two, and yet so many years of her life had already been spent hunched over one fabric or another, her focus unwavering. A simple dress could take a hundred hours to make. A beaded gown could run over a thousand, sometimes two. But she never met the clients.

Outside the Columbus Circle station, the morning seemed vain and preening. The endless green of Central Park was edged with the gilt of fall. Swarms of fat yellow cabs circled. As Kate passed the long row of livery carriages getting ready for the day, the drivers placed garlands of plastic flowers over the horse's heads. The beasts were stoic, as if resigned to their lot in life. Every now and then, there'd be a shake of the head or a snort. But they never bayed or bucked. The blinders they wore narrowed their world.

Kate loved horses ever since she was a child. On the Great Island, in Cobh, on the coastline of County Cork, wild horses lived along

the beach. If you were gentle, and had an apple in your hand, sometimes they'd let you get close enough to lasso them. If you were
careful, you could slip onto their backs and they would gallop full
bore along the brilliant sapphire sea and you could lean into them,
listening to the beat of their untamed hearts. But you had to be
gentle and very careful. And Kate was both.

City horses were very different. They wore hats and walked
round and round all day. Of course, so did Kate.

Clip, clop, she thought.

From the street, Chez Ninon was nondescript at best. The dress
shop was a series of second-floor windows in a Park Avenue office
building that could be easily overlooked—and that was the point.
Discretion was essential to their business. Most of Chez Ninon's
clients were part of the Blue Book society, the old-money crowd.
The owners, Sophie Shonnard and Nona Park, were Blue Book, too.
They were also glorious crooks.

Kate had been told that Miss Sophie and Miss Nona's evolution
into the life of artistic larceny was a gradual process, a matter of supply and demand. For nearly forty years, "the Ladies," as they called
themselves, had run a custom shop in Bonwit Teller that produced
only original designs. But as time went on, more of their fellow
Blue Book friends wanted French fashions without the French price
tag. And so, in the spirit of friendship and a healthy bottom line,
every season Miss Sophie and Miss Nona flew to Paris to pilfer the
very best designs from the finest runway shows.

Chanel, Lanvin, Nina Ricci, Cardin, Givenchy, and Balenciaga—the Ladies would carefully watch each collection and then run to the nearest sidewalk café to sketch the garments from memory. Once back in New York, they would create fifty designs or more but make only four copies of each. For special clients, like the First Lady, they would offer exclusive copies of the pieces they knew would be of interest, with exclusive price tags to match. No matter what couture house the Ladies had stolen their designs from, they would put their own label on the finished clothes. *Chez Ninon. New York, Paris.* When a collection was ready, the Ladies would pop champagne and open their doors at precisely three p.m., from Tuesday to Thursday. Everything was sold on a first-come, first-served basis. By invitation only.

Every season, the Chambre Syndicale de la Haute Couture et du Prêt-à-Porter forced Chez Ninon to pay a "caution fee" to the French designers. The Ladies always pronounced it *cow-see-on*—the fee was so exorbitant, they could pronounce it any way they pleased. If they didn't pay, they couldn't attend the runway shows. But they always paid. There was no way to ban them.

Miss Nona was more than seventy years old, but how much more was difficult to determine. She was always red-carpet ready, dressed in the originals that she so shamelessly copied, and demanding front row seats at all the best runway shows. Macy's, Marshall Field's, Ohrbach's, even Bonwit Teller—if Nona wanted a buyer's seat she'd take it. She had sharp elbows and the air of a deposed duchess; no one dared refuse her. Her partner, Sophie, only slightly younger, tagged along behind her, apologizing and wielding her Southern charm with the precision of a surgeon. The Ladies would not tolerate being ignored or silenced. They were always exacting and always in the way.

"Wonderful and pixilated," an editor at *Vogue* once called them. Carmel Snow, the editor in chief of *Harper's Bazaar,* considered them the most "discerning American buyers of Parisian fashion." Miss Nona was even featured in a nail polish ad. They were charming pirates, but they were pirates nonetheless.

Luckily for Kate, they never came in until after ten.

Morning light streamed in through the large windows. It was early. The sewing machines in the Ready-to-Wear Department were, thankfully, quiet. Black-and-gold enameled beasts—they still had treadles. The machines were noisy and burned the girls' arms and hands if they overheated—and they always overheated. The Ready-to-Wear girls were the mice of the back room, pumping the treadles of their machines like the pedals on a pipe organ. Laughing and gossiping, they hummed with life. Most wore their hair in curlers or shaped into spit curls that were taped into place. They were young and always ready for a night out. Their quick eyes and even quicker hands stitched without care. Kate never understood why a seamstress with as much talent as Peg Harris had spent her days running off dozens of dresses on a machine, but Peg clearly had loved doing it. "Clothing the masses is noble work," she'd tell anyone who asked. Kate agreed, but she would certainly rather dress the First Lady.

She tossed the newspapers on her desk and put the kettle on for tea. She could hear Mr. Charles on the telephone behind the closed door of his office. Noel Charles was the in-house designer at Chez Ninon and Kate's direct supervisor. Silver haired and impeccable, he was manicured down to his buffed fingernails. He had an accent that was somewhat European. He always spoke of Belgian roots, but to Kate he sounded neither French nor Dutch. He had a vague Continental air; his accent was chameleon-like and shifted depending on whom he was speaking to.

He hoped to open his own shop soon and talked of taking Kate with him, as a partner. It was such a grand scheme—it didn't matter if it was truly possible or not. Kate just liked sitting in the quiet workroom with Mr. Charles early in the morning. They would have tea and talk about important things, like current events. It was civilized.

The kettle whistle blew. There was some Barry's Gold Blend in the cupboard, which Kate had found in a specialty shop downtown. She'd paid a dear price for it, and it was stale, but stale Barry's was better than A&P tea anytime.

She carefully trimmed the photos of the First Lady from the newspapers that she'd bought at the subway station. One copy was for her scrapbook and the other she tucked into her weekly letter to her father, along with half of her salary, twenty-six dollars. The Old Man never mentioned the clippings at all, and so she never did, but it was interesting to Kate to see if the gossip columnists recognized that the Dior gown was not really a Dior at all. And there was something so wonderful about seeing the way a gown was worn—the way the shoulders turned, the head tilted, or the iridescent beads caught the light. Even after all this time, seeing her own work worn still thrilled her.

Fashion is the art of the possible—Kate was quite fond of saying that, but it was true. With a needle and thread in her hand, anything was possible, especially when it came to the First Lady, because Kate's sister, Maggie Quinn, and the Wife were exactly the same size. Kate couldn't help herself. On a rather regular basis, she turned her own sister into a "Little J," as everybody in the neighborhood called her. There was no harm done. The muslin patterns were often tossed away, so Kate just plucked them out of the trash. Her sister was a little younger than the Wife, but their coloring was very similar. And they were both Sunday-china beautiful. Kate always tried to be respectful about it. She never made the exact same outfit if she could help it. She'd usually try a different fabric entirely, although sometimes it would be a similar color. And she never had the hats made up—even though Schwinn, one of the boys at the shop, who always rode a bike to work, was a very fine milliner.

"It's like waving a flag," Kate told Maggie. "Without the flag. It's patriotic."

It was Kate's way to honor Inwood, tucked away in the northern part of Manhattan and her adopted home. Irish, mostly. In Inwood, the President was a local boy made good. He took his first Holy Communion at St. Margaret of Cortona in Riverdale, right next door, and that made him one of their own.

And even though Kate thought of the Wife as having a bit of a swayback from all that horseback riding—and she had that French last name—the First Lady was still a Lee from County Cork. Her mother was the granddaughter of Irish immigrants who came across during the potato famine in the 1840s. And Kate was from County Cork too—Cobh, specifically. "Cove," in English. The village was the last place the *Titanic* laid anchor before beginning its voyage across the Atlantic, the last place the Lees saw before they left Ireland forever. And, although the Lees were actually from the country, according to her father, their people knew each other—although the Old Man was always a bit sketchy about the details. So Kate liked the Wife, no matter what anyone said. And Kate had to believe that, even with all those French mannerisms, she must long for the Island. Kate did.

The day she left, her father was in the garden, going at the red roses with the kitchen knife and then his teeth. He was like a mad dog. The thorns left a thin trail of blood. Kate knew the boat would not wait. He knew that, too. Rose after rose—so much went unsaid. Finally, she picked up her suitcase and walked to the gate. "You can press them into a book for luck," he shouted after her.

Kate stopped and turned.

That helpless grin. The fistful of ragged red roses. The Old Man had refused to take her to the docks. It wasn't that far, just around the hill and then along the unfurling edge of the deep-water port—just a couple of miles or so. But he wouldn't do it. *Or couldn't,* Kate thought.

He'd already lost Maggie and her husband to the promise of America—and now Kate. He had no more children to lose.

The Old Man pressed the battered roses into her hands. Behind him, a thick fog hid the lush green all around them. There was some mercy in that.

"Keep one," Kate said. "We'll match the dozen when I get back."

"When you get back," he said, "we'll plant a few more. Your mam would have liked that. You and me, digging around." Then he turned and went inside. He had never left the Island in his life; he had no words for such a thing.

Kate picked up her suitcase again. A rose petal fell at the gate. Then another. And another. She was late. She didn't stop to pick them up.

Petal by petal, Kate ran down the long, winding road, dragging her suitcase behind her. She ran along the water's edge where lovers often lingered and then down the high street, past the pubs with their doors thrown open wide and the rusting cars careening this way and that, then onto the tangle of docks filled with suitcases and the sorrow of leaving, and, finally, onto the boat waiting in the harbor, a harbor whose motto was *Statio bene fide carinis,* "A safe place for ships," and, aboard that boat, into the vast sea itself. Petal by petal, Kate left a trail, just like a young girl with bread who does not think of rabbits and foxes, but only of home.

It was just six years ago when she left, but it felt like a lifetime.

Kate was nearly finished with her tea when Mr. Charles finally emerged from his office. She'd rearranged her desk at least twice, moving the series of framed pictures of her nephew, Little Mike, from the left to the right and then back again, waiting for him to finish his call.

"I thought I would grow old on that telephone," Mr. Charles said. "Miss Sophie can certainly talk a blue streak." He was wearing his best suit: dove-gray waistcoat, black pinstriped jacket, and the gray trousers with knife pleats. He was also holding a large envelope with a presidential seal. "And what do you think this is?"

"I can't imagine."

But she could. Kate could imagine all manner of wonderful things in that envelope—from an emerald full-length ball gown completely covered with Austrian crystals to a pure-white silk cocktail dress with a black satin bow. When it came to the Wife and Maison Blanche (as everyone called the White House), the possibilities, and budget, were limitless.

"It's a love letter," Mr. Charles said, and opened the envelope. Inside, there was a watercolor sketch, a clipping from *Life* magazine with four women modeling the same Chanel suit in different colors and variations, and a letter from a secretary on the embossed stationery of Maison Blanche. The entire room was suddenly filled with the scent of Chanel No. 5. The clipping from *Life* was about Chanel's comeback. The French designer, who was now about Miss Nona's age, had come out of retirement to create the "must have" suit for every proper country-club lady. And the Wife wanted one.

As with nearly all of the First Lady's custom orders, she'd sketched out her version of how the suit should look. She was quite a talented designer and painter, too. The watercolor was exceedingly cheerful. The Wife was holding one hand out as if a tray balanced on it had just been whisked away. The other hand was firmly on her waist. Maison Blanche was set in the background, but it loomed over everything. The Wife looked like a society girl soon to be trapped in a tornado of history. Her smile was mischievous; her eyes were wickedly playful. She was wearing a pink pillbox hat that sat back on her head—it didn't hide her beautiful face, as hats sometimes can. A note on the drawing read, *If it is another godforsaken pillbox, please make sure that it does not appear to have been stolen from an organ grinder's monkey. It should be a non-hat hat.*

Kate knew that there was a new man at Bergdorf Goodman's assigned to create hats for the Washington crowd. Mr. Charles said that Halston—one name only—was very meticulous. He'd come from Lilly Daché and had the same head size as the Wife and would try her hats on and look at them with two mirrors so that every angle was right and the fit was perfect. Kate couldn't imagine how silly he looked in some of those hats, especially a summer straw he'd recently made with a large green polka-dot bow. But he got the job done, and that was all that mattered.

While the sketch was playful, the Wife's instructions for construction were quite precise. She was mad for fashion and had been designing her own clothes since she was a young girl. As a college senior, she'd won *Vogue*'s Prix de Paris contest with an essay that began with a sense of whimsy—*If I could be a sort of Overall Art Director of the Twentieth Century, watching everything from a chair hanging in space*...She was all about the details.

"Why is this a love letter?" Kate asked.

"The President wants her to have this. He wants Chez Ninon to make it happen."

The back door suddenly opened. Schwinn saw the envelope immediately. "Is it Christmas?"

"It is Christmas," Mr. Charles said.

It was always Christmas when an order came in from Maison Blanche.

Schwinn was slight and freckle faced, with sun-washed blond hair that seemed to be styled by a series of cowlicks. He always wore the same clothes: a neatly pressed white cotton shirt, black trousers, and a black tie. He worked in the front, with the Ladies, but instead of wearing a suit jacket, he wore a windbreaker that made him appear as if he were just stopping by for a moment on his way somewhere else. Kate had never met anyone like him. He seemed to be about her age, about thirty years old, but he could have been older or younger. Unlike most men, he liked bicycles, not cars. He knew so much about them that some of the Ready-to-Wear girls thought he might have been part of the Schwinn bicycle family, perhaps a son. But Kate thought that Schwinn was just a nickname. She asked him about it once, and he said, "Schwinn is good enough for a bike, so it's good enough for me." Kate wasn't sure what he meant by that, but that was just his way.

Schwinn was a salesperson, but his formal title was "stylist," which seemed to mean that he helped women accessorize clothes but he was also a designer himself. He had a nice business on the side, making hats for some of the clients. Kate thought that the Ladies probably knew but looked the other way. Everyone liked Schwinn, especially the clients. He was funny and enthusiastic about everything. And he was Catholic, which Kate liked, too.

But there was also something about him that seemed deeply wounded. His eyes were gray with bits of green, and he never looked at you directly. He was secretive, too. In six years, Kate had only learned two things about his past—he'd been an art major, and he'd dropped out of college to serve in the Korean War. He'd told her that those were the only two things worth knowing.

Schwinn picked up the drawing from the Wife and studied it carefully.

"He wants her to have a new outfit," Mr. Charles said. "That's a first."

"Even the President can be a man in love. It's probably a peace offering for the way the press savaged her during the election for wearing all those French clothes."

Everyone was still trying to figure out who told *Women's Wear Daily*, a small industry newspaper, that the Wife had spent $30,000 during the campaign on clothes in Paris. "Smart and charming," they wrote about the future president and his wife, "and running for election on the Paris Couture Fashion ticket."

The average American salary was $5,600 a year, and so when the story broke, Mrs. Nixon began harping on the Wife's un-American clothes. She went on at great length about how she only bought her clothes off the sales racks in moderately priced department stores.

The Wife had planned to ignore it, but when the Associated Press ran the piece, suddenly everyone wanted to read *Women's Wear Daily,* and the scandal grew. She was then forced to counter the speculations with an exclusive quote in the fashion section of the *New York Times*—"I couldn't spend that much unless I wore sable underwear"—which was followed by a statement from the campaign office stating that the Wife was "distressed by the implications of extravagance, of over-emphasis of fashion in relation to her life." The situation spiraled out of control, and newspapers around the country began to run unflattering articles about the Wife's "balloon hair," and worse. Finally *Women's Wear Daily* apologized to the family and dubbed the First Lady "Her Elegance." After seeing what pain they'd caused, they vowed never to criticize her again. But the damage had been done to the Wife's image. Even eight months after the election, the press still hovered like vultures, waiting for her to make the same mistake again.

"This pink suit could be a very bad idea," Mr. Charles said. "It's clearly French. Maison Blanche wants us to pay Chanel for the right to make a line-by-line replica. If that gets out—"

"It won't matter all that much," Schwinn said. "The suit is American if we make it. The reporters can't touch her for that. If we make it, she's not taking jobs away from anyone. She can wear French without the criticism—it's the gift that keeps on giving."

If Schwinn was correct, it was a very clever gift indeed.

The rest of the back room arrived, squawking like geese. Then came Maeve, late as always. Maeve was the fitter. She was an Inwood girl, like Kate. Somewhere in her late fifties, she was un married. Irish, of course. Her hair was the color of iron. She was broad shouldered, nearly square.

"Christmas?"

"Christmas," Mr. Charles said.

She looked at the sketch Schwinn was holding. "That woman is a fine doodler," she said. "But Chanel is not going to like this at all—it's exceedingly pink."

CHAPTER TWO

"Pink is the navy blue of India."
— Diana Vreeland

The suit was not actually pink, but raspberry. That was what Coco Chanel had named the color, and so the Wife had taken to calling it that too. Chez Ninon, however, referred to it as "pink." Pink. Pink.

That vexed Chanel. Everything about their request vexed Chanel, especially the Wife's tinkering. Now they want it licensed as if it is original.

It was late in the day when the telegram arrived in Paris at the offices of 31 rue Cambon. The designer was six floors up, in her private atelier, on her knees with her small gold scissors hanging around her neck on a black velvet ribbon. She was basting a length of wool crepe onto a malnourished model. Her assistant, who was dressed in far too much black cashmere for such a warm day in such a warm room, read the telegram from Chez Ninon to Chanel again. Chanel sighed. She shook her head but said nothing.

"Raise your arms," Chanel said to the model. "Good. Lower your arms. Good. And again?"

The workroom walls were banks of mirrors so that Chanel could watch the way the black wool responded to movement and how it looked in the light. The model had been flapping her arms up and down for at least an hour, maybe more. Chanel was trying to get the armhole of the dress absolutely perfect.

"And again?"

The model was on the verge of tears.

Seventy-eight years old and still working, Chanel seemed relevant and ancient at the same time. She was dressed as she often was—in a hat and suit. The hat was black and Spanish, inspired by the cowboys of Seville. Its crown looked like a layer of a cake. The suit she was wearing, which she wore nearly every day, had lost its buttons and was held together with safety pins. It was thinning under the arms, but she loved it. Made from her own signature fabric—number H1804, from Linton Tweeds—it was an ecru wool-and-mohair blend. It appeared as if it were dyed two slightly different shades of the same color, but it was not. It was like a magic trick. The yarns took the color differently, and so the mohair seemed to be a darker shade of white than the virgin wool, giving the suit a white-on-white checkered look. It was that sort of subtlety that Chanel adored. She was wearing pearls, as always. There were so many ropes wrapped around her neck, they seemed to elongate it, making her look a bit like an ostrich.

The dress was driving Chanel mad. "And once more," she said to the model. The girl raised her trembling arms over her head again. The room was overheated. Chanel's assistant looked appropriately bored as he stared at himself in the banks of mirrors. He wore a gold pince-nez, which set off the sharp angles of his face but served no practical use. No matter how warm he was, he would have to stand there, sweating, waiting for Mademoiselle's response—no matter how long it took. The man held the telegram with two fingers, away from his body, as if the paper were dripping wet.

The fitter, who was also dressed completely in black, handed Chanel pin after pin. He too was sweating and pale. Chanel didn't seem to notice anyone's discomfort. She was always cold, so the heat of the room suited her. The enormous length of black wool overwhelmed the model, blended with her black hair, and served as an alarming counterpoint to her shocking green eyes. Chanel draped the heavy wool around the girl's frail body and over her head, creating a monklike cowl. The wool intensified the heat of the room, but no one offered the pale model a glass of water or a moment to collect herself. The cowl would not sit properly, and the armholes still would just not lie flat. Chanel's hands shook slightly as she reset the pins again.

"Once more. Arms straight up. Hold."

The dress was meant to be that year's Little Black Dress—the "LBD," as Chanel called it, as everyone had called it since 1926, when Chanel declared that black should not be for clerics, maids, and nuns alone. But after dozens of fittings over the course of four days, the dress was still far from complete.

Chanel was intent on fixing the armhole, no matter how long it took. With the gold scissors hanging around her neck, she snipped away at the basting she had just laid in.

"The telegram. Once more," she said to her assistant. The man read in a neutral voice: URGENT NEED OF LICENSE FOR MAISON BLANCHE STOP EXACT LINE BY LINE REPLICA OF LIFE MAGAZINE SUIT

STOP PINK STOP SEND TOILE STOP NEED PINK FABRIC AND FINDINGS STOP MUST BE PINK STOP HOW MUCH STOP.

To which Chanel said, "Stop."

She was usually quite flattered when her work was copied. Chanel reveled in the irony when suits she'd designed for champagne lunches at La Grenouille were mass-produced for office girls who ate from brown bags in badly lit rooms. However, because of politics, always politics, this "Chanel" was to be American made, a licensed "line-by-line" using Chanel's own fabric and trim. In pink. It was to be pink. Pink. Pink. Pink. Not raspberry, as the color was actually named.

"These people are annoying," she told her assistant. The man, in his ironic pince-nez, nodded.

Chanel had never worked with the Ladies before, but she certainly knew them. She was still angry that Chez Ninon told everyone that their copies of her clothes were better than the Chanel originals. They were total fakes, never authorized, but they made this claim to all of her best customers. "Their clients in New York receive four fittings and Chez Ninon thinks that makes them superior. We only need one; we do it properly the first time."

This suit was not just a personal favorite of Chanel's, but groundbreaking. The *Life* photo spread honored it as a "crisply tailored figure-fitting shape." And yet, it was forgiving. You could be fat as a fig and still look wonderful. The double pockets on each side drew the eye in and made the jacket look fitted, although it was not. It was modern and timeless.

One can always design fashion, but to design beauty is another thing entirely. Chanel had closed her shops in 1939 and had been in retirement for years; the rumors of her collusion with the Nazis were difficult for her public to understand. But now, with this suit, Chanel had returned. She was forgiven. She was relevant again. Revered. With this suit, she could not be denied her place in history.

Chanel walked around the model. Looking. Measuring. Considering. She was like a scientist at work.

"Why do these Americans always want to know how much?" she said. The model held her arms steady over her head, but the heat was quickly becoming too much for her. Chanel pulled at the fabric hard. The girl tried to stay steady, but she leaned forward a bit. Chanel roughly moved her back into place.

The model moved her head slightly, as if to attempt to straighten her spine.

"Am I boring you?" Chanel said.

"No, mademoiselle."

"Good. That's good to know. Straighten up."

"Yes, mademoiselle."

"Yes?"

"*Oui.*"

"*Oui.* Very good." Chanel was not being unkind but instructive. "French is the language of diplomats. You will never be in demand if you do not learn it properly. Now put your hands down—but slowly."

"*Merci.*"

"And now put them up again. Slowly. And down again. And again."

Despite her great discomfort, the model never showed any emotion. She stared straight ahead. The assistant adjusted his pince-nez glasses—he did that quite frequently, as if to draw attention to them—and then cleared his throat. "Mademoiselle, what should our telegram say in return?"

Chanel closed her eyes for a moment, as if to shift her thoughts. Then lit a cigarette. The Wife was a very good customer, and so very lovely, but things had become ridiculous after the election. For a time, Chanel went along with the ruse of selling dresses to the Wife's sister for a "friend's cousin," some unnamed "Sicilian noblewoman" who had the same exact build as the First Lady—a five-foot-eight boy's body with broad shoulders, big hands, and size 10 feet. The two also had the same taste. "We must pretend her husband is the president of France," the sister would say.

Of France?

It was positively insulting. Once the clothes were finished, they were sent by special diplomatic courier to Washington—as were frequent shipments of Chanel No. 5. Not only the parfum, with its rich bourbon vanilla and bougainvillea overtones, but also the eau de parfum, with its forward notes of may rose and ylang-ylang, and even the eau de toilette, which was heavy with sandalwood. The supposed Sicilian noblewoman bought Chanel No. 5 in all its variations and complications for morning, noon, and evening—and the bill was mailed to the First Lady's father-in-law in Hyannis Port. It was laughable, at best.

This request from Chez Ninon for a muslin toile, a test garment, was tiresome. While it was not unusual to create line-by-line replicas of designs—they were even regulated by the Chambre Syndicale de la Haute Couture et du Prêt-à-Porter as a way to appease the International Ladies' Garment Workers' Union—Chanel was always reluctant. To make a copy was one thing—it would always be inferior—but to give the ability to replicate exactly her work, her vision, and her art was completely another. Why should she allow another name to be put on her work? She'd resigned from the Chambre Syndicale in 1957. They had no jurisdiction over her. She could do what she wanted, and she simply did not want to.

Although it was interesting that the request did not come from Oleg Cassini, who was now ordained her official "dressmaker," as he had said. *That is good,* Chanel thought. *Maybe there is a falling-out.*

Everyone was shocked when the editor at *Harper's Bazaar,* Mrs. Vreeland, championed Cassini to the First Lady. Why Vreeland promoted a man with such a playboy reputation was beyond understanding. His first press conference was held in New York and made headlines. At the Pierre Hotel, with a cocktail in hand and a crooked, debonair smirk, he announced that there would be two press showings a year featuring the First Lady's wardrobe, but the press would not be invited. The events would be held exclusively for the New York Couture Group, the garment manufacturers in the city.

"Press knows nothing about fashion," he announced. Everyone gasped.

His cologne was overwhelming, too.

It was the first, and also the last, press conference Mr. Cassini ever gave. How could the First Lady, a woman who was such a devotee of Chanel and French couture and, more important, the chemise—which Cassini openly ridiculed in a fashion show by making a version in burlap and having the model litter the runway with potatoes—how could this particular woman have chosen such a man as her designer?

Inexplicable. A falling-out would be very good, indeed.

"We are done," Chanel said to the model, and then smiled, charmingly. "See you tomorrow, then?"

"*Oui,* mademoiselle. *Merci.*"

"Good."

"The telegram?" the assistant asked again. "And what shall I answer, mademoiselle?"

"I am going home to think."

Hôtel Ritz had been Chanel's home on and off for decades, since the beginning of World War II. It was right across the alley from her shop. Her room was unlike any other. It was not opulent but small and tucked out of the way, in the attic. It was just a bed with white sheets in a room with white walls. The only decoration was a spray of wheat, which her father once told her was a talisman that would bring her luck. The room was profoundly quiet, much like the convent school where she spent her youth. It was a good place to think.

Chanel washed her hands and face with lye soap; she hated the scent of skin. She lit another cigarette and went out onto the rooftop with a glass of red wine and looked out over Paris. From that height, the city seemed to be made of buttercream—but yellowed and dusty, as if sculpted for a cake that would not be eaten, just remembered in one's dreams. It was no longer the city of her youth. There were so many people; there was so much noise.

"Americans," she sighed.

When the moon rose pink over Paris—at least, that was the way the Ladies would later tell the story—Chanel finally decided that they could have the suit. However, if this particular Chanel was to go to America, to be made by American hands, there would have to be restrictions and agreements set in place. Especially if Cassini was to be anywhere near it. The man's aesthetic was vulgar, or, as he called it, "sexy": all high slits, low necklines, and high drama. No subtlety. No sensuousness.

As for the question of how much, Chanel wrote down a very large figure, indeed.

When Chanel's telegram arrived the next day, Sophie showed the ransom note, as she called it, to Nona, and they laughed. Their reply went out an hour later: *Sharpen your pencil and recalculate.*

While Chanel, the person, was not easily copied, the same could not be said for the suit. It was a very simple design. The finished product might not have all the Chanel touches, nor the exact fit or feel, but it would be similar and could be made in half the time and at a fraction of the cost. A copy of the blouse alone would cost only $3 to make, but the Ladies could charge $300 for it—and everyone would be happy to pay. Purchasing the toile and license was ridiculous and impractical, but Maison Blanche insisted. Chez Ninon would also be forced to pay Chanel for the right to use the material, the signature gold chain that would be sewn into the hem to help the jacket hang properly, and the gold "CC" buttons. The buttons alone would be $250.

Chez Ninon usually charged $3,500 for one of their "Chanel" suits, which were made from similar-looking fabric and buttons but run off on machines with a very limited amount of hand finishing. Unfortunately, Maison Blanche had made it quite clear that the entire suit couldn't cost more than $1,000, preferably $850 or less. There wasn't even a way to take a shortcut or two. The pink suit was to be a line-by-line copy and so must be entirely sewn by hand. It would be impossible to make a profit or break even—perhaps that was why Maison Blanche did not ask Cassini—but the Ladies could not turn it down. To dress a socialite was one thing, but to dress that same socialite when she became the First Lady was an honor they could not easily pass up.

Miss Nona marked the suit in on the production schedule.

"That's just eight weeks to delivery," Sophie said.

"Chanel will give it up in the end," Miss Nona said, but she didn't sound sure.

When a week passed without a telegram or phone call, without any response at all, Miss Nona's confidence waned. She began to wonder if asking for a discount from an icon might be perceived as—she couldn't think of the right word.

"Unseemly?" Sophie said. "Insulting?"

Miss Nona was hoping for "amusing."

She knew that this could be a very expensive miscalculation. Miss Sophie had already ordered the fabric from Chanel's supplier Linton Tweeds, in Cumbria—the price of the yardage nearly made her heart stop. They should have waited for Chanel to agree. They couldn't use the fabric at all without her consent, but they were running out of time. The suit was to be worn the first week in November, just seven weeks away. The President was planning a family weekend. It would be the first time they would visit Camp David—and there was a very good chance that it would be the last. The Wife had already rented a place in the country near Washington, where she kept horses. It was quite clear to the Ladies that the Wife needed this pink suit to convey a strong sense of cheerful femininity—and an unflagging reasonable nature—so that when the First Lady announced that this camp of David was too backwater, she would be photographed looking reasonable.

Miss Nona couldn't wait any longer. "I'm going to call Chanel."

"Paris? It's six dollars a minute," Sophie said.

Nona had the call put through anyway. Each ring sounded like the rattling of tin cans.

Then finally a voice: *"Allo, oui?"* It sounded so very far away.

"For Mademoiselle Chanel. Chez Ninon," the overseas operator said.

"Non."

"Non?" Miss Nona couldn't believe it. "Ask them if I can leave a message. *Pouvez vous prendre un message?"*

"Non."

The line went dead.

CHAPTER THREE

"Clothing is the fabric that defines and measures time."

—Oleg Cassini

$\mathcal{A}$t 4:30 a.m., Kate's alarm clock fell to the floor, still trilling like a five-and-dime hummingbird. She'd rolled over to turn it off but accidentally knocked it over to where it now lay, insistent. *Friday.* Every bone ached, every muscle felt sore. The list of what had to be done was long and began with Kate hemming a tea-length chiffon cape for a fifteen-year-old girl who would probably be miserable wearing such a creaky old thing. There was also Mrs. B's lace ball gown, which needed adjusting: the lace was Spanish and delicate, very prone to unraveling, so it was difficult to tell how long the task would take. And then, maybe, one or two alteration jobs that Maeve couldn't get to because the fittings were overbooked. Two days' worth of work needed to be stuffed into eight hours.

It took Kate another moment to realize that her front door was open.

"Hello?"

She distinctly remembered locking the door the night before. At least, she thought she did.

"Who's there?"

Light from the street lamps shone though the thick tatting of the lace curtains that she'd made and illuminated the front room. Everything seemed fine. Kate got out of bed and took a quick look around. The tiny white kitchen was still immaculate. Her mother's bone china teapot, a Belleek with tiny shamrocks, was still gathering dust. Kate took all her meals downstairs with her sister and her family—that was part of their agreement. Fourteen dollars a week, and Kate made all the clothes for Maggie and her two Mikes, both big and little, in exchange for room and board.

Next to Kate's kitchen, the old door that served as her worktable still held the muslin skirt pattern Mr. Charles had made for her. Floor length. He told her it would be "positively enchanting" for New Year's Eve. Next to it, there were the two bolts of matelassé silk, hand loomed to look like a bed of white roses, that she'd planned to make it with. The skirt would be too fancy for the dance at the Good Shepherd, but Kate was going to wear it anyway. The bolts were beautiful but flawed. Some places were stained and some were snagged. In a few areas, the quilting was so sloppy that it would have to be redone. It would take Kate weeks to work around the imperfections, but the skirt was worth it. It was always worth it.

If someone was hiding in her tiny apartment, it would be difficult to imagine where. There was barely enough room for Kate. Everywhere one looked, things were stacked upon things. There were dozens of boxes filled with zippers that were grouped according to color—and the same was true of rickrack and lace. Kate prided herself on having thread of nearly every single shade ever made; she had eleven variations of violet alone. Buttons were kept in old mason jars that lined the windowsills. Patterns were filed in a battered four-drawer cabinet that she'd found on the street. Fabric was piled everywhere. It was mostly bolts and swatches from Chez Ninon's remnant room—the girls always took their pick. Even though that was somewhat frowned upon, it wasn't really stealing. It was certainly nothing to bother Father John about in confessional. The Ladies eventually threw the excess away. It was "liberating the fabric," as Maeve said. Kate couldn't help herself. When it came to fabric, she was obsessed by the touch, color, and the promise that it held.

Some of what Kate took from Chez Ninon was for personal use, but a few pieces were remnants of history. There was a half yard of the bride-ivory satin from the inaugural-gala gown. And then the Renaissance red wool that turned out to be "the perfect thing" for an upcoming televised tour of the Maison Blanche renovation. Kate was loath to remember the thick chain stitching that outlined the standaway neckline and the hem of the skirt, a signature of the Christian Dior house that had nearly made her go blind. Her favorite was a small snip of Chinese yellow silk from Nina Ricci for a state dinner held in a room that was quickly painted off-white by the staff so that the brilliant-yellow and deeply black gown could not possibly go unnoticed. They were all reminders that beauty was calculated—nipped, tucked, pulled, and pleated into life.

What time did I get in? she thought. Too late, of course. And no dinner. Again. September meant back to school, and that meant new wardrobes for everyone. All the girls at Chez Ninon worked late, and Kate was no exception. But still, leaving the door open was inexplicable. And now she was wasting time. She'd be late. She was never late. *Ever.*

Kate quickly took the curlers out of her hair; her head was raw from the bristles and clips. She put on her favorite suit, the gray tweed one. Mr. Charles had made it for her. The heather in it set off the strawberry in her skin—at least, that was what he said. He was quite the flatterer, with his Frank Sinatra ways, but Kate liked him all the same.

The morning was bleak. There was a dull, cold rain. Kate pulled out her umbrella and put on her cashmere beret instead of her hat. She left the matching mittens behind and wore a new pair of soft gray kid gloves because one doesn't wear mittens in the city. She wasn't even sure who'd told her that. Probably Miss Sophie—she was always giving the back-room girls tips on how to improve themselves.

By the time Kate arrived for six o'clock mass at the Good Shepherd, the rain was furious. Her hair was soaked, the curl gone. The beret and gloves would probably shrink. Kate's only comfort was that at that hour, not many from the neighborhood would see her. Pete the Cop, maybe. He was everywhere. But he wasn't really from the neighborhood and wasn't Catholic, so he didn't count. Father John, of course. But he never cared about that sort of thing; he couldn't even match his own socks. Father John had been an esteemed member of the famed Cork Gaelic footballers. He wore the red and white of the Blood and Bandages, as the team was called. He was a man who knew both God and greatness—and so that was more than enough. And he had such a beautiful voice. Soaring.

Christe eleison.

The first mass of the day was always a Low Mass. It was simple, the way Kate liked it. No choir or organ music. Just Father John, chanting in the ancient darkness. Two candles on the altar—and nothing more.

Christe eleison.

Indolent clouds of sandalwood and frankincense hung low overhead. Everything seemed preserved in amber.

Kyrie eleison.

Kate's voice echoed in the rafters. The church was nearly empty. For a moment, she thought she heard Patrick Harris somewhere behind her in the darkness. Pitch-perfect and humble, as usual. He wasn't showy, like some who had good voices.

Kyrie eleison.

It wasn't possible, though. It was Friday. Patrick Harris was a Sundays Only Catholic—which was not his choice. He'd told Kate that many times. He'd go every day if he could. Patrick made it quite clear that he wasn't one of those Poinsettia-and-Lily Catholics or Christmas Bunnies—but he had a butcher shop to run and no one to help him anymore. All of his people in America were gone. His father went first, with a heart attack. Then, two months ago, Peg, with the same. So Patrick had to be at the shop every morning, even on Saturdays, because the pig men at the slaughterhouse delivered at the crack of dawn. Two squat men with a couple of skinned beasts slung over their shoulders—Kate had seen them often.

Kyrie eleison.

But it did sound like Patrick. Kate turned around to take a quick look, but the church was too dark. Still, it had to be him. While there were nearly twenty thousand parishioners at the Good Shepherd—priests said nine masses in the church every Sunday and five more for the overflow crowd at the school—she knew that voice very well.

Kate usually stopped at the butcher's on the way home if the family needed something—and sometimes, even if they didn't. Patrick Harris still had a bit of that particular Cork accent, that music, to his voice. It was lovely just to hear him talk. It was, in a way, like being home again.

People were lining up for communion. Kate looked over her shoulder again; she still couldn't see him.

"The body and blood," Father John said as he held the host out for her: a small, white, round wafer in his huge pink hands.

"Amen."

Kate scanned the church again. All around her, people had their heads down, praying. Standing. Kneeling. Patrick Harris didn't seem to be anywhere. Communion continued on, pew by pew.

"Amen," Mrs. Flaherty told Father John.

"The body of our Lord," Father John said to Mrs. Kilpatrick and then to Mrs. O'Hara and then Mrs. McNamara.

Patrick Harris was still nowhere to be seen.

After the service, Kate took a moment and lit a candle for Mrs. Harris. Peg had always been so very kind to her.

Outside the Good Shepherd, the rain had not stopped. She stood on the church steps under the shelter of the roofline. The subway station was across the street, just a quick dash, but it felt like it was miles away, given how hard it was raining. Her umbrella was still wet. Her hair—she didn't even want to think about her hair. The train would be leaving in just a few minutes. Traffic was backed up all the way down Broadway, so Kate made a run for it, dodging between stopped cars. She jumped over a puddle, pushed through the glass doors, and then ran down the stairs and through the turnstile. The station, thankfully, was nearly deserted. There was just a handful of people. It was not quite rush hour.

The express train began at 207th Street. The conductor leaned out the window of the train, red faced and cheery. "Raining, is it?" He wasn't from the neighborhood. He had a smart word for everyone.

Kate shook out her hair, pulled out her compact—and that was when she saw him. Patrick Harris. He was standing on the platform with his umbrella in one hand as if waiting for her to arrive.

Kate let out a little yelp. "You gave me quite a start."

"Sorry."

Patrick must have been in church after all. He was dressed in a suit and dark overcoat. He'd shaved, and his silver tangle of hair was finally trimmed into place. He was only three years older than Kate, but, unlike Mr. Charles, he'd gone gray early. Kate had never noticed how blue his eyes were before. He looked handsome, actually. He was wearing a tartan tie, the Irish National. And he wasn't even damp.

"I was wondering if you'd like to have some cake with me," he said. "I made it myself. Peg's recipe."

"I have to go to work."

"Just a quick bite. Father John and I are having cake in the rectory. In honor of Peg. Mam. It's her birthday."

Kate had completely forgotten. She was glad she'd lit the candle, and would dearly love a bite of Peg's cake, but the A train was ready to leave: two bells.

"I have to go."

Patrick seemed slightly embarrassed, as if he'd overstepped some invisible line. "Of course. Certainly. Peg would not want you to be late, especially not on her birthday." He turned to walk back up the stairs.

"Aren't you coming downtown?"

"No. Pete the Cop let me jump over. I told him I had to ask a girl about a cake. I think he thought it was a code for something. He laughed, slapped me on the back, and gave up a wink."

"Hopeless romantic, is he?"

"Or dirty old man."

The subway doors were closing. Kate jumped on board the train.

Patrick smiled, but he also looked sad standing there on the platform, all alone.

"What kind of cake?" she yelled after him.

He didn't hear her. She hoped it was Peg's yellow crumb.

When the White House called Chez Ninon later that day, the toile from Chanel had still not arrived. It had been eight days since Miss Nona's counter offer had been sent via Western Union. When Maison Blanche called, it was usually Kay McGowan, Cassini's showroom director, who coordinated fabrication and acquisitions for the state wardrobe. But this call was not from an assistant or a secretary or an assistant to a secretary but from Her Elegance, as *Women's Wear Daily* called the Wife. The childlike whisper, the patrician tone—Miss Nona's hands began to sweat.

"I'd like to see the toile," she said. "I'm not sure if the weight of the fabric will be right for casual wear."

"Of course," Miss Nona said. "Would four o'clock work for you?"

It would.

As soon as Miss Nona hung up the telephone, Miss Sophie said, "I suppose you have a plan?"

"I have her dress form, muslin, drafting tools—and Kate."

"Then you have a plan."

CHAPTER FOUR

"I captured the synthesis of her elegance."
—Oleg Cassini

$\mathcal{M}$r. Charles had the skills to make the toile, of course, but he was too valuable to lose. Women came every day from all over Europe to have suits made by him. The Ladies couldn't whip up a toile themselves, for obvious reasons. It had to be Kate, they explained. Kate was the only one the Wife had never met and would never see again. That was the way it was with back-room girls—they were invisible. So if Kate made the toile, and the Wife discovered that it wasn't a Chanel, the Ladies could make a great fuss and say that a mistake had been made and that the girl, Kate, had obviously forgotten to order the toile and would be fired. Then they could reschedule the appointment for the following week, by which time the Chanel would most certainly have arrived.

"Fired?"

"Don't get stuck on the details, Kate," Miss Nona said.

"We'd never fire you," Sophie said.

"Of course not."

Everyone else had been sent home early. "No witnesses," Mr. Charles said and laughed as he and the girls piled out the back-room door. And so, their reassurances were not entirely comforting. Sitting on the edge of the Ladies' silk settee, with the huge crystal chandelier creaking overhead, Kate felt abandoned. The Ladies, ancient and gilded, were perched at their Louis XIV desk—a fake, of course. The walls, ceiling, and floors were glass and perfume-bottle blue. It was a room designed for dreaming, not living. Behind the Ladies, walls of windows framed a Park Avenue skyline buffeted by rain.

"And when will they be here?" Kate asked.

"Soon," Miss Sophie said.

"Too soon," said Miss Nona.

The gilt, the azure, the women—it was like a Byzantine mosaic, Kate thought. "Byzantine" was Mr. Charles's latest design inspiration. "Delightfully complicated," he explained to Kate. Now everything seemed Byzantine to her. "Couldn't we simply tell the Wife that the Chanel is in the mail?"

The Ladies chuckled.

"But it is coming soon, isn't it?" Kate said.

Miss Nona patted Kate's hand gently. "We have all the faith in the world in you."

"But they'll wonder where everyone is. Mr. Charles. You. Schwinn."

"Tell them that I took ill," Miss Nona said. "Everyone rushed to the emergency room to be by my side."

"She's at death's door," said Sophie. "But resilient."

"My recovery will be amazing. Everyone will be overjoyed."

"And surprised!" Miss Sophie said.

It was almost too believable. Perfume could no longer hide the acid of Miss Nona's aging; twilight followed her wherever she went. The Wife would honestly think that Nona was dying—Kate sometimes did.

The directive was delivered, and so the Ladies stood. Time to go. The floor was always a little slick, especially when it was raining outside, because the delivery boys sometimes tracked in water. Miss Sophie took Miss Nona by the arm.

"Watch your step," Kate said.

"You are a dear girl."

"She is, isn't she? A remarkably dear girl."

As the two old women shuffled across the blue floor, they seemed smaller, slower, more stooped, as if already a memory—and that made Kate's heart hurt. But they were absolutely Byzantine.

Kate knew she'd grown exceedingly fond of that word, but it seemed to apply to nearly all the goings-on these days. At the request of Maison Blanche, the Ladies were now "importing" Hubert de Givenchy's couture originals from Paris. It had become part of Kate's job to remove his label, stitch in one from Chez Ninon, have Maeve alter it to Cassini's specifications—put a bow on the back, or a dart here and there—and then ship the clothes on to the Wife. And then to do the same for the Nina Ricci shipments and the Dior—and all the rest.

There was such an alarming amount of French clothing being imported and altered by Chez Ninon that Kate began to wonder if her immortal soul was in peril. Father John told her not to worry. " 'Thou shalt not commit chicanery' is merely a suggested commandment," he said, but made her say two Hail Marys just to be on the safe side. Now there was the matter of a faux Chanel. Kate wondered how many Hail Marys and Our Fathers it would take to absolve her of this particular bit of creative endeavor. She didn't even want to think about it.

Since the elections, fittings with the First Lady had become a nightmare. The press stood outside the door to Chez Ninon all day long, nearly every day, hoping to catch the Wife coming or going. Fool's errand that was—since the campaign, she barely came in at all. But the press was unrelenting. In an effort to throw them off the scent, the Ladies bought a department-store mannequin that looked exactly like the Wife. Miss Sophie told everyone that it was a seamstress dummy and that their important client, who was so important that her name could not even be said aloud, wouldn't need to come in for fittings anymore.

No one believed her.

Now, months after the election, when the Wife felt that she absolutely needed to come in, which was very rare, the Secret Service would drive only as far as St. Patrick's, a few blocks away, where Her Elegance would put on her lace chapel cap and walk into the church and keep on walking to the sanctuary and then down into the catacombs. There, in the presence of the holy dead—specifically, all the archbishops of New York—she would take off her cap, put on a scarf and her sunglasses, and make a run for it with the Secret Service in tow.

New York is filled with tunnels, and under St. Patrick's there's one that ends up at the back door of Chez Ninon.

At least, that was the story Miss Sophie told the girls in the back room.

It sounded a bit like a fairy tale, but it wasn't Kate's place to speculate, and so she didn't. Kate was in charge of finishing—not questions. She was one of the "kippers," just as her mother had been, back home in Cork, one of the back-room girls with a knack for Milanese buttonholes. However, if asked, Kate would say that she could understand why such a very important client and her bodyguards would be running through curtains of cobwebs in the abandoned service tunnels under the streets of Manhattan, past rats and the watchful eye of the holy dead, to shop at Chez Ninon. It is exceedingly difficult to find a good dressmaker. There was no wonder at all in Kate's mind why she and Mr. Charles were drawn to the word *Byzantine*.

Kate tacked the Wife's sketch onto the wall, next to Mr. Charles's cheeky cartoon of the designer Charles Frederick Worth outfitted as the Patron Saint of Chez Ninon. Worth, the creator of haute couture, had a tape measure in one hand, a bolt of silk in the other, and French francs raining down on him, piling at his feet. Kate didn't find it funny at all when Mr. Charles first showed it to her. "Shame it always comes down to money, isn't it?" she said.

"It's a shame when it doesn't."

Kate now understood. Fifty-two dollars and twenty-five cents a week doesn't go very far, especially when you send half of it home.

She laid everything out the way her mother had taught her. *Mise en place* style—that was what her mam said they called it at John W. Dowden & Company Limited. *Mise en place*, as the chefs say—"every element within reach":

Dress form.

Sewing machine.

Tailor-point scissors.

Shears. Bias tape.

Pins. Thread. Muslin.

Pencil. Paper. Iron.

The one-inch grid ruler.

The set of French curves.

Creating a toile took logic, math, and nerve. It was always thrilling.

Ninety minutes was all Kate had. First—muslin. The muslin for the toile had to be the exact weight and texture as the bouclé. But what weight would that be? Since the fabric hadn't arrived from Linton yet, it was difficult to know. The bouclé was handmade; its weight could vary greatly. The Wife would certainly suspect if Kate made the wrong choice.

She rummaged through the boxes of feelers from Linton, looking for a similar bouclé from another season. As big as a hand towel, a feeler was a sample sent out to clients to be squeezed, and twisted—it was the only way one could tell how a fabric would perform when worn. Everyone got them. Even Queen Elizabeth was sent boxes of feelers each season so she could twist and squeeze and then smooth them.

Kate's father worked at the woolen mill; it was his job to pack up the yearly shipment of cashmere feelers for the Queen's consideration. She was very concerned about wrinkling. He carefully wrapped the feelers in tissue paper sprayed with the powdery spicy scent of carnation—L'Heure Bleue by Guerlain, her favorite fragrance. No expense was spared in trying to garner the coveted title of "Royal Purveyor to Her Majesty The Queen." Although the Royals never bought their selection, it was always gratis. It was their country, after all. They owned it. Everything was theirs.

"Free Ireland," the Old Man would always say when he spoke of it, but Kate knew that was just pub talk. Her father knew nearly as much about the young Queen as Kate did about the Wife.

"You and I work in the shadow of greatness," he once wrote her. "And that's both a blessing and a curse."

Today, clearly, it was a curse.

Twist and smooth—sample after sample. Kate really had no idea what she was looking for, exactly. Just something that seemed similar. Most jackets would have a heavy toile made from twill muslin, but Chanel jackets were always as light as mohair.

At the bottom of the box, there was a bit of the ecru wool-and-mohair blend, the white-on-white tweed: Chanel's favorite. Pattern H1804, designed by Mr. Jamison, chief man at Linton himself. *Good a guess as any,* Kate thought.

Second—the pattern. Kate rolled brown paper out on the cutting table. How much she needed was a matter of math. Cassini's notes were taped to the back of the Wife's dress form:

Bust: 35½"
Waist: 26½"
Upper hips: 34½"
Lower hips: 38⅛"
Waistline from hem on side: 25¼"
Three-quarter sleeve from neck: 21¼"
Neck to waist: 17½"

Shoulder from center-back to armhole: 7¾"
Five feet seven inches tall

Thirty-six inches of brown paper would be just enough to sketch the skirt on. The jacket—that was more difficult. Twenty-two inches long, or twenty? If the jacket was to hit exactly at the hip, the Wife's imbalance would have to be accounted for. Chez Ninon adjusted for that when she came in for fittings. Chanel, on the other hand, always figured it in. The Wife would instantly know the toile was a fake if this wasn't right. Kate closed her eyes and tried to imagine the last hem she'd done for Maison Blanche. An inch and a half lower on the right side—that seemed to be correct. The Wife's left shoulder would also be more forward than the other.

Kate visualized the line as she imagined it to be—not a hard edge, but an edge that was soft enough for "forgiveness," as Mr. Charles always called that sort of cut.

She marked four points on the brown paper. Kate slipped her favorite drafting tool, the French curve, in place—the edge of it touching each point—and ran her pencil along it. As she traced the line, she imagined the story behind the suit, the details of how it really came to be. It helped Kate to know why something was being made. All clothes told a story. A wedding dress could tell the tale of a marriage of convenience or fairy-tale love by its color alone—off-white raised eyebrows. *Maybe,* Kate thought, *the story of this pink suit is one of forgiveness.*

Chanel had certainly designed every element of it with an eye to that—every seam in the jacket could be adjusted for a comfortable fit. The Ladies said that when the Wife wore the pink suit, she would be forgiven for not wanting to spend her vacations at Camp

David. And Schwinn had said that the Husband wanted the suit to be a real Chanel, so that he could be forgiven for putting his wife through the unbearable scrutiny that a president's wife had to face on a daily basis. *A gift of forgiveness is what it is,* Kate thought. It was a noble story. Inspiring, even.

You would think the First Lady would own a watch. Or that someone in that entourage would. The waiting was killing Kate, but she should have expected it. Even before Her Elegance was the Wife, she was late for all sorts of odd reasons. Once it was because she accidentally set the backseat of her little red convertible on fire with a cigarette and was trying to find someone on Park Avenue who had enough ice water to put it out. "Firemen are always so much of a bother," she said.

She knew that from experience, according to Mr. Charles. "But she's such a lovely person."

And he'd know. He not only spoke to her personally, but he also knew exactly how warm she needed the room to be before she stripped down to her knickers.

Kate looked at her watch again. The lace ball gown for Mrs. B still needed to be delivered that night. There could be no excuses. Mrs. B was a secret partner in Chez Ninon, but it wasn't much of a secret—her work always went to the front of the line. She'd recently lost weight—illness again—so there had been a slight gap in the neckline that was easily fixed by inserting an elastic stay. To get to her building during rush hour would take at least thirty minutes, which was thirty minutes more than Kate would have if all those security people and assistants and secretaries and all the rest of that entourage did not arrive soon.

Two hours and twenty-two minutes late, Kate thought. She's probably at St. Patrick's *now*. The ice in the champagne bucket had melted completely. The single crystal *coupe* looked forlorn. Kate sat in the showroom, fidgeting. Ankles crossed. One hand over the other? Hands in her pockets?

It was one thing to honor the Wife by copying her clothes for Maggie Quinn; it was another to meet the real deal. Kate thought of all the things that could go wrong. She could be sweaty, and that would ruin the toile. And all that smoking—Kate did not care for anyone who smoked. After fittings, the Wife's dressing room was like the inside of a gray cloud. What if the Wife cursed? That would be awful. The more Kate waited, the more she was convinced that nothing good could come of this meeting. She closed her eyes and pictured the Wife's face—that smile, the faint freckles across that nose, and the dark hair. Perfectly Irish, perfectly beautiful. Perfect—not human. And that was the way Kate preferred her.

Kate pulled the champagne bottle out of the bucket to take a good look at it. Was there a trick to opening it? She wasn't much of a drinker, but the color of champagne was an important factor in her work. When a champagne *coupe* was held, it became an accessory. The color of a gown must be chosen based on the type of champagne served. If the champagne was vintage, even if it was only aged a year or two, it would have a golden cast; Dom Pérignon was usually the color of new gold. But if it was aged more than five years, then it was the color of autumn leaves. Taittinger, which was the drink of the moment, was always "cathedral gold" because it was the color of the gold leaf in St. Patrick's.

Moët & Chandon was what the Ladies left for this particular meeting. It was what they always served. Non-vintage. Miss Nona bought by the case. When poured into crystal *coupes* it cast the world in the shade of tattered moonlight, which made everything feel both unbearably beautiful and unbearably sad. Details like that made a difference; they separated dressmakers from seamstresses.

Cut. Trim. Baste. Tuck. Pin. Trim. Stitch. That was what most people thought sewing was about, but they were wrong. It was really about perfection. Each stitch must be exactly like the one before it; each must be so small that it seems part of the fabric. A ribbon is sewn into the waist of a skirt to help keep the blouse in place. Zippers are either placed on the side, for comfort, or in the back, to emphasize the elegance of a line. Each tuck and pleat carefully disguises any flaw in the wearing or the wearer—small breasts, uneven hips, thick waists, and, of course, waning youth.

There were always so many elements involved, so many things to consider, and so many variables. From what Kate could tell, the same dress, or even a similar one, could not be worn Opening Night at the Met and also to the New York Junior League Winter Ball—the guest list was nearly identical. But a dress worn to the Kentucky Derby could be dyed another color and worn again in the same season. At the Derby, the "Horsey Set," as Miss Sophie called them, spent so much time looking at each other's hats, they never noticed the dresses at all.

Finally, at 6:46 p.m., when there was no hope of getting Mrs. B's gown to her at a reasonable hour and there'd be all hell to pay, the phone rang. A secretary. Reschedule.

"I see."

Kate's knees stopped shaking. That was fine. Better she didn't come.

Kate threw the toile in the trash.

CHAPTER FIVE

"Elegance is innate. It has nothing to do with being well dressed. Elegance is refusal."
— Diana Vreeland

It was nearly ten p.m. when the train pulled into Inwood. Maggie Quinn had long since cleared the supper plates and put her Little Mike to bed, so it was too late to root around in her sister's icebox. And Kate would not make the same mistake she'd made the night before. She was determined to have a proper dinner, but it was difficult to tell where to go.

The Hedgehog, the Last Stop, Erin's Isle, Chambers', McSherry's, the Lounge, Grippo's Torch Café, on 207th near Broadway—that was close—Doc Fiddler's, Cassidy's, Jimmy Ryan's, Keenan's Corner, Dolan's, the Pig 'n' Whistle, or Minogue's. Those were just some of the choices. *There's a reason why Walter Winchell calls it Ginwood,* she thought. There were seventy-three pubs in the Inwood neighborhood, and they could be divided into three categories: Greenhorns, Far Downs, and all the rest.

Greenhorns were for men from the old country. Green to America, they were not afraid to work and fiercely longed for the habit of home. Each of the pubs was connected to a particular town or county and took its name as a way of advertising—like the Lakes of Sligo, on 228th, where one could always raise a pint to the dark mist of the Northwest Coast. Their jukeboxes were filled with songs by Carmel Quinn and Dennis Day, who were always caterwauling on about Mother, Dear Mother, and Dear Mother Ireland. The songs were so maudlin that Kate hated to even walk past those pubs.

The Far Downs were for the Irish Americans, the children of the Greenhorns. Elvis was on their jukeboxes—"All Shook Up" and "Fever." Kate thought the man sounded like he was suffering from malaria.

At the Far Downs, no one cared whether you were from Cork or Dublin. The only thing that mattered was that you were a good Democrat and that, like all good Democrats, if you were called to the war you'd go gladly to protect your new homeland and make Ireland proud.

The other pubs were just that—other. Nobody cared about them.

Maeve always said that you could judge a place by what kind of beer they sold. Her father had owned a pub in Dublin, and she was always going on about Miller High Life. If an American bar served High Life, they probably served food, and good food, too. It was the champagne of bottled beers—Kate saw that in magazines—but it seemed to be the kind of thing sold on Park Avenue. Inwood was not a champagne kind of place.

Rheingold Girls? Schaefer beer? Knickerbocker or Piels? The signs were everywhere. And, of course, the ever-present "Ice Cold Beer." Kate wondered what her father would think about all these beers. Back home, beer was served cool, not cold—and never to women alone. If a pub did serve ladies, they'd have a snug, a separate room, for the women to drink in with their girls. Respectable men and women never drank together in public.

Cobh was such an entirely different place from Inwood. On the Great Island, pubs were at the center of daily life. In Newtown, on Cobh, Kate's family lived in the seventh of twenty cottages that were built around Fogarty's Pub. They were lined up in two rows, one on either side of the pub, on the top of the hill overlooking the endless sea. You'd get the news at Fogarty's, and anything that came by post. You'd take a phone call there or send a telegram. And there was drink—they stilled their own whiskey—and music. There was also a lovely snug for the Ladies so they could sip a halfie in relative peace.

Cobh was an old-fashioned place—solemn and silent, too. In Kate's New York neighborhood, it was always loud. There were sirens. And shouting. And praying. But it was the music that wore on Kate. Not just the screeching of jukeboxes, but all the rest of it. Most apartments had stoops. Most people in Inwood were homesick—music was to be expected. It could be very lovely, especially when accompanied by button accordion, harp, pennywhistle, or drum. And you could often hear bagpipes; there were several piper bands in Inwood.

It was the opera that she hated. Nearly any hour of day or night, you could hear one aria or another. So many singers from the Met lived in the neighborhood, and they kept such odd hours, that there always seemed to be opera in the alleyways. Even at that moment, on a Friday night, Kate could hear the howling heart of opera, with all that wailing about love lost and found. She'd been in love before with a couple of boys back home, but it was not like that. Opera made love seem histrionic and best avoided at all costs.

"You people need to calm down. All of you," she said to no one in particular. *New York would be a wonderful place if only it could keep quiet, just for a moment. No wonder we drink so much,* Kate thought.

The rain had stopped hours ago. Kate stood outside the train station. She didn't like to walk aimlessly, especially at night. *Through the park? Or up Step Street?* Kate wasn't sure which way to go. The steps were quicker, closer, but went nearly straight up. There were 120 steps, and her shins were aching. She'd delivered Mrs. B's gown herself—the Ladies hated to pay for night deliveries. Kate thought about the Capitol Restaurant, just across the street; the Greeks were good about keeping open all night, and they had a respectable fish dinner with two veg and rolls and butter, but it seemed like too much food. Still, she walked across and looked inside the window. She could see there was no room at the counter or at the small booths, either. Everybody in Inwood was hungry. Even at that hour.

Bickford's, maybe. That was close, too. You could get a simple scrambled egg with an English muffin and real strawberry jam. It was not as good as Peg Harris's jam, but it was passable. They served breakfast all night long, and so until the pubs closed, it was a decent place. After closing time, the hooligan crowd took over.

Kate walked past the Good Shepherd and blessed herself—a quick sign of the cross—and then stood on the steps and looked up and down Broadway. Dyckman Street, this side of Broadway, seemed to be the answer. There were plenty of choices there, although Kate knew that F. W. Woolworth's and the soda shop next to the Dyckman Theater would be closed. Nash's Hungarian Pastries, the German pork store, and even the broasted chickens that spun on the rotisserie at the delicatessen were probably gone for the night, too.

Still, Dyckman it was. Kate wanted to walk a bit to shake off the day. A few blocks more one way or another wouldn't make that much difference on a cool autumn night. But a few blocks later, and a few blocks more, she knew that Dyckman was as bad as Broadway at that hour. The only things open seemed to be the pubs, and none she knew of served food.

Kate noticed that there was still a light on at Patrick Harris's shop. She crossed the street and knocked at the door. His butcher shop was next to the Knights of Columbus supply store and across the street from the telephone company, a good location. He stayed open late, usually until nine p.m., so the telephone operators could pick up a fresh chop or two, then hop the train home. Through the large front window, Kate could see that Patrick was cleaning up. He was so focused that he didn't hear her. She knocked again. He looked up, surprised. Patrick was still in his whites, stained from a day of good sales. His white wool fedora was tilted at a rakish angle. He wiped his hands on a clean towel and opened the door.

"Cake's all gone," he said.

Peg's cake. Kate had nearly forgotten. "Was it good?"

"Solid effort. I used the last of Peg's raspberry jam in the center, which was brilliant, but the buttercream melted. I suspect the problem was the butter. I really like butter, but you can't use extra butter, can you? Then I put in too much milk because I put in too much butter. Father John didn't mind, though. Man will eat anything."

"And the crumb?"

"Wasn't Mam's. Wasn't bad. But not our Peg's."

Yellow butter cake with raspberry jam was a Peg classic. "I'm sure it was lovely."

"Dry. Father John slathered it with his own jam from the cupboard. Then he ate it with his hands as if it were a scone."

Kate laughed at the thought of it. "It may have been a bit on the dry side, then. Have you had supper yet? I'm famished and could use some company, if you've a mind."

"Excellent." Patrick put an arm around her shoulder, gave it a squeeze. "We'll go together. I'm finished here."

A group of young girls whom Kate knew from the Good Shepherd passed by the open door. They'd obviously been bowling. They swung their bags as they walked along. They reeked of beer and fried food, which made Kate's stomach growl again. When they saw Kate, one of them giggled. The other three laughed out loud. They passed by quickly but kept turning around to look back, laughing. Kate's ears went hot.

"What are they on about?"

"Nothing."

"You're not a very good liar."

"We'll talk about it over dinner."

"Lovely. You'll have a halfie and discuss my personal failings."

"We can start with mine first, if it makes you feel any better."

"What will we save for dessert?"

"There's always football. Our blessed Father John has written the Gaelic Athletic Association, telling all about the wonders Mike Meehan has been doing for our parish club."

"Would they care?"

"Of course not, but it fills Father John with glee to tell them."

Patrick Harris still lived in the large apartment above the butcher shop that he'd shared with his parents ever since they came to Inwood. Kate hadn't been up there since his mother had died. Sometimes, after church, they would walk back together, and Mrs. Harris would invite her up for Sunday tea. After tea and Peg's exquisite cake, Patrick would pull out his guitar and Peg would bring out her button accordion. They'd all sing together. Kate, too. With their eyes closed in reverie, their voices twining like ivy, they would sing until Peg would start crying. No matter how hard Peg tried, the music of home always overwhelmed her.

"You're a good girl to stay," Patrick would say to Kate when he walked her home. "Most girls don't have the time for the old ways." But Kate loved to sing, and she most certainly loved the cake. And it was always nice to hear Patrick's lovely voice. Now, with Peg gone, those Sundays were just a memory.

"I'll be ready in a minute," Patrick said.

"No hurry," Kate said, but the smell of bleach was overpowering. She began to cough and couldn't seem to stop. Patrick ran back to the stainless sink and poured Kate a glass of tap water. He watched her closely, like a mother hen. She drank it all, quickly. She hadn't realized how thirsty she was.

"You've had nothing today, have you?"

"Tea. Cream. Two sugars. It was Barry's. I found it in a tourist shop in the city. Gold Blend. Wasn't the same, though."

"Never is, is it?"

"Never. Tasted stale."

Kate leaned against the white tile wall as Patrick Harris took off his stained apron and butcher's coat. He had on the same shirt he'd worn that morning. It was a very nice shirt—department-store brand, but it had a fine fit for being mass produced and was properly tapered at the waist.

Patrick took Kate by the hand. It was nice when they walked like that. Hand in hand, like children. The pub wasn't far. There was no sign outside, which made it look more like a private social club than a common pub. Kate had never really noticed it before. There was no reason to. Back home, the pub was the link to the world outside the Island. In America, it was the link to the ruination of your liver.

Patrick opened the pub door for Kate, but she hesitated.

"It's a respectable place. The Browns were good friends with our dear Peg. They're looking out for me now."

The room was dark, long, and narrow. Men were playing darts in the corner. It didn't seem like a very friendly place, but Kate had no choice. She was hungry. She felt dizzy. Patrick helped her with her coat, quite the gentleman, and then hung it on the rack by the door for her. Kate pulled off her gloves; they had indeed shrunk a bit from the rain that morning. She took off her hat. Patrick led them to a booth near the wood-burning fireplace. The scent of wood smoke was comforting. Kate closed her eyes for a moment, and it felt like Fogarty's Pub back home, and that was lovely.

"We'll get you some good grub," he said. "Mrs. Brown feeds me as an act of mercy, which I pay for with steaks, chops, and the occasional chicken."

"That's lovely."

"I must be the only butcher in town who doesn't cook."

Patrick had gotten quite thin since his mother's death.

The bartender brought Patrick a pint and Kate a half. "Much obliged, Mr. Brown," Patrick said.

The slight, wrinkled man seemed irritated by the sight of Kate. "You're lucky," he said to her. "Mrs. Brown says there's just enough fish for the both of you. Ten minutes." Then he left.

"He's really quite kind," Patrick said.

Kate didn't know the Browns. They were Sundays Only church-goers. She didn't know what to make of the husband. She pushed the beer away. "He's very presumptuous. Maybe I don't drink. Maybe I don't eat fish."

She noticed a sign over the bar—NO LADIES ALLOWED—that could certainly account for Mr. Brown's lack of enthusiasm, and the lack of a proper snug. But the sign seemed silly. On any given Sunday, rows of baby carriages were lined up outside the pubs on Dyckman Street. Inside, couples dressed more finely than they were at church sat huddled together with children in their laps, out for a nip and a little gossip.

A sign is just a sheet of paper, after all, Kate thought. Still, it was uncomfortable.

"Maybe I should leave," she said.

Patrick caught her by the arm. "Sit down. Think about it. Bright red hair. Pixie of a girl. Big gold cross. You are clearly an Inwood girl bearing the sorrows of your people's history. Of course you eat fish, especially on Friday. And of course you're going to want a hal-fie to wash it down. It's Inwood."

"I haven't been a girl for a very long time, Patrick Harris."

"In Inwood, you'll always be that green girl fresh off the boat. Drink up. It's good for you."

Kate took a sip. The beer was dark.

"Like Murphy's back home," he said. "Do you remember it?"

Kate took another sip. It was. Murphy's was a point of pride for her father—a Catholic-owned brewery. It was the beer of the working class. If a pub didn't brew their own, they always had Murphy's. The beer had a thick creaminess with a bit of a sweet edge.

"Makes me homesick," Patrick said. "That's why I love it."

The food felt like it took an eternity. Ten minutes turned to twenty. They talked at length about the football finals at Croke Park—Offaly's chances versus Down's.

"My money's on Down," Kate said. "Two goals in three minutes from James McCartan and Paddy Doherty against Kerry last time out—and Kerry was undefeated."

"Paddy's a fine man. A fine captain. But Offaly—"

"Has no chance."

Mr. Brown, the bartender, brought them each another beer. When the talk turned to committee work for Good Shepherd's Harvest Festival and Dinner Dance, the fish-and-chips finally arrived. It was nearly midnight by then. Mrs. Brown brought the meal out herself, as if the delivery of food were a command performance at the Gaiety. Her makeup was bright. Her hair was whipped into a fresh bouffant with a bow at the crown. There was an air of Evening in Paris and Niagara Starch about her. Kate could not believe that she'd freshened up, as the Ladies would say, to deliver fish.

"Here we go!"

The woman was beaming, cheery—at midnight. That was a feat that was worthy of a standing ovation. Kate could barely keep her eyes open.

The fish was the classic "one and one," one cod loin and one serving of chips, served on top of brown paper bags. A mason jar of onion vinegar was placed between them; a handful of pickled pearl onions floated to the top. Just like at home.

Once she had served them, Mrs. Brown didn't leave. She stood for a moment, smiling. She seemed to be waiting for something.

"Thank you," Kate said. "Looks absolutely delicious."

"So, how is Her Elegance these days? Taking to the mantle well, is she?"

Kate was used to people asking her about the Wife. "She's lovely. Quite well. Busy, obviously."

"Obviously."

Mrs. Brown looked so very pleased, as if she had been given an unexpected gift. "Well. Eat up, then," she said, and left them to their dinner.

Patrick shook his head at Kate. "She nearly died of joy, chatting you up about the First Lady. You shouldn't have on with people like that. She's quite dear."

"It made her happy."

"And you, too. You're positively glowing."

Kate had already put a chip in her mouth and burned the roof of it. She didn't care. The chip was fried perfectly—crisp on the outside and soft on the inside. She took another sip of beer and broke the fish apart with her hands. The cod was sweet and fresh; the batter was golden and crisp. The vinegar provided the right sharp note of acid.

"You eat like you've been in prison," he said.

"Let us just say that our dear Maggie Quinn cannot be accused of being a good cook."

"And you?"

"Runs in the family, I'm afraid."

Mr. Brown delivered yet another round of beer. Patrick leaned back in the booth and smiled at Kate. "It's nice to eat together again. I miss those Sundays when Mam would have you come around."

"I miss the cake." Kate looked at her watch. "Almighty. I have to go to work in four hours. Saturday is always busy."

"Finish your beer."

"I may be drunk."

"That will be two of us."

"What would Father John say?"

"He'd order me a whiskey for courage."

The words made Kate's hands sweat. Patrick took a long pull of his beer and then put it down. "We should do this more often," he said. "On a regular basis. I've been thinking about it."

"And why?"

"Why?"

"Yes. Why have you been thinking of it? You're between telephone operators, aren't you? Another tossed you aside?"

"Kate, you're not making this easy."

"Patrick, you're making no sense. We see each other nearly every day. That's pretty regular."

"This is why I should have ordered the whiskey," he said. "Look. Yesterday, Maggie Quinn stopped by for a dice of pork and told me that your Mr. Charles wants you to start a shop with him. A mom-and-pop sort of thing, she said. The kind of thing married people do."

"Married?"

He raised his hand to silence her. "And when I heard that, I suddenly thought, I've lost her."

"Maggie Quinn has a very big mouth."

"Have I lost you, Kate?"

"Am I yours to lose?"

"I thought we should figure that out."

"You did? So it's decided, then? Just like that? We suddenly need to figure this out?"

"I thought you'd be pleased."

"And why exactly is that?"

"Well. You know. You have nobody. I have nobody. We're not getting any younger."

Kate felt embarrassed and angry—not prideful—that was what she told herself later. This was not about her vanity or her pride.

"So you feel sorry for me?"

"No—"

"Did you ever think that maybe I like the way my life is? I don't have to answer to a husband. I have a perfectly wonderful life, you know. Extraordinary, even."

Later, Kate blamed the beer. She wasn't used to drinking. But it really didn't matter what her reasons were.

"The Wife," she said. "Maison Blanche. Her Elegance." That's how the story began. Kate's lie was brilliant with imagined detail. "We're just like a couple of girls together. Chatting away." She didn't recognize the sound of her own voice. "I've known her for years, you know. Made her clothes forever. "

When she finished, Patrick Harris said quietly, "I'll take you home."

"Probably best," Kate said.

He knew, of course. There was no mixing—the Ladies were quite firm on that. Peg would have told him. It was a stupid lie.

Yet the Ladies got away with such grand stories—totally unbelievable and usually about their Blue Book friends—and no one seemed to care at all if a story was true or not. Why should Kate be any different? *No harm done,* she wanted to say.

But downtown was clearly not Inwood.

"I'm sorry," she said.

A stray lock of gray hair had fallen across Patrick's eyes, shading them. She couldn't tell what he was thinking, but Kate felt his disappointment as if it were her own.

It was after one a.m. when they left the pub. Patrick put his arm around Kate as they walked down the street. He was shaking. She hoped it was just the cold.

They stopped at his shop. "I need to get my coat."

Kate was surprised that she followed him inside and then up the stairs. She told herself that she didn't want to stand in the dark, waiting, on the street. Something could happen. People might see her. People would talk. People always talked. But she knew that wasn't the reason she followed. And so did he.

They walked up the dark stairs together in silence. The scent of bleach and blood was now faint. Kate held the rail to steady herself, even though she no longer felt drunk. When he opened the door to his apartment, the stairs were flooded with soft light. He stopped on the landing and turned to her, and held out his hand for her to take.

Kate stood on the landing. Peg had been gone for two months, but the apartment looked as if she'd just gone round to the shops. Her white sweater was folded on the back of her easy chair. Her button accordion was nearby. Kate had never seen so lonely a place.

Patrick kissed her with passion.

She kissed him back: embarrassed and chaste.

It was very awkward. They stood there for a moment, half in the light and half in darkness, unsure of what to do next.

"We are like fallen angels, you and I," he said. "That's what the poet would say. Not wise enough to be saved and not wise enough to be wicked and banished forever."

Patrick leaned in to kiss her again, but Kate turned away, just slightly.

Everything was moving too fast. *We're just friends,* she told herself, but knew that wasn't exactly true—probably never was true. More than anything, Kate wanted to lean in again, she wanted him to kiss her one more time—just so she could be sure that what she felt was not friendship but heat—but the moment had passed. He straightened his tie and stepped back.

"Well. Tomorrow, then," he said.

"Tomorrow."

As Kate walked down the stairs, Patrick Harris began to softly sing. *God save our gracious Queen. Long live our noble Queen.*

He sounded more sad than cruel, but the song was such an odd choice for this moment. The Queen lorded over everyone. Poor Ireland. Poor us.

Kate should have been angry. "Free Ireland," her father would have said.

She stopped at the bottom of the stairs with her hand on the door. She could still feel the warmth of his kiss. She hesitated and looked up at him, standing on the landing, singing. He was watching her. Light flooded over him, a store-bought sun, softening the lines in his face.

God Save the Queen, he sang, and his voice cracked, just a little. It took her breath away.

Patrick went into the apartment and gently closed the door behind him. She could hear him walk across the floorboards and then stop. Kate imagined him standing over Peg's chair, with its small, white sweater, a sleeping ghost.

Kate walked out into the cold night of Inwood alone, longing for the heady scent of peat smoke, the soft stars, and the damp air of a homeland that seemed now to be just a dream.

CHAPTER SIX

"Shocking pink was an invention of [Elsa] Schiaparelli and a symbol of her thinking. To be shocking was the snobbism of the moment."
— Bettina Ballard

$\mathcal{I}$t was Friday again. An entire week had passed, and Kate had not seen Patrick. Another day at Chez Ninon was nearly over. The scent of raw silk—the particular stench of dried mulberries and sea air, of heat and rot—clung to Kate's hands and hair. She'd spent the day making "feathers" from rare wild silk for Mrs. Astor's new gown.

"It must be completely covered," Mr. Charles said. "Miss Nona insists."

The project's impossible architecture was overwhelming, and Kate was happy for that. She hardly thought of Patrick at all that day. The silk was as iridescent as pearls; it didn't even seem to be real. Kate took a match to a thread just to make sure. True silk burns slowly. And this had. Then she had checked the bolt for its voice, the silk voice. Real silk sings in a very particular manner when the pieces are rubbed together. And it sang. It sang with the softness of wings. The silk was real—and daunting.

Raw silk stains easily and absorbs any bit of water, even humidity. The requirements of the project were completely absurd. Each "feather" must look absolutely real. It must be soft as down, which meant it had to be sheared and scissored into life by hand. Each feather needed to be so small that it would appear to have fallen from a chick. And there was very little silk on the bolt, so there could be no staining or waste.

Kate had worked since early morning, and there were still about 426 feathers left to make. When she was finished, the feathers had to be sewn onto chiffon with stitches so fine, they would be invisible. Mrs. Astor was coming by for a final fitting the next morning—and Mrs. Astor could not be denied.

Neither, though, could the Ladies. Miss Nona and Miss Sophie apologized profusely as they pulled Kate away from the project.

"We need to see you in the office."

"It's urgent," Miss Sophie said.

Kate never liked the word *urgent*. It always had an ominous ring to it.

The day was cloudy. The blue office had a murky cast. Kate sat gingerly on the edge of the pale settee. She had silk dust all over her. The light from the crystal chandelier overhead covered her in rainbows, but she was clearly in need of a bath.

Miss Sophie and Miss Nona were both dressed in Chanel suits—real Chanels. Miss Sophie's was black bouclé with a mandarin collar trimmed in gold braid. Miss Nona's was white and gold tweed, and a gold chain hung around her tiny waist. Gilded, as always, the two sat side by side at the faux Louis XIV desk and volleyed the conversation back and forth.

"We need you to tidy yourself up—"

"Yes. Please. Tidy up—"

"And then run to The Carlyle—"

"But you'll have to tidy up first—"

"The First Lady is at the hotel, waiting with a reporter. They're waiting for us—"

"They'll be very disappointed it's not us, so go into the sample room and choose something nice to wear. Something that says, 'Please don't be furious—'"

Kate had no idea what they were going on about. "What are you saying?"

"We trust you," Miss Sophie said.

When it came to the Ladies, *trust* was the only word that was more ominous than *urgent*. Miss Nona smiled and patted Kate's hand gently. "We trust you implicitly, but do find a nice outfit to wear in the sample room. Make sure it's something smart. And fix your face. You need to charm them."

"You want me to be interviewed?"

"No!" They nearly screamed the word.

"Heavens, no," Miss Sophie said. "We just want you to say you were sent to do the fittings."

"We'll call later and tell them we misunderstood."

Kate did not like the sound of this at all. "Couldn't you just tell them no?" The Ladies both laughed. Apparently, they could not. They also could not honor the request for a feature story about the Ladies themselves: "A personal look into the lives of the women behind the Woman."

The Ladies explained that they had led colorful lives—too colorful for some of their Blue Book society clients. Kate suspected that for once the Ladies were not exaggerating. They were not.

In 1928, Nona Hazelhurst McAdoo De Mohrenschildt Cowles Taylor Park and her partner, Sophie Meldrim Coy Shonnard, opened Chez Ninon because they were between husbands—and broke. A dress shop was the only solution. Both loved fashion, especially French fashion. Both had lived in Paris. Both were Blue Book. They knew everyone and knew what they wanted—but their collective pasts were dicey, at best.

Miss Sophie was the first wife of Ted Coy, one of the greatest football players to ever play the game and a literary model for F. Scott Fitzgerald. After a whirlwind romance—they met while skiing—Miss Sophie and Mr. Ted eloped. That act prompted Miss Sophie's father, Civil War veteran General Peter W. Meldrim, a self-proclaimed Southerner of the old school, to announce that theirs was a family not keen on eloping. Sophie was forced to promise her father she would not make that mistake again—and she did not.

In 1925, Miss Sophie became engaged to the elderly publisher Frank Munsey. Unfortunately, she was still married to Mr. Ted when she decided to give marriage another try. In a stroke of exceptionally bad luck, days before her divorce was final, the pending groom died, leaving Sophie relatively penniless while the bulk of his fifty-million-dollar fortune went to the Metropolitan Museum of Art.

Soon after, Miss Sophie married Munsey's equally elderly stockbroker, Horatio S. Shonnard. It was a church wedding. "I promised my family," Miss Sophie told the press. Her father was not amused.

Miss Nona, on the other hand, was the second daughter of

William Gibbs McAdoo, the Ku Klux Klan–endorsed California senator, Teapot Dome scandal participant, and forty-sixth secretary of the treasury, who saw World War I on the horizon and closed the U.S. stock exchange for four months, saving America from financial ruin. He'd had three wives, one of whom was President Wilson's daughter Eleanor Randolph Wilson.

Miss Nona married her first husband, a Russian diplomat, in 1917 at St. John's Church in Lafayette Square, in Washington, D.C. The *New York Times* reported that the bride's gown, which she designed herself, was "handsome enough for a presentation at court with a round skirt covered in tulle falling in billows from the waist to the floor." The church overflowed with lilacs and dogwood. Most of D.C. society was in attendance, including the President and the second Mrs. Wilson, as well as Vice President and Mrs. Marshall. The *Times* pointed out that Mrs. Wilson, who had just lost her mother, "lightened her deep mourning" for the occasion and wore a small black straw hat trimmed with the wings of dead magpies.

Not surprisingly, a hat made with the wings of dead, black birds, no matter how small the wings, is not easily overlooked at a wedding. Newspapers also reported that the tiny flower girl, Miss Sally McAdoo, dressed in a sweet gown of "frilled white organdy," wept continuously, copiously, disconcertingly, and violently throughout the ceremony. The groom died two years later.

Miss Nona's next husband was the faith healer Dr. Edward S. Cowles, psychiatrist and founder of the Body and Soul Clinic at St. Mark's-in-the-Bouwerie. While they were married, Cowles was tried for murder and arrested for operating a medical clinic and foundation without all the proper licenses but at a tidy profit of five hundred thousand dollars a year.

The rest of her husbands were unremarkable—but, given the combined backgrounds of Miss Sophie and Miss Nona, it was understandable that the request for an interview would be met with alarm.

"Isn't she usually at the Plaza?" Kate said.

"She should be in Washington," Miss Nona said.

Miss Sophie picked up a small, thin box covered with red stickers: PAR AVION—BY AIR MAIL. It was the Chanel. Finally. Kate wondered when it had arrived.

"Take pins. Remember, you came to do the fitting for the pink suit. If she asks, say we thought that she was kidding about the interview. We are uninteresting. We are boring. Do you understand?"

The address on the box had that particular handwriting of all Europeans. All those loops, always the same exact size, fascinated Kate. The perfect line through the sevens. French. Belgian. Italian. There was nothing to distinguish the personality of the sender. The penmanship was precise and uniform—like stitch after stitch. Chanel herself could have written that address.

"Kate?"

"Understood."

Kate had never worn anything from the sample room before. In fact, she wasn't sure if any of the back-room girls in the history of Chez Ninon ever had. The sample room was a walk-in closet nearly the same size as the showroom. It was stuffed with sample clothes from each season. There were plenty of choices for Kate, ranging from Charity Lunch dresses to Dinner with the In-Laws suits. Nothing, of course, said Lying to the First Lady While Look-ing Smart day dress. There was, however, an entire section marked MAISON BLANCHE. The samples were knockoffs of the Wife's knock-offs. That seemed like a good place to start. There was the salt-and-pepper wool tweed after Spring–Summer model number 3270 by Hubert de Givenchy, with its fringed neckline, three-quarter-length-sleeve jacket, and pencil-thin skirt. Then there was the navy-blue silk shantung with the three-button jacket—Mr. Charles de-signed that one. Very nice, indeed. But stuffed between the rest was Kate's favorite of them all—a vibrant blue-and-black checked tweed suit. The blue was so deep that it was nearly purple, and when set against the black, it was impossibly bright. The Wife had worn one just like it for a tour of a porcelain factory in Vienna that summer. The electric colors stood out in the Viennese factory that was filled with the pale pink and green porcelain that the country is known for.

Next to it was another copy, made in a tweed of emerald green set against a deep pearl gray. This suit, which was made for Miss Nona, would be perfect with Kate's gray Lilly Daché hat, her shoes, and the matching kid leather gloves. And, unlike the suit she had worn to work that day, it would not stink of rotting mulberry and raw silk.

Kate slipped on the jacket and looked in the three-way mirror. The color suited her very well. The gray brought out the pink in her cheeks and the deep auburn of her hair. She had finished the suit herself but never thought that she'd be the one wearing it. The en-tire time Kate was working on it, she imagined Miss Nona in Paris, sitting at a sidewalk café along the Champs-Élysées, madly sketch-ing the floppy bows, swooping hats, and leopard prints that she'd committed to memory at the Yves Saint Laurent show. The suit lent itself to the elegant practice of fashionable hoodwinking. It was perfect for Kate's visit to The Carlyle.

The back-room girls had their own powder room, but Kate used the one in the showroom. *Just this once,* she thought. Its counters looked like the cosmetics department at Bonwit Teller. There were lipsticks and powders in nearly every shade—and so many French perfumes. Kate wanted a splash of Chanel No. 5 to cover the scent of raw silk that clung to her, but there was none. So she dotted a little Je Reviens behind each ear and in the crook of her elbows. Then she frosted her lips pink, just because. *I look lovely,* she thought. And that made her blush.

The two-story penthouse at The Carlyle was a holdover from the President's bachelor days. Kate knew that from the movie magazines that some of the girls brought in to read with lunch. Marilyn Monroe had been seen there recently—that was the talk, but Kate would hear none of it.

The hotel wasn't far, just a short walk down to Fifth Avenue. She went through the revolving doors, and that was confusing to Kate. She expected the doors to open out into a lobby, but there was a bar and a café and a restaurant with white tablecloths, and no front desk. Kate couldn't even find an elevator. Finally, a doorman discovered her wandering around—"This will not do," he said—and took her by the arm and led her to the front desk. A call was made to the manager.

"Chez Ninon," she told him. "I'm expected."

"For?"

Kate took a deep breath. "A fitting."

The manager phoned the penthouse. "She said a fitting. Yes." He covered the phone with his hand. "You are not here for an interview?" he asked Kate.

"Tell them the Ladies sent me," she said.

"She said she is a representative of some women." The manager listened for a moment, then said, "Yes. As you wish." He hung up the phone. "They'll sort it out upstairs," he said to the bellman, and didn't address Kate at all. The sour-faced man then escorted her onto the elevator. He was not willing to let her out of his sight. He reminded her of a toy soldier, with his uniform and wooden air of authority. On the way up, Kate tried to be pleasant. "Must be like living in a movie, with room service and all the rest," she said.

The man looked at her and then through her. "Tradespeople normally ride the freight. Keep that in mind for your next appearance."

Kate felt sorry for the joyless people of the world.

The elevator doors opened, and the bellman walked Kate all the way to the apartment, holding her arm tightly, as if she were going to run away. He knocked on the door and waited for it to open before he turned to her and said, "The freight elevator is on your left."

Kate longed to smell the scent of silk on her skin again.

A tall man had opened the door. Blond. Nondescript. Secret Service, clearly.

"I'm Kate. From Chez Ninon."

The man wrote her name down and told her to wait in the entryway. It was a room by accident, a marble alcove surrounded by a series of white French doors that led into the penthouse. With the doors closed around her, it was like standing in a small white box. There was no place to sit. The air was stale and smelled of old cigarettes. The perfume Kate had taken from the Ladies' powder room quickly became cloying. It reminded her of a funeral home—that stale air of old lilies, starched dresses, and face powder—but she waited. She held Chanel's box in front of her like a Christmas gift.

Every now and then Kate could hear muffled voices behind the door, and she'd think about the reams of impossible silk waiting for her back at the shop. No one had even bothered to take her hat or coat. Kate pulled off her kidskin gloves; they were still a little stiff from the other day, when she was caught in the rain, but they felt as though they'd stretch back into shape eventually. She was wearing a beautiful suit, and that was all that mattered.

Kate looked at her watch again. It was now nearly five p.m., but still she had to wait. Just wait—that was what she was told. They knew she was there. She couldn't just leave, despite the fact that there were 426 silk feathers waiting to be made. She tried to imagine how long that would take, how many feathers an hour she could create without getting sloppy.

And then there was Patrick Harris. Standing there waiting, with nothing to do, made it difficult not to think about him, too. It was awful that they'd parted so badly. She could hardly believe that it had been an entire week since she'd seem him, since they'd had dinner at Mrs. Brown's pub. Kate had been so embarrassed. She even went to church late on Sunday. She stood in the back, by the marble of St. Patrick himself, a very popular spot with the old-timers, just to avoid being seen.

Kate told herself she didn't really miss him—*We're just friends*—nor did she miss Mrs. Brown's kindness, nor the quiet of the secret pub, nor the onions in the vinegar and the way the fish was fried so that it was crisp, golden, and still moist.

All these thoughts piled up one on top of the other, and her heart began to race. "I need to leave," she said, which surprised her. Her knees were aching. Her shins again, too. Her hands were swollen. She wanted to just sit somewhere, anywhere. Kate felt a crushing panic, and so she did the one thing she knew she shouldn't do. She knocked.

"Anyone there?"

The man was back again.

"They'll be with you shortly."

"May I sit? Maybe just move a chair out here?"

He acted as if he didn't hear her. He turned to close the door, but Kate caught his arm. "My knees feel older than God. You must know how that feels. Don't you?"

He frowned and removed her hand. *Another joyless man,* Kate thought, but he led her into another white room, and this one, thankfully, had chairs. She could sit.

"Don't touch anything," he said. "Don't get anything dirty."

"Surely not," she said, and sat on the edge of a soft chair with her hands on her knees, Chanel's cardboard box perched on her lap. Although the room was quite large, it felt cramped. There were boxes from all sorts of stores piled along all the walls. They were from all the best places—Bergdorf's, primarily. Kate tried not to count them. *They can't all belong to the Wife.*

The room reeked of cigarettes; the ashtrays were overflowing. *They could be anybody's cigarettes,* she told herself. Although she knew that probably wasn't true.

The room was dramatic. The windows were two stories high and overlooked the city. In sheer contrast to the piles of boxes and overflowing ashtrays, the decor was a designer's attempt at pristine elegance. The pale-yellow walls were trimmed in white. The furniture was all white. Even the carpet was white. It was not the kind of room you could live a life in. It made Kate feel hollow.

She looked over her shoulder and out the windows. All of Manhattan seemed to be moving toward the end of its day. Cranky yellow cabs, sleek black sedans—from that height, the city seemed to whisper below her.

Suddenly Kate could hear the voices in the next room. And then she heard that laugh, so like a little girl's. The Wife.

"In fifth grade, 'Behave or Else' was my middle name," she said.

The reporter was a man. "I don't believe it," he said.

"It's true."

They must have stepped away from the door for a moment. She could hear them talking, but not clearly. And then Kate heard, "Thoroughbred—that's what they called me. I was brought up to be like a racehorse, but I was too wild and good for nothing."

A few minutes passed and the door opened. It was the Secret Service agent again.

"You're no longer needed," he said.

Kate scanned the horizon. As the sun slipped behind the graying buildings of New York, the edges of them seemed to catch fire. Kate had waited all that time. Again. And was stood up. Again.

What about the Chanel?

"Miss, I have to ask you to leave."

"Yes. Of course." The room was very quiet. "Please tell her that Chez Ninon can start the fittings tomorrow. For the Chanel suit."

"Tell the secretary on your way out."

"Of course," Kate said, but there was no secretary to tell.

She found the freight elevator without a problem.

CHAPTER SEVEN

"Fashion anticipates... elegance is a state of mind."
——Oleg Cassini

*O*n the way home, Kate couldn't stop thinking about it. *Thorough-bred?* The thought of people raising children to think of themselves as beasts infuriated her. She couldn't imagine saying something like that to Little Mike. What good did all that racehorse training do? That willful girl may have grown up to become the most famous woman in the world, but she sounded so sad and lonely.

Unfortunately, Kate didn't finish Mrs. Astor's gown that night. She would later say that she wasn't exactly sure why. She'd run all the way back to Chez Ninon from The Carlyle with every intention of working for as long as it took to make up for her absence. But when she arrived, she looked up and could see that the shop was dark. The entire second floor of Chez Ninon was deserted. There wasn't even a light on in the back room. Kate looked at her watch. It was half past nine. *Everyone's home,* she thought, *except me.*

For a while, Kate stood outside, looking at the building. It seemed to be just another building on another street crowded with offices and shops. It didn't seem to be a place where dreams were sewn one stitch at a time or small miracles could be made with lace on lace. She couldn't bear to leave the Chanel behind in those darkened rooms, and so she didn't. Kate began to walk.

The clouds that she'd seen roll in cut the city off at its knees. The a cappella music of night, the insistence of sirens and sorrow—the push, push, push of it all—seemed closer and louder, like a heartbeat in her head. Street by street, corner by corner—Kate wasn't above it. She was part of it. The texture of the city, the warp and weft of it, was hers. The turned-up collars of couples rushing to the subway, the worn cotton shirt of the grocer rolling down the heavy metal gate as he closed for the night, the girls on the way to Times Square—coatless, without gloves or a hat, their dresses so tight they could barely move. This was Kate's world now, all of it. Her home was no longer Cobh. Nor was it the New York of those who stood before the mirrors at Chez Ninon, impatient and squirming, eyeing themselves three times over and thinking about the next beautiful gown and then the next. Kate's world was that of the hot dog vendors, with their torn peacoats, the carriage drivers, in their fraying top hats, and the police, in their rough wool and scuffed shoes.

Life under the clouds. It was tattered and dirty—and yet, somehow beautiful. It was her world, with all its pulse and pain. Tomorrow she'd have to explain what had happened at The Carlyle. What had happened was simple—Kate sat down. For the first time since she'd left Cobh, she'd sat down like a lady, not like a back-room girl. And when Kate sat down at The Carlyle, everything changed. Miss Nona would not understand at all. Miss Sophie would think that Kate had truly lost her mind.

She didn't mean to sit. She was on her way out. Kate had taken the freight elevator, as she was told to. But the room the elevator opened onto was so elegant, with a large, gilded mirror and a crystal chandelier. It felt like a small parlor in a great country manor, like the Fota House, back on the Island, with its botanical gardens, exotic zoo, and tales of its city of ghosts. She wanted to sit for a moment in a beautiful place in her beautiful borrowed suit. The chairs were soft leather. The logs in the fireplace burned without smoke. There were fresh red roses in Chinese vases on small, dark wood tables.

Kate had sat in beautiful rooms in Cobh, even in Dublin, and no one had ever denied her entrance. She certainly didn't intend to spend the entire evening there. She just wanted to collect herself. The room was warm. She slid off her coat. She placed her Lilly Daché hat, so very French, and her kidskin gloves on the table next to her. They looked so grand there—like they belonged. She kept Chanel's box on her lap—it wouldn't do to lose it.

"Tea?"

The young man wore a handsome tuxedo, European cut, with thin satin lapels. He served her tea from a silver pot and poured it into real china cups with saucers. There was a silver pitcher of cream and perfect cubes of sugar on the tray as well.

"Cake?"

Of course, cake.

"And sherry?"

Kate thought of sherry as something that went into a trifle along with Bird's custard mix, but she was certainly willing to try it. She moved Chanel's box from her lap and placed it behind her like a pillow. She draped her coat over it.

"May I take this?" he asked.

"No. But thank you for asking."

"Very well."

The waiter went back into the dining room and returned with a small white linen tablecloth, which he placed over the back of the chair, covering her coat and the package from Chanel.

"This will be our secret," he said.

The tea was lovely: a smoky, solid black. There was plate after plate of so many delights: tiny jam tarts with butter-cookie crusts, small chocolate cups filled with some sort of raspberry brandy, and exquisite white cakes covered with pink almond paste and topped with the most delicate sugared violets. Kate had never seen anything like it before. And the sherry was very smooth.

A woman in a beautiful suit can go anywhere, Kate thought.

She knew she should leave. She still had so much work to do. But just one more. One more cup of tea. One more small cake. One more splash of sherry. One more moment. It wasn't so much the food and drink but the world of that room that kept Kate firmly in her chair. Fabric, line, color—the very spark of life swirled around her. Men. Women. Children. Some seemed to have tumbled out of a fashion magazine; they had a liquid grace about them. Some skittered across the room in heels so high that every step pitched them forward, closer to the ground.

He who seeks beauty will find it. Schwinn said that. He could see beauty where no one else could. To him, age didn't matter. Looks didn't matter. It was line, color, and movement that mattered. Fabric and texture that was stylish or interesting captured his heart. It didn't matter who wore it or why; all that mattered was beauty and grace. *Clothes are the only armor the body has.*

The girls called his sayings "Schwinnisms." Most laughed at him, but not Kate. She understood. Beauty was everywhere—especially in this room in The Carlyle. It was in a chinchilla wrap with red leather gloves, and in a full-length black sable with black velvet pumps. She could see the hours that went into each gown and dress and jacket, all that close work, all that puzzling over one thing or another, all that skillful stitching and well-thought-out design. Kate had never seen so many lovely pieces in one place. So many hours went into each piece, so many lifetimes.

"Mademoiselle, will there be anything else? Will you be joining us for dinner?"

On the silver tray, the young man was carrying a single glass, a *coupe*—although it wasn't filled with champagne. Kate wasn't sure what it was, but it was such a beautiful color. Rose? Peach? It was difficult to decide what shade it was. She wasn't even sure what kind of drink it was.

"It's a Pink Squirrel," he said.

"And that is?"

"Apricot. Cream, mostly. Would you like one?"

Kate could think of nothing more lovely. She took the glass from his tray. Took a sip. The man looked alarmed. Kate reassured him.

"It's just wonderful. I've never had anything this wonderful before. Please thank everyone."

She patted his hand, and the man stiffened.

"What room, mademoiselle?"

Room?

He wanted to put her charges on a room. Kate was mortified. At Chez Ninon, everything was given to the Ladies. Cakes and champagne—it was all a gift. Kate had $2.03 in her purse.

"The room, mademoiselle?"

"Penthouse."

The young man looked uneasy. Kate fled. She grabbed her coat and Chanel's box and ran out of The Carlyle, into the city. She couldn't bear to go back to work, and so when she finally found herself sitting on the A train, her heart was racing. She didn't know what to do.

Last stop. In spite of the kiss, or maybe because of it, Kate needed to see Patrick. The Carlyle, the Wife—the whole evening had been so confusing; she felt lost. She just wanted to hear his voice; it always calmed her. But as soon as Kate opened the door to Mrs. Brown's pub, she knew she'd made a mistake. The pub was a completely different place than it had been the week before. It was smoky as a dream and reeked of stout. There were so many people. Couples everywhere. The sign that read NO LADIES ALLOWED had been replaced with another—SESSIONS NIGHT.

Back home at Fogarty's Pub, every Thursday was sessions night, which meant that everyone who could play the old tunes came together to do so. The place was always packed. In America, the tradition continued; there was barely enough room to stand. The pub was stifling.

Kate took off her coat, but there was no cloakroom to check it in, like there was at The Carlyle. There were no quiet waiters either. There was no quiet, at all. In the center of the pub was a man sitting on a chair with a *bodhrán,* a drum as round as a plate. Kate had never seen a grown man playing a drum like that before. It was the sort of thing young boys back home carried in parades. It sounded like distant thunder. Around him there was a fiddler, a flautist, and a somber man playing shinbones like ivory castanets. The man with the drum had a voice as deep as church bells. The floors and the windows shook. Even the beers on the bar seemed to hum.

Mr. Brown recognized Kate from the Friday before and poured her a half pint without asking. Some of the musicians were obviously from Cork. Their accents were unmistakable. She took a sip of beer and noticed that Patrick Harris was leaning on the bar farther down. He stood next to a woman that Kate hadn't seen before. Her platinum-blond hair was swept into an updo. A chain of fake pearls clipped her black cashmere sweater around her neck. She was probably a telephone operator; she looked like a tarted-up alley cat.

Kate had not expected to see Patrick Harris with another woman. The cream. The apricot. The sherry. The cakes. Even that sip of beer. It had all been too much, and Kate felt it rise in her throat when Patrick leaned in to the woman and whispered something. Kate tossed a nickel on the bar for Mr. Brown and was turning to leave when Patrick saw her. He smiled, which confused Kate. He seemed pleased to see her in spite of the other woman and pushed his way through the crowd. The woman at the bar watched him go. She had on thick eyeliner and frosted white lipstick—*What a sight,* Kate thought.

When Patrick reached Kate, he pulled her close. Chanel's package was wedged between them.

"This is a stunningly pleasant surprise," he said, and leaned over the box and kissed Kate on both cheeks. It was as if the other night had never happened. Kate wasn't sure what kind of welcome she expected, but now she felt foolish. Patrick was wearing cologne that smelled like something her father would wear to church: old-fashioned and lush with sandalwood. It wasn't something a butcher would wear, Kate thought. The woman at the bar was watching them so intently, as if they were the finals at Croke Park. *Down or Offaly?*

"I should go," she said, but Patrick couldn't quite hear her. The music was too loud. Even the floor was shaking.

He shouted over the din.

"Did you get my peace offering? Am I forgiven, then?"

"What?"

"Slipped it under your door. Let's go outside. I can't hear."

The musicians slid from a ballad into a reel. The crowd erupted into dance. They were boisterous and bumping against Kate and Patrick.

"I have to go," Kate said, and clutched the Chanel box even tighter.

Patrick stepped back a moment and looked at her closely. "Have you eaten? You're looking a tad nawful."

"Not like that prostitute, I suppose?"

Kate didn't mean to say that out loud, but the woman just wouldn't stop staring at them.

"That was uncalled for."

Kate suddenly felt ill. She pushed past Patrick and into the bathroom. He followed her in.

"A little privacy, please," she said.

"Kate. This is the Gents'."

Chanel's package fell onto the floor. Kate tried to pick it up, but the room felt as if it banked hard to the right. Kate dropped her coat and leaned over the sink. *Óinseach. What a fool.* Patrick Harris rubbed her back gently. "Cough it up, girl. You'll be fine." He wetted a paper towel and placed in on the back of her neck. It felt good. "You know, you're very pretty when you're jealous."

She gave him the surly look that he deserved, and he laughed, obviously quite pleased. The water on the back of her neck made her feel a little better. Or maybe it was just the sound of his laughter. "You don't have to enjoy this so very much," she said.

"Been a long time since a girl fancied me enough to heave. It's quite a touching gesture."

A man opened the door and saw the two of them leaning over the sink.

"Give us a minute?" Patrick said.

The man closed the door quickly. Kate felt even worse.

"Wonderful. I'm sure this little event will be in the church bulletin now."

"Probably right under the photos of the Knights of Columbus pancake breakfast."

Kate wasn't quite in the mood for jokes. She was sweating hard. She took a handful of cold water and drank it. "I'm sorry. Your girl must think I'm quite the sow—"

"She's not my girl. She's just a girl. Actually, I was hoping you'd come."

Kate leaned up against the wall. Patrick picked up her coat from the floor, shook it out, and folded it gently over his arm. He picked up the Chanel box and blew on it just to make her laugh. He stood there smiling at her like Peg's boy, a good boy, the kind of boy who doesn't forget his mother's birthday. He was an old-fashioned boy, always courtly, even in the Gents'.

"Patrick," she said. The rest of the sentence was more difficult to say; there were so many choices for how it could end: "I don't want to lose you" or "I don't want to lose myself" or "I don't know if I have time to love anyone properly" or "I'm not the sort of person people love." But the way Kate said his name seemed to tell Patrick everything he needed to know. She could see it in his face—a trace of disappointment, and then that smile.

"We're fine now, Kate?" he said. "Sorry I overstepped."

Friends again, she thought. But wasn't sure that was what she wanted at all.

"Well, then," he said. "Nice suit. How have you been?"

He was trying to make her smile, but she couldn't. He put his arm around her. "Let me walk you home. Where's your hat and gloves?"

The last Kate remembered, they were on the rosewood table in front of the fireplace at The Carlyle, looking as if they belonged. But they didn't belong, and neither did she. And now her very best hat and her beautiful, soft kidskin gloves were gone. She took the package from Patrick. "I'll be fine. Go back and have fun."

Kate gently pushed her way past him, into the crowd and then into the night, alone.

CHAPTER EIGHT

"You gotta have style. It helps you get up in the morning. It's a way of life. Without it you're nobody."

—Diana Vreeland

A hot bath was what Kate needed, a good, long soak, but it was little comfort. Steam filled the small, white room: a poor heaven. Windows kept the stars at bay. She couldn't imagine what Mrs. Brown thought of her going into the Gents'. Patrick's peace offering made her feel even worse. It had been slid under her door. Inside the large manila envelope there was a poem by Yeats that Patrick had copied out carefully, calligraphy style, on cream parchment paper with deep, black ink. No one had ever done such a lovely thing for Kate before.

Had I had the Heaven's embroidered cloths,
Enwrought with golden and silver light

Kate hadn't thought of Yeats since her days at National School, when she'd had to memorize one of his poems. She'd chosen this very one because it was short, although at the time she'd thought it was overly grand. *Enwrought* was just a fancy word for *embroidered,* after all. As soon as she'd passed her exams, she'd forgotten it.

> *I would spred the clothes under your feet.*
> *But I, being poor, have only my dreams:*

Now she couldn't get it out of her head. Outside Kate's window, the pub crowd was stumbling home. William Butler Yeats as a way of apology. Only Patrick Harris would do such a thing.

> *Tread softly because you tread on my dreams.*

Kate's heaven was poor indeed. There was no fabric embroidered with golden or silver light. Water pipes ran from floor to ceiling, exposed and rusting. The painted cast-iron bathtub was peeling. And yet, there was Yeats and his exquisite vision of the world; there was some comfort in that.

Kate meant to close her eyes for just a moment but slipped into sleep. Then slipped further, nearly under the water. It was a laugh that woke her—slurred and squealing outside her window. Maggie, very late and quite drunk, was coming home with Big Mike in tow. Kate jumped out of the cold tub. She couldn't stop shaking. Her thin terry-cloth robe smelled of bluing and was stiff. It felt harsh against her skin. She put it on, tied it tightly, and sat on the chipped bathroom floor.

The bare lightbulb, the stained walls, and the rusting pipes that moaned nearly continuously—*This is my life,* she thought. *Life under the clouds.* It suddenly did not feel beautiful and broken, but merely broken. That was when Kate decided that she would copy Chanel's toile even before the suit was made. It wasn't done, but she didn't care. If the Ladies found out, she could be fired. If she ruined the toile accidentally, she could be fired. But to make the pink suit for Maggie was an irresistible challenge. This pink suit was real art, after all. Not a copy of a copy. *My brush with greatness,* she thought.

She didn't have much time. Kate cleared off her worktable by the fistful, heaping things upon other things. She put on her white cotton gloves, the ones she always used when handling fine fabrics, and rolled up the sleeves of her old bathrobe.

Chanel always worked in a suit, with hat and pearls—the Ladies had told her that, but Kate didn't have time to care. Chanel's box had been opened by the Ladies and resealed with just a single strip of cellophane tape. Kate pulled the tape up carefully. The muslin toile was still wrapped in white tissue paper embossed with Chanel's name and the double-C logo. There was a wax seal. If Kate was very careful, no one would know that she'd opened the box. She gently slid the toile out of its wrapping. The seal remained unbroken.

Good. Fine. Perfect.

It was difficult to believe it was really Chanel's toile in her hands. At Chez Ninon, they'd never received a line-by-line replica of Chanel's work before; there was something about it that was profound. It had gravity to it. Kate now knew that her copy of the toile wasn't even close, was a cheap imitation. *Eegit,* she thought. She'd felt so unbelievably proud of what a wonderful job she thought she'd done. But now Kate could see that the Wife would have known immediately that Kate's effort was only an imitation. She was, after all, a very good client of Chanel.

The toile held a faint, musky scent of roses and cigarettes. The muslin was a very particular weight and was the color of old ivory. Chanel probably had her own muslin made especially for the bouclé. It was basted together with golden thread. *Enwrought*, Kate thought. Holding the Chanel in her hands, she suddenly realized that she was no better than a trained monkey. If a designer always used a particular stitch, then Kate used it. If a designer rolled the collar in a certain way, Kate did that too. At Chez Ninon, you did whatever it took to make a garment seem "real." But in the end, even if the copy you made looked exactly the same as the original—with the same material and the same perfect stitch—a suit, like this pink suit, was only nearly right. *Knockoffs*, as they were called. *Off*, like meat left lying in the sun.

What made a Chanel was Chanel. It was, quite simply, the woman herself. This pink suit was not just a suit: it was Chanel's vision. It was complicated and yet seemingly simple. It was art: beautiful, and overwhelming.

Kate held the toile to her face for a moment, weighing it and committing the weight to memory. In order to create a proper pattern, she would have to adjust the cut of her own toile accordingly and make allowances for her own fabric, which was rough and cheap. *The world is filled with so many things that back-room girls can't even imagine,* she thought. Things like a toile that is soft as cashmere.

Kate dismantled Chanel's toile, the test garment, so very carefully. Every stitch—and there were hundreds—she snipped with her sharp scissors. When finally done, she ironed the pieces flat.

Each part was like a piece of a puzzle. She placed them over a few yards of yellow calico that she'd been saving for a summer dress. It was not the right weight at all, but it was all she had. Kate pinned the pieces down and sharpened her scissors again. She had to be careful. One snag. One stain. One slip. The muslin could be ruined so easily. But Kate cut. And cut.

The heavens' embroidered cloths,
Enwrought with golden and silver light.

While she worked, Kate could hear everything in the apartments above and below her. The restless, creaking floorboards, the soft vibrato of sleep, the words of lovers scattered like dice—there were no secrets at that hour. Kate could hear the rasp of her own breath and the newspaper boy's swing and thud. The milkman's truck was a rattle of glass bottles. Then doors clicked. Dogs barked. Brakes squealed. It was morning.

You tread on my dreams.

Kate basted Chanel's toile back together as quickly as she could, but she made sure that each stitch removed was replaced exactly. There could be no mistakes. It was bad enough that the gold thread Kate had was not exactly the same; it wasn't silk, but it was the best she could do. The Ladies would not be pleased if they thought Kate had copied the toile. It wasn't done, especially with a toile as important as this one. But Kate couldn't help herself. It was such a beautiful suit, and a Chanel. Kate had to understand it stitch by stitch.

When a taxi stopped outside the building and gave two honks,

Kate finally finished. She carefully folded Chanel's toile and slipped it back into the tissue paper and into the package. And then she fell fast asleep.

Miss Sophie was not angry—she said that repeatedly—but she was surprised.

Kate was late for the first time. *Ever.* And Mrs. Astor's girl was furious about the dress. She actually wagged her finger at Miss Sophie when she came round and found that it was unfinished. "It was like a little fat sausage in my face."

Miss Sophie had missed her breakfast, so the temptation to lunge was apparently quite keen.

Then there was The Carlyle. There had been a delivery that morning—on a Saturday morning, no less. It was addressed to Kate. It was a box marked PERSONAL.

"Kate. What has gotten into you?"

That seemed to be a very popular question.

The Ladies sat in their office at the faux Louis XIV desk, with the box from The Carlyle between them. Mr. Charles sat next to Kate on the silk settee, his perfectly manicured hands folded as if in prayer. He was Kate's boss, after all. Miss Sophie had made everyone tea, but it had grown cold.

"Man trouble, is it?"

"No."

"The butcher? Peg Harris's son?"

"Patrick?"

"Yes."

"No."

"Are you ill?"

Another very good question. Seeing the box from The Carlyle had made her breathless.

"No."

"This is addressed to you."

"Yes."

"Kate, you can tell me if something's wrong. You really can. Mr. Charles, Miss Nona, and I will always help you."

Kate believed her. Since the beginning, everyone at Chez Ninon had been so kind. Still, she picked up the box and stood. "The tea was lovely, thank you."

"You didn't drink it."

"Mrs. Astor's gown won't sew itself."

Kate turned to walk back to her desk.

"Kitty?" Mr. Charles said.

She wanted to stop.

"Kitty?"

Kate knew that if she didn't turn around, Mr. Charles would be cross with her. Maybe even send her home. *Kate. Just Kate. Not Kitty.*

Box in hand, Kate walked down the long, narrow hallway that separated the Ladies from the back-room girls, past the rows of empty dressing rooms, richly appointed with an eye to serene elegance, and through the staging room, filled with racks of clothes waiting for delivery or a final fitting, past the sample room, where the green tweed suit she'd borrowed for The Carlyle was back on its hanger for a good airing out, and into the back room, with the rest of the girls. The closer Kate got to the workroom, the louder the hum was. When the carpeting ended and the floor turned to concrete, she felt she was where she belonged. The clattering of dozens of sewing machines, the gossip and laughter, the din of work—it was such a comfort. In the back room, Kate wasn't a second-class citizen. No one had the touch like she did. If the Ladies and Mr. Charles were angry, they'd get over it soon enough. She might not be Chanel, but they needed her.

Kate placed the box from The Carlyle underneath her workbench; it could wait. Maison Blanche could not. She turned the iron on. Mr. Charles had asked her to press the toile. Maeve was busy with another fitting. The first fitting for the pink suit was in ten minutes. At least, it was scheduled to begin in ten minutes. So much would depend on traffic, and the Holy Dead of St. Patrick's, of course.

Our Chanel, Kate thought as she ironed the toile into place, seam by seam. The loosely fitted box jacket with matching blouse and A-line skirt were more complicated than she had even imagined. When finished, the front of the jacket would appear to be made from a single piece of fabric—but it was actually a series of rectangles pieced together. Since the bouclé was handmade and easily unraveled, given to shedding with the least provocation, construction would be a daunting task. With Chanel, nothing was ever easy.

Chanelisms, Chaneleries—the fashion magazines all had their name for them; her construction techniques were legendary. The jacket would take more than seventy hours to make. The lining must first be quilted to the fabric before it was cut. Then there were the buttonholes. To be Chanel, they had to be sewn twice. Each one must be embroidered on the bouclé side and then bound on the lining side. Then the two must be basted together. It was insanely difficult to do properly because each side must be sewn with a very fine silk thread. The thread was so fine, and so fragile, that you couldn't pull it through the eye of a needle unless you dipped it in beeswax for strength.

The buttons themselves were also a surprise. They looked manufactured but were actually made by hand. Each was an ornate metal cap set in a fabric-lined ring. Each had to be tacked in with stitches so fine, they would be invisible to the naked eye.

And, finally, the fabrics were always difficult, at best. The blouse was to be made of a very particular silk charmeuse that was too delicate to be made into a shirt, and impossible to sew without damaging, but would feel wonderful next to the skin. For the suit itself, the bouclé was so loosely woven and very fragile —too fragile to wear often. But the softness of the cloth was incomparable, so it must be stitched together with magic and hope. When photographed, Kate knew the suit would appear practical and durable. It would appear conservative. But in reality, it was incredibly fragile and decadent. Everything about it was luxurious and sensuous—and that was its secret.

Copy or not, to make it one time was impossible. To make it twice was unimaginable. Wonderfully unimaginable.

CHAPTER NINE

"The planning was constant, the logistical invasion of every country she visited, every party she attended—the cloth, the weather, the sensitivity of the people and what they wanted to see her in."
—Oleg Cassini

*W*hen the Wife finally arrived, only two hours late for her fitting, Mr. Charles told Kate that she did not look like a Thoroughbred at all. Her fingernails were bitten down to the quick. Her thumb was ragged and bleeding. Barefoot, she fidgeted in the loosely basted toile. But as soon as she stood at the three-way mirror, everything changed. The elegance. The bearing.

"There must be royal blood somewhere," he said.

Cork, Kate thought. In ancient times, it was a place overrun with kings. High kings, they called themselves. There were so many of them, and so few commoners, that King Niall of the Nine Hostages traveled to Wales to kidnap some people to rule over—including St. Patrick himself.

What kind of place has to steal its own saints?

"Cork," Kate said.

"Cork?"

"Very royal."

Mr. Charles laughed for a long time.

The Secret Service, pigeon gray from head to toe, arrived first. The Holy Dead of St. Patrick's catacombs had been forsaken that day. The Wife stood at the front door, wrapped in the silk air of Chanel No. 5 eau de parfum. The scent of ylang-ylang and may rose made Kate long for spring. The press was waiting in the hallway, of course.

The back-room girls were hovering by the dressing rooms. "Clever," Maeve said. "Putting on a public show about buying American."

"I need all of you to get back to work," one of the agents said.

It could have been the same man from The Carlyle. Kate wasn't sure. They all looked alike. *How could the Wife tell them apart?*

"Girls. Now. Back to work," he said, and clapped his hands as if corralling children.

"Give it a rest," Maeve said. "What are we going to do? Hem her?"

In the showroom, the Ladies were holding the front doors open for the Wife's grand entrance. Miss Nona was shouting at the press, "Shoo! Shoo!" Miss Sophie was laughing. Behind her was Mrs. Molly Tackaberry McAdoo, the Wife's saleswoman and Miss Nona's niece. Miss Molly was blowing kisses in the air at the press while her tiny black-and-white fluffy dog, Fred, circled the crowd, looking for treats. *Such a circus*, Kate thought, but the Wife seemed quite calm about it all. She looked like she always did in the photographs: the hair, the eyes, and the smile. She rarely changed. Everyone was gawking. Kate didn't know why she was gawking at her, too. She knew the Wife's face as well as she knew her own. Didn't everybody? Although, truthfully, Kate preferred the photos with the husband in them, too. They always seemed to be on the verge of telling each other a secret, leaning toward each other as if in orbit, one drawn in by the other's gravity.

The Wife stopped in the doorway for a moment. She moved her right foot slightly forward. Straightened her back. A quick tug adjusted the line of her camel coat. Chin down. Eyes up. A tilt of the head. And then she smiled. She turned her head slowly, panning from left to right, like a cat following the sun. Cameras flashed. And the world had another twenty pictures exactly like the previous twenty.

"Show's over, girls," the agent said.

"It is a bit of a show, isn't it?" Kate whispered to Maeve.

"It's as if the Virgin Mary herself is shopping for a little splash-out."

When the Wife finally made her way to the three-way mirror with Mr. Charles, Mrs. Molly Tackaberry McAdoo and the tiny black-and-white dog in tow, she told the Ladies how lucky they were that they weren't in the gift-wrap business. She'd written an article about that once, back in her days as the Inquiring Camera Girl for the *Washington Times-Herald*.

"Do you know it takes three people to gift wrap a baby grand piano?"

"Fascinating."

"Amazing."

"True?"

"True."

Kate suspected that it wasn't true, but the Ladies loved the story so much that Miss Nona told it to the back-room girls several times before she and Miss Sophie left for the day. What was true was this—the Wife had been at Chez Ninon for about an hour, but that was the only thing anyone could agree on.

She seemed taller or much shorter than usual; she was more tired or well rested.

She whispered like Marilyn Monroe or growled like Katharine Hepburn.

She had clearly put on at least five pounds or had absolutely lost ten.

She flirted with Mr. Charles shamelessly or ignored him completely.

Even the color of her lipstick couldn't be agreed upon. Pink? Red?

Chanel No. 5 eau de parfum—that was all Kate knew for sure. The toile, still warm from the heat of her body, reeked of it.

"Lucky toile," Mr. Charles said.

The fitting had taken much longer than usual. Maeve's marks were off. Mr. Charles was gracious about it, though. It really wasn't Maeve's fault, at least not the way she told the story.

"Like a wasp, she was. The sheer buzz of her—it was unnerving. Moving back and forth from one foot to another. My mouth was full of pins—you can't chalk a Chanel, as you well know—so I'm pinning and basting and rebasting to get the marks right, and she never stops moving. And there's ashes from those infernal cigarettes tumbling down my smock—it's just like cinders rolling down your back, mind you—and I've got this needle in my hand, and she never thinks for one moment that just one bit of blood would ruin the entire thing, just one drop from a pinprick, and we'd all have to start over again. Does she think that?"

Maeve always provided her own answers, so this really wasn't a question.

"Of course she doesn't."

Everyone nodded. It was always best to agree with Maeve.

After the Wife left, they sat around the long cutting table in the back, going over the details of the suit. The workroom was stuffed with dozens of dressmaker's models; each one was the correct size and shape for a Chez Ninon client. Their names were written across the backs of the mannequins in huge block letters: PALEY, BRUCE—and all the rest. These Blue Book–society mannequins—silent, headless, and in one state of undress or another, with their sleeves hanging undone or their hems ripped away—lurked in the workroom, making the place feel crowded and small. But they were a necessary evil, the only way to get the clothes fitted properly and with minimum fuss. There was an entire storage room filled with them. Kate hated to go back there; it was like some sort of nightmarish cocktail party. Mannequins were grouped not alphabetically, but according to what page they appeared on in the Social Directory, which was exceedingly difficult, because the section called *Married Maidens* was cross listed by both married and maiden names, just in case of divorce.

The Ladies never worried about filing the Wife's; it had been in perpetual use since the campaign days.

"Let's get started," Mr. Charles said, and cleaned off the cutting table. Kate made tea. Maeve liberated, as she liked to say, another box of "Ladies' chocolates" from Miss Nona's office.

"Maeve, that's the second box this week. If Miss Nona finds out—" Kate said.

"She won't notice. How many times did she tell the same piano gift-wrap story? Four times? The old bird is slipping a bit. It's bad for her diabetes, anyway."

Schwinn unrolled the sketch the Wife had made of the suit. Kate laid out Chanel's notes next to it.

Mr. Charles began. "Accessories, Schwinn?"

"No hat at first. Most women buy a suit and then find the hat. Not many can afford both a hat and a new suit. But a hat, later, is a must."

"Halston?"

"Of course."

"We should have him make two hats. When she sweats her way through one of them, the backup will match. It would be nice if one had contrasting piping trim around the crown, but that's my take on it. He'll have his own."

Maeve closed her eyes, as if about to nod off to sleep. It had been a long day for everyone. Kate warmed her tea. These meetings could go on for hours.

"She asked for three blouses," Mr. Charles said. "Each one needs to be a different style, but all should be of the same fabric. She wondered what I thought about black instead of the blue that we ordered. What do I think about black?"

Schwinn looked at the sketch again. "I like the blue best."

"But with her skin," Mr. Charles said, "the black could work, too."

"Agree."

"But the blue *is* better."

"Absolutely."

"Softer."

"Yes."

"Kate?"

Kate liked it when Mr. Charles called her by her real name instead of "Kitty," which was an alarming habit he'd recently picked up. "Black is for beatniks."

"Unless you're Chanel."

"Kate has a point, though," Schwinn said. "That photograph of the Wife reading Kerouac on the campaign trail raised enough eyebrows."

"Agreed. Three blue blouses—all a slightly different cut. Kate, can you look into something you think will work? Thumb through the magazines—don't limit yourself to Chanel. Keep in mind that she's considering wearing the pink suit in India. We'll need a blouse design that will stand up to the humidity."

"Does she want to pick up the gold from the suit buttons? We could do a gold trim on a blue camisole. The women there wear camisoles under their saris, so no one would think it scandalous, and it would be more comfortable."

"Camisole, yes. Not sure about the gold trim. She's very concerned about how much embellishment one can wear in India."

Schwinn took a chocolate from the box. "Gold brocade was invented in India. I think the sky is the limit."

"True, but the photos of the Wife are for Americans."

"Our Miss Molly told me they'd been discussing Mughal illustrations. Very primitive style. Vivid. Very bright."

"Yes, the Wife is very keen on them," Mr. Charles said. "I hear our dear First Lady has actually put Kama Sutra prints on the dining-room walls of their country home. How can guests even focus on the food?"

Kate had no idea what Mr. Charles and Schwinn were talking about, but it sounded like something untoward. They both rolled their eyes.

"Whatever we do," Schwinn said, "we have to keep in mind that Indians love marigolds. Whatever color she chooses must match marigolds."

Kate took the blue fountain pen from her desk and began to sketch. "Let's say that the first blouse should be a chemise with a simple V-neck that will lie underneath the jacket and go unseen when it is buttoned up. That way, she can have a normal-to-long décolleté line when she wants to look youthful."

Kate held her sketch so that everyone could see it. It was just a quick line drawing, but it was clear from the sketch that the V-neck would make her look even more swanlike.

"I like that," Mr. Charles said.

Kate began to sketch again. "The second could be a basic jewel neck that her single strand of pearls would lie against, just as she sketched it for us." Kate's drawing was a close-up of the neck detail, with small dots for pearls.

"Of course. Always give Her Elegance what she asks for."

"Always. But for the third, why not do what Chanel asked for?"

Kate picked up the *Life* magazine clipping of the four women wearing Chanel, standing on the street corner. "This seems to be a modified cowl, doesn't it? The silk collar is gathered high, so it drapes. Given how it's gathered, it would probably drape no matter how high the humidity." Kate quickly drew a blouse with fabric that appeared to be twisted around the neck.

"Very old crone," Maeve said. "Even my mam wouldn't want to be seen in that."

"Exactly," Kate said. "After being caught reading Kerouac, she now knows what doesn't play in Wisconsin. If she loves the suit, she'll want to wear it for all sorts of audiences—including the conservatives."

Kate put her sketches next to the Wife's. Mr. Charles leaned in to study them all. "Well, what do we think about our Kitty's idea?"

Kate, she thought.

"Swell," Schwinn said.

"Sure," Maeve said.

"It's settled, then," said Mr. Charles. "I'll sketch these properly, and we'll send them on to her for approval."

"What about Mr. Cassini?" Kate asked. "Doesn't he get final say?"

"Not this time. This is our suit. Cassini will have nothing to do with it."

"He'll come sniffing around, though," Maeve said. "Mark my words."

Kate was refining the lines in her sketches. "Will we be making all of these at once?"

"She wants three. She gets three," Mr. Charles said. "The carpenters at Maison Blanche just enlarged her closet. It's now twice the size of my apartment."

Maeve reached across the sketches to take a few more chocolates, and put them in the pocket of her smock. "For the bus ride home," she said, and put on her coat. "All I have to say is that this pink suit will be very pretty on her."

"This isn't about what's pretty, Maeve," Mr. Charles said. "It's about perfection. The First Lady is the best of us. She's who we all aspire to be. She must be perfect at all times."

"Don't let him fool you," Maeve said to Kate. "She sweats like the rest of us too."

"Perspires," Mr. Charles said.

"Perspires, then," Maeve said. "She perspires like a bloody racehorse."

As soon as Maeve left, Mr. Charles started sketching—five quick lines for that long, thin frame, the hair in a flip, and freckles across the nose. A suit, very Pierre Cardin–like in design, was starting to take shape. "Miss Molly said that there was another order placed today," he said. "The First Lady has requested that I create a piece especially for India. She wants me to do it personally."

Mr. Charles kept on drawing; he didn't look up. He'd waited until Maeve had left to tell Kate and Schwinn. Kate knew this would not turn out well. The last time this happened, it was the Paris trip. The final dress, which bore the Chez Ninon tag and no mention of Mr. Charles, was a navy-blue silk shantung suit with a matching overcoat. Its twin now hung in the sample room. Based on the clean lines of Givenchy, with a slightly flared skirt, the ensemble was a huge success. The First Lady adored it. As soon as she returned from Paris, she wrote Mrs. Molly Tackaberry McAdoo about how enchanted she was. "Practically a uniform—there is never a day, or an occasion, where I can resist wearing it."

Stories about the navy-blue silk suit appeared in all the news-papers, not only in New York and Washington, but all over the country, in places where Kate didn't think people even cared about fashion, like farm country and the high desert and the rugged coast. Mr. Charles's drawing was often on the front page, usually in the lower left column. But his name was never mentioned. The credit line was *Supplied by Chez Ninon.* He was upset for weeks. And now he would be upset again.

"What color should we make this one?" he asked, but he didn't sound entirely pleased.

Schwinn patted him on the back. "It can wait until tomorrow, Noel." He never called Mr. Charles by his first name. No one did.

"I just want to get the ideas down," he said. "She needs to see the sketches in a week."

"How about white on white?" Kate said. "Like Norman Hart-nell's depiction of India on the Queen's coronation gown. He did a single lotus flower inlaid with mother-of-pearl, seed pearls, and rhinestones. It looked like diamonds and pearls in an ocean of dia-monds."

Mr. Charles frowned. "But how would it photograph? White on white could get lost or flare in the light of flashbulbs."

"Can't some things just be beautiful?"

"Of course not. It's just as I said to Maeve. The First Lady is our perfection."

"I understand that, but everybody likes something beautiful—"

"This is not everybody," Schwinn said. "This is the Wife." He leaned over the table and added a few faint freckles to the forehead of Mr. Charles's drawing. "Marta at Bergdorf once showed me one of her orders. It was a series of drawings with swatches for an entire wardrobe of hats—all of them were carefully designed to photo-graph perfectly. She even indicated camera angles. For a woman like that, beautiful is never enough."

Schwinn took a chocolate-covered cherry from the box, popped it in his mouth, and smiled at Mr. Charles with that country-boy grin of his. "Let's do this tomorrow."

"She is our perfection, though. Isn't she?" Mr. Charles said.

"She's our dream."

Kate wasn't sure if Schwinn had answered the question, but he picked up his rusting bike to carry it down the stairs. "Night, all," he said. The door slammed behind him.

Mr. Charles kept on sketching. Kate poured the remaining tea into his cup. She wanted to say something to console him, but she had no idea what. The fluorescent lights hummed above them. The radiator knocked and hissed. Her hands still held the scent of the toile—of Chanel No. 5—but it was quickly fading.

"I should go, too. I promised that I'd be on time tonight. My sis-ter's been after me. I'm already late, of course."

Mr. Charles looked up from his drawing. "Have you thought about the shop?"

"Of course."

"Of course, yes?"

"It's a mad scheme."

"No. It's a business proposition. I'm offering you a share of the profits. I'll also teach you how to design couture."

Her sketches of the blouses lay on the table next to him. "Don't I design now?"

"Not exactly. You have very nice ideas. I perfect them. What I do requires skill."

Kate wasn't going to let that annoy her. "I think we're all tired," she said.

He rubbed his eyes. "I can't stay at Chez much longer, Kitty. You don't know what it's like to design things and not get the credit."

I most certainly do, she thought, but said nothing, put on her coat.

"Don't forget your box," he said. "It isn't every day that a back-room girl gets a special delivery from The Carlyle hotel."

Kate had forgotten it completely.

CHAPTER TEN

"A new dress doesn't get you anywhere; it's the life
you're living in the dress, & the sort of life you had
lived before, & what you will do in it later."
—Diana Vreeland

Kate made it all the way to Central Park before she opened
the box from The Carlyle. Inside were her hat and gloves—of
course—and an envelope. The amount on the bill was shocking.
Even though it was late, and a Saturday night, Kate walked all the
way to the hotel. She thought that maybe if she explained that she'd
made a mistake, things could be worked out. Maybe she could do
some sewing or darning in exchange for the bill.

When Kate turned onto Madison Avenue, she turned back
around again. She couldn't do it. She could see the elegant hotel
on the corner of East Seventy-Sixth, but it was so very East Side to
her. Limos were pulling up; women in their furs were sliding into
them. Kate didn't want to face the humorless doorman again. She
didn't want to give him the distinct pleasure of showing her where
the service entrance was. *Another time,* she thought. Maggie would
be furious enough as it was.

Her sister's apartment was dark when Kate arrived. Even though it was the weekend, Big Mike was on the night shift. The dining room table had been cleared, and plates were piled in the sink. The place smelled of meatloaf and tea. Maggie made a particularly wretched meatloaf. She always used too much oatmeal, so Kate was somewhat glad she'd missed it, although she hadn't missed it by much. The teapot was still warm.

There was a light on in the back, in Maggie's room. Kate took off her shoes so as not to make the carpet dirty—beige was such an impractical color for a rug—and walked carefully past the plaid colonial furniture that Maggie Quinn had once loved so much and now desperately hated. The door to Little Mike's room was ajar. Kate looked in to find him sleeping. The boy still was Gerber Baby sweet; he hadn't quite outgrown that yet. Kate dreaded the day when that would happen, when his arms and legs would go long and his shoulders would broaden and he would understand what the word *secret* really meant and collect them as he now collected rocks, thinking them to be precious and worth keeping.

A kiss would wake him, even a careful kiss, so Kate let him be. She was taking him into the city in a couple of days. She would hold his sticky hand then, and be happy that it still fit in her palm.

At the end of the hall, Maggie was sitting in her bedroom, cross-legged on the floor, surrounded by long cardboard boxes from Chez Ninon. *Just a girl and her little coffins,* Kate thought. That was what the boxes were called. Couture clothes are so delicate that hanging pulls them out of shape, dust destroys—but, wrapped in tissue, coffins will always keep them safe.

"I'm sorry," Kate said.

Her sister was clearly upset. Maggie ignored Kate and continued arranging her coffins in chronological order: Campaign Trail, Inauguration, Day Wear, Dinners, Receptions, Private Parties, Travel, and Horseback Riding. Kate was surprised by how many there were. She'd clearly lost count.

"I really am sorry I missed supper."

Maggie looked like a little girl building a fort. Her blue housecoat was thin, starched and pressed, but worn. Big Mike's black sweater was wrapped around her. She looked as if she'd been crying. Kate sat down at the edge of Maggie's bed and watched her slowly arrange and then rearrange the boxes. She was not hurried or frantic. Every time she picked up a box, she appeared burdened by the weight of it. With her unruly tangle of smoky hair, the impossibly green eyes—Kate's sister was beautiful even when she was furious.

"I left a plate for you in the icebox," she said finally.

"You're angry."

"No."

"Disappointed?"

"Patrick Harris was here. He came for dinner."

Kate's face went hot. Patrick had given up a night's business from the telephone operators to have dinner with Kate—even on a Saturday night, that must be quite a loss. Not to mention missing the opportunity to bask in the adoration of all those pretty operators, fawning over blood pudding and pork steaks.

"You should go over and talk to him now," Maggie said. "It's not that late. He was worried about you. Apparently you put on quite a show last night."

It wasn't even eight o'clock, but it had been such a long day. Kate was exhausted. She knew if she went to the butcher shop, it wouldn't be for a simple chat. Not now. Not anymore. Not with Yeats looming over them.

"I'm sure he'll still be worried tomorrow."

Kate opened the box, marked DAY WEAR. Inside, carefully folded in tissue, was a day suit in ivory wool in the style of Christian Dior. The ivory was more flattering on Maggie, much more so than the red the Wife had chosen.

"This one gave me fits," Kate said. "The collar was maddening."

Kate had placed three large, black buttons on the side to give it that fitted look that the Wife liked; it suited Maggie as well, but Kate couldn't remember the last time she saw Maggie wear that suit. In fact, she couldn't remember the last time Maggie wore any of the Wife's clothes.

"You should wear this on Monday. Come with us to the zoo. We'll take pictures. Little Mike will cherish them forever. It's very lovely on you."

"To the zoo? People would think I'd sprung a leak. It's too fancy for the zoo, Kate."

"The Wife would wear it. You could wear black flats to dress it down. Gloves would still be nice, though. A hat, of course."

Maggie took the box from Kate and looked at it oddly, as if she'd never really seen it before. "What was this for again?"

"Day Suit. That's what the Wife called it."

"Just something to wear around the house?"

"Well, something to wear in the day. Out to lunch. Shopping. The zoo." Kate tried not to look at the holes in Big Mike's sweater that left Maggie's elbows exposed. "The Ladies were just told that the Wife might wear hers on a Valentine's Day television special about Maison Blanche. Did I tell you that? Hers is red, not ivory like yours. Very clever of her to wear red on that day; makes you think of sweethearts."

"Patrick Harris told me that you came to his pub last night. You called his friend a prostitute."

"You two certainly talk a lot."

"He said you took sick. Are you sick, Kate?"

"I'm fine."

"I don't think you are."

Maggie took the ivory day suit from Kate and held it by one arm as if it were a white flag and she wished to surrender.

"Here, let me fold it," Kate said. "I'll put it away."

Maggie threw it on the ground. Kate leaned over to pick it up. Maggie kicked the pale suit away, just out of Kate's reach.

"Leave it. It's mine, and I want it on the floor."

Kate had worn cotton gloves to make that dress so that she wouldn't get it dirty. The material was very fragile.

"That's uncalled for," Kate said. "I'm sorry I missed dinner, but—"

"Dinner. That's always quite the occasion, isn't it? Something to get all tarted up over." Maggie opened the box marked STATE DIN-NER. "Maybe I should have worn this, then."

It was an evening gown. The original was a Nina Ricci with a deep brown sleeveless bodice and a full yellow silk skirt with a large silk bow at the waist. The Wife hated brown, and so Chez Ninon re-created it in black, but Kate loved the original so much that she made Maggie's exactly like it. She had even hand-knotted the large, yellow sash as Nina Ricci had required. It took her over a month.

"You could have worn it tonight, just for the fun of it."

Maggie threw it on top of the ivory wool. Kate couldn't believe it. All her hard work.

"If you're not going to respect these clothes—"

"Then you'll stop making them? Because that's what I would like. I would like you to stop doing this. I have told you over and over again. These clothes are too much. All of this is too much."

"You can dress them down—"

"Kate, these are clothes to go horseback riding in and to dance all night in, at balls at foreign embassies."

"And they're beautiful."

"People laugh at me. They laugh, Kate. And sometimes to my face."

At that moment, Maggie was not Sunday-china beautiful, like the Wife. She was wild, untamed. She had the kind of beauty that drove ships onto the rocks. She stood on top of the mound of dresses with her dirty shoes. *The ivory wool,* Kate thought, *the yellow silk.* It was unbearable to see her do this to such beautiful things.

"Maggie. Please."

"What you said about Patrick's friend, and you being sick in the Gents'—that's too much. You were drunk. People talk, Kate."

"Did Patrick say that?"

"No. He said you were overly tired, which is a polite word for *drunk.*"

"Why are you so angry?"

"Because you behave as if there aren't rules. But there are rules for people like us, Kate."

Kate noticed that the ivory dress now had a scuff on it from Maggie's shoe. It pained her.

"Think about Little Mike," Maggie said. "Children are cruel. He goes to school this year. We can't have the others picking on him because of the Wife, because of you."

It felt as if the world had suddenly been put on pause. That night when Patrick sang "God Save the Queen." And those girls laughing when they saw her outside the butcher shop. And even Mrs. Brown—she seemed sincerely interested in Kate and the Wife, but you never knew.

"Everyone laughs?"

Kate heard the hurt in her own voice. Maggie heard it too, and that softened her a bit.

"Not Patrick," she said. "He doesn't laugh."

But you, Kate thought, *you do.*

There was nothing more to say. Kate closed the door gently behind her, leaving her sister standing on the most exquisite clothes in the world, surrounded by a fort built from the coffins of another woman's life.

On Sunday morning, Kate went to mass alone. She then took the train to Grand Central Station to eat at the Horn and Hardart, the Automat. Maeve said it was a good place to go when you had nothing to do, and so Kate spent most of the afternoon watching travelers drop a nickel in a slot, turn the knob, open a tiny door, and take their food. It was very clean and brightly lit. It was the sort of place where you could have your coconut custard pie and hot tea without anyone knowing you or talking to you or being disappointed by who you were.

On Monday, when Kate arrived to pick up Little Mike, Maggie's apartment smelled like fresh porridge and burnt toast, although neither was offered. The little coffins were lined up by the front door, in alphabetical order, with CAMPAIGN TRAIL on the top. That box held a copy of the double-faced scarlet wool "lucky" coat. The Wife's version was clearly a Paris original from Hubert de Givenchy, just as *Women's Wear Daily* had claimed. The fine craftsmanship was evident in the welted seams. However, the First Lady issued a statement saying it was bought at Ohrbach's department store. As soon as she said that, Ohrbach's coat suddenly became so popular that women fought to buy it even at forty dollars. So Chez Ninon knocked it off for the ready-to-wear set, just for good measure. The coat was a knockoff of a knockoff. Piling it in the hall was punitive. Everyone in the country had one.

"Maybe you know someone who'd like these," Maggie said.

"I thought I did."

"I'll stack them in your kitchen while you're gone."

"Lovely."

Maggie never even asked where she'd been on Sunday.

Little Mike was in a quiet mood, or maybe he was just trying to match Kate's. He was only four years old but he was a very serious child, the kind of child who, if not taught an appreciation for foolishness, would grow up to be an accountant more prone to enumerating the days of his life than living them. Or maybe he would grow up to be like his mother, so filled with regret. Or, Kate thought, maybe he'll grow up like me—apparently, horrible. *Well, at least according to Maggie.* Clearly, Kate and her nephew were in need of fun.

They took the A train into Manhattan. To celebrate Little Mike's fourth birthday, Kate had taken the day off so they could visit the new children's zoo in Central Park. They'd planned to pet Whaley, the smiling gray fiberglass whale that looked big enough to eat them both, and then to walk down the plank to Noah's Ark to feed the ducks and maybe end up chasing the White Rabbit down Alice in Wonderland's tunnel. From there it was only a short walk along Park Avenue to Chez Ninon, so the back-room girls could give Little Mike a tour—they'd seen so many pictures of him, they felt as if he were one of their own. Kate had promised her nephew all of this—but only if he took the subway and only if he was a little gentleman and if he didn't cry.

Ice cream, too?

Ice cream, too.

It was morning rush hour when they boarded the train. The crowd pushed in around them. At least the day was cool and the car was not dark or dirty but clean, and smelled of office workers and their dime-store perfumes.

"Who looks smart?" Kate whispered in Little Mike's ear. It was a game that she'd taught him. "Who is the most stylish?"

The boy pointed to two people who had just entered the train at the Dyckman Street station, the stop after hers. Their skin was black as river stones. Instead of a hat, the woman wore her hair wrapped in vibrant scarves, intricately patterned and in shades of orange and red and that particular burnished gold that reminded Kate of Egypt and its queens. The man's suit was perfectly cut and fitted. He wore a fine cotton shirt and a brilliant blue tie. He had the air of an intellectual, but Kate could see by his overcoat that he was a traveler, or a preacher, perhaps. His clothes were road weary but had a dignity that was undeniable.

"Very good," she said, and kissed Little Mike on his forehead. The boy needed a trade, after all.

Kate had never seen the couple before. *They must have come from the Dyckman Houses,* she thought. The new housing development was on the other side of Broadway. Very nice: lots of families were moving there. It was a massive place. In the 1930s, before the project was built, it was the Dyckman Oval, the legendary sport complex that had served as the home of the New York Cubans, part of the Negro leagues. The team had brought Satchel Paige and the Pittsburgh Crawfords to their collective knees. All of New York had loved the Oval—"Harlem's own"—even Babe Ruth, who played an exhibition game there. He was an old, bleary drunk by that point, with cow eyes; the world was woozy around him. The Sultan of Swat, the Behemoth of Bust, the Big Bam, the Caliph of Clout, the King of Swing, the Colossus of Crash—Bambino—that day he took swing after swing and then, miraculously, his lumbering body finally remembered what to do, and the ball soared out of the park without looking back and nearly touched the ragged clouds, just as it did in the days when Ruth was the Babe and was every boy's dream, back before the women and the booze and the car accidents, and the too-much-of-everything, including life. At the crack of that bat, the splintering of it, ten thousand fans did not just cheer, they screamed. There were no newsreels or cameras or mayors or aldermen to preserve the memory of that swing, but for a moment, the Dyckman Oval was the finest ballpark in all of Manhattan, maybe the world.

Now it was gone.

Kate and Little Mike sat side by side on the subway bench. Their knees knocked into the backs of the legs of the people standing in the aisle: sleepy, arguing, whispering, shouting, praying to their own gods, bobbing above the crush of their own lives. Rocking back and forth and moving in and out of darkness. Kate knew that trains frightened Little Mike, but he would have to learn how to ride the subway eventually. She held his hand tightly. Not because she was concerned that he'd run away or get lost—he was a smart boy, a well-behaved boy, anybody could see that—but because she liked the feel of his hand in hers.

An elegant man with a cane boarded at the Harlem stop. He had a thin mustache and skin like midnight. He looked like he came from Sugar Hill. "Clothes are like maps," Kate whispered to Little Mike. "They tell where a man has been and where he can go."

The boy had no idea what Kate was talking about, but he stared at the tall man in his beautiful clothes, and he said, "Pretty."

"No. *Handsome.*"

Sugar Hill was an expensive neighborhood, made up mostly of musicians like Duke Ellington and all the rest. The man touched the rim of his gray bowler hat and nodded to the couple. He seemed surprised to see them.

"Brother Taj," he said. "Honored."

The man in the bowler sat across from the couple. He held his ebony cane between his knees. His tie was red raw silk, probably from Florence, as it had that particular sheen of Italian silk. There were tailors in Harlem who'd learned their trade in Italy and catered to the music crowd. Leighton's, Cy Martin's, and House of Cromwell—they were the best of the best. Kate had seen their work on the train before. "Fine vines," as they were called. Like all couture, they were handmade. Silk and mohair suits, cashmere top-coats, and alligator shoes in every color of the rainbow. The Blye Shop had the softest alpaca sweaters, softer than any other, any-where. Nat King Cole wore them on his album covers.

The man in the bowler kept staring at the couple, and so Kate did too. After a while, the preacher began to look very familiar to her. She'd seen him before but couldn't remember where—maybe the newspaper? Finally, the man from Harlem leaned in and said, "Thank you, Doctor. Thank you for it all. You're a good man."

Then Kate knew. He was that preacher who was trying to ban segregation on buses. He was a good man. And brave.

At the next stop, two college students huddled onto the train together. Kate noticed that the girl was neatly dressed, in pearls and patent-leather shoes: Columbia University. The boy—he really seemed to be a boy—was wearing wrinkled, ill-fitting khaki pants. His coat was secondhand and needed a good cleaning. City Col-lege, of course. There were no seats available, which seemed to make the young man upset. The two wrapped themselves around the pole next to Little Mike. They were dangerously close to toppling over onto the child. Kate pulled her nephew closer and looked away, out the window. The world flashed by as if they were in a silent film, the frames slipping, then catching, then slipping again. No piano to accompany the scene, just the rhythm of their breaths.

"Last stop, Africa," the young man said.

He was clearly trying to make a scene. Kate pretended not to hear it. The man in the bowler looked as if he were about to say something but had thought better of it. The wheels on the train sparked against the rails. Kate pulled her nephew onto her lap, out of the way, just in case. The train was flooded in sunlight—this was the part of the route that Little Mike liked the best: it was all aboveground. Kate pointed out the train window. "Look, birds," she said. "Seagulls."

"Hawks?" Little Mike loved hawks.

"Just gulls," Kate said.

The child seemed disappointed but leaned in to her to look out the window, his arms around her neck. The river was far below them, and a few men in overalls stood on the shore. "Do you think those men are lawyers?" Kate asked.

Little Mike shook his head. "Union."

Big Mike had apparently given the boy a lesson or two of his own.

"Union is good," Kate said, and focused on the cold blue of the river beneath the train, the workmen, and the squawking seagulls. The preacher turned and smiled at her. Kate smiled back. "That's a very nice tie you have on, sir," she said. She didn't know what else to say.

"Thank you. They are my weakness."

When Kate and Little Mike finally reached Chez Ninon, the back room was filled with headless mannequins, but no one was working. The pink bouclé had arrived from England. Across the work-table there was an ocean of bouclé in shades of pink. Everyone was leaning in to get a closer look. They all glowed pink.

"Pretty," Mike said.

"No," Kate said. "Stunning."

On the end of the yardage, there was a brown cardboard tag from Linton Tweeds. It was used for inventory control. In neat block letters, someone had written a piece number and a pattern number. The customer was identified as Chanel, as she'd granted the rights. There was also the name of the "warper," who was Ann. She had signed the card herself. As did the weaver, who was Susan. Finally, there was the darner, whose name was signed in joyous, loopy letters and quite wonderfully was Kate.

CHAPTER ELEVEN

"The most difficult thing...was restraint."
—Oleg Cassini

$\mathcal{B}$y Friday, it was snowing pink in the back work room. The bouclé did not just shed, it came undone. *Bouclé* means "to curl" in French, and so the soft wool curled and snagged even after they had had the yardage dry-cleaned. It was imprudent in its color and insolent in its impossible weave, and every time scissors were sharpened and then taken to it, puffs of cloth floated like dandelions in the wind.

When Kate touched her hair, the pink hid in her bangs. If she rubbed her eyes, it hung from her lashes. It made her sneeze. Made her cough. Made her itch. It had the scent of old sheep and coal fires. There were tiny piles of fluff on her table and on her lap. Pink tumbled toward the floor, catching on her nylons, hanging on her shoes. Even her navy wool coat, which she had hung on a hook by her desk, was covered in pink. Pink had worked its way into cups of tea—tiny puffs floated on top of thick cream. And into sandwiches—pink stuck in the grape jelly. Chewing gum. Chocolate. Doughnuts. Pink had even found its way into her coin purse and buried itself among her subway tokens. It was the dust over everything.

Chez Ninon worked with Linton's bouclé on a regular basis, but this particular yardage was reckless, improbable, and not merely pink but a tweed of pinks—it was ripe raspberry and sweet watermelon and cherry blossom running through an undercurrent of pink champagne. In full light, it was like a vibrant wall of fuchsia growing wild in the Mexican sun. In half-light, it reminded Kate of Japanese peonies blooming in the winter: the iridescence was intense but fleeting. It was like the memory of roses; it was the kind of pink that only the heart could understand.

This pink-on-pink weave was not just unruly—it was unnervingly insistent. Like most couture fabric, it would require twenty stitches per inch at the beginning and end of each seam and twelve stitches per inch everywhere else. Not the usual SPI of nine. And everything had to be sewn twice—every seam, every cuff—first in a straight line and then in a zigzag line, to reinforce the seam. Given the maddening nature of this particular ream of fabric, instead of taking eighty hours to sew the jacket, it would now take ninety. The skirt would probably take thirty.

Only Kate had that kind of skill. She didn't usually do the fabricating, but since the suit was for Maison Blanche, the Ladies thought it would be best. By the end of the day on that Friday, Kate was covered in pink.

Pink took the train home with Kate and followed her into the 207th Street station. When she waved at Pete the Cop, a few stray tufts caught on the blue wool of his coat sleeve. When Kate walked across Broadway and then past the Good Shepherd Church, to the river's edge, to stand on the dock and watch the hawks flying low, she left a trail of pink behind her.

At that hour, Inwood seemed not like a part of the city of New York but like the Island, more like Cobh. That evening the sun set, ripe as a persimmon, staining the horizon and river below it. At the moment when it seemed to slip into the darkened water, a handful of bats flew out of the caves that lined the river. Small and black against the red sky, they banked left out of instinct, then swooped low over the water for a drink, and then swirled up into the red clouds as if toward heaven. The rest then followed: ten, twenty—and then hundreds. They poured out from the caves like a waterfall into the river and instinctually banked left, into the deep blue of the ultramarine sky. It was nearly October; they were mi-grating to Mexico for winter, as they always did.

Winter, Kate thought. It was such a lonely word.

She walked along the edge of Inwood Hill Park and decided that she would rather be hungry than face Maggie, especially covered in whorls of pink. When she reached Broadway, she could go either left or right. If she went right, her copy of the Chanel toile would be waiting for her on her sewing table. If she went left, there was Patrick.

Kate was beginning to envy the instinct of the bats. Free will was entirely overrated. At the children's zoo, a volunteer had told Kate and Little Mike that bats exit caves by flying left first, out of in-stinct. So Kate turned left.

Harris Meats was still open. The white-tiled store looked clean and comforting. Patrick was behind the counter in his old-fashioned white fedora and white butcher's coat. The bell on the door jingled when Kate walked in. He looked up and smiled. "I'll be right with you," he said. Then he winked, which made her blush. Patrick was packing an enormous order for a middle-aged woman Kate had never seen before. She had dyed black hair, wrapped into a chignon, and bright red lips. He wrapped the last of his pork chops and ribs in white freezer paper and marked it with a black wax pencil.

"That side of bacon, too?" she asked.

She looked like a telephone operator. She had an independent air about her and wore the kind of impractical shoes, high heeled and strappy, that someone who sat all day could wear. She smiled at Kate. "I'm afraid I've nearly cleaned him out. Sorry."

In the glass case, there were a couple of smoked fish and a few links of black-and-white pudding, but that was all that was left. The woman leaned over and picked a bit of pink from the shoulder of Kate's coat. Patrick walked around the counter with the bag. "It's heavy, Mrs. Strout. I double-bagged it, but be careful on the way home."

"See you Monday."

"Monday."

He opened the door for Mrs. Strout. The bell jingled. "Have a good night," he said. The bell jingled again. And then he turned to Kate and said, "Would you like a ride?"

"A ride?"

"It's Friday night. I've got a car. What do you do in America on a Friday night? You ride around. So why not?"

Why not, indeed?

It only took Patrick a few moments to clean up. The car was in a parking garage around the corner, where telephone company executives parked. Patrick's Oldsmobile was new, a red-finned boat of a thing with a matching carpet and a cream leather interior. It was a convertible. "A Ninety-Eight," he said. "The Ninety-Eight was the pace car at Indy."

Kate had no idea what he was talking about, but even in the fluorescent light of the parking garage, the car shimmered.

"Can you call a car beautiful?" she asked.

"Rose is the very picture of Oldsmobility," Patrick said.

The car was named Rose, after the President's mother. Kate had never heard of anyone naming a car and talking about it so indecently, as if it were a real, living thing. It was daft, but Patrick looked so proud, she couldn't bear to tell him that "Oldsmobility" made Rose sound like she was fast, and no one wanted to think of the President's mother as being fast. He patted the car door lovingly and settled Kate into the passenger's side.

"Peg loved the real Rose, you know," he said. "Only seemed proper to name her after the great matriarch. I couldn't name her Peg, could I? That would be strange. 'Mam' would be awkward, too."

There was an odd sort of logic to that which Kate felt she nearly understood. The car was immaculate. There were rubber mats on the floor. The front bench was cream leather but wrapped in plastic, which Kate was grateful for, because once she took her coat off, she was still covered in pink tufts.

"Should we put the top down? We could turn the heat up," Patrick said.

Why not? The night sky was freckled with stars. While Patrick took the top down, Kate took off her hat and gloves. She ran a quick brush through her hair. There was pink wool in the bristles, but she tried not to worry about that. Kate was about to shame her entire family in a way that would give Maggie fits, and, frankly, she didn't care. Maggie was correct—there were rules. One was, You don't ride around with the top down past Labor Day. It was as bad as wearing white. But Kate didn't care. Patrick was handsome. He was happy to see her, even though Kate was covered in pink.

"People will talk," he said.

"That they will."

Kate shrugged and squeezed his hand as a friendly gesture. She was surprised that he held it tightly as they pulled out of the parking garage and onto Broadway, where people in the streets were going to dinner or movies or bowling or the pub. They turned to look as Rose passed by. Some turned all the way around. Some of them even pointed as Kate and Patrick passed. *Poor Little Mike,* Kate thought, but knew there were worse things in life than having an aunt who didn't always obey the rules—like having an aunt who mindlessly obeyed them. *What a frightful way to be.*

Above them, a stainless steel moon, utilitarian and common, shone bright enough. The air carried the rusted scent of Indian summer. Patrick continued to hold her hand as they drove down Broadway. Bagpipes, Elvis, and opera—the music of the street—provided the sound track. Kate was nervous. She couldn't seem to stop talking as she picked away at the pink that had stubbornly clung to her nylons.

"It's the poetry of sheep. That's what bouclé is—"

"Poetry? Yeats, then. Less bleating."

Patrick was nervous, too. He wouldn't let Kate finish a single sentence.

"But this wool is—"

"It is just hair, isn't it? Sheep's hair. Odd, when you think about it that way. That's probably why no one ever says, 'That's a fine bit of sheep's hair you're wearing, Mrs. Miller.'"

They both laughed, although Kate was only trying to be polite. It was, after all, Chanel's bouclé, Chanel's poetry.

"Her tweedmakers are always invited to her shows, you know. Second row. Right next to the movie stars and jet-setters."

"The Ladies told you this?"

They did. "They see it every season. After the show, Chanel holds court with the *fournisseurs*—that's what they're called—the suppliers of tweed and braid and buttons. She ignores everybody else. She once pushed a photographer all the way down two flights of stairs so she could talk to the *fournisseurs* alone. One by one they tell her how very wonderful she is. And she tells them the same story about Churchill—'Currkell,' as she'd say. She tells the one story over and over again."

"Currkell?"

"Yes. Currkell. Chanel speaks in this slipstream of words and dreams, and the only way you can tell she's done with you is that she's suddenly talking to the person behind you as if you've disappeared. She'd just start the Currkell story all over again—"

"Not Churchill?"

"No. *Currkell.* But it doesn't matter. She could read a grocery list to them if she wanted to. The tweedmakers are honored that Chanel speaks to them alone. That kind of respect means more than money."

Most of the pink was gone from Kate's nylons. Just a few whorls remained.

"What clever crows the Ladies are," Patrick said, although his voice was not unkind. "I suppose this story first came up when you'd asked for a raise."

It did. It didn't matter, though. Kate liked the story anyway.

"You tell me a story, then."

"I don't know any grand people."

"About Peg."

Kate did know a lot about Peg Harris. Kate's and Patrick's mothers had both worked together in the back room at John W. Dowden & Company Limited, in Cork City, when they were young girls. It was a high-society shop for the posh—"Like Chez Ninon, but utterly huge," Peg once told her. Kate's mother's stories always began with Peg bewitching one delivery boy or another. They were cautionary tales. Mrs. Harris, in her day, was quite a looker, and that was a sorrowful thing, according to her mother.

"Those kinds of girls, the pretty ones, even if they are dear like our Peg, breed trouble," she'd say, but she sounded wistful about it, too.

"Tell me something noble about Peg."

"Noble? It's Mam. She put up with us. That's noble."

"True. But what about her work?"

"She worked hard."

"She loved it, though."

"She loved the check."

"And the Ladies, of course."

Patrick laughed hard. "Mam did not love the Ladies. She liked the other girls, though. Maeve in particular. 'The Great Conspirators,' my pop called them. Mam and Maeve would sit on the back stoop, drinking gin in teacups, and go on for hours about the Olé Chez. They called it that, always with a hard *z*."

"But she loved the Ladies. She told me they were wonderful,"

"Mam was just luring you in. The shop needed another good kipper, and you fit the bill."

"She lied?"

"If you think they're wonderful, then it wasn't exactly a lie, was it?"

Kate picked a bit of pink from her skirt. *That's the problem with cars,* she thought. *You sit too close. You tell secrets no one wants to hear.*

The stars were not shy about shining, and so the ride was quite lovely. The street was quiet; not many families had cars. Only the occasional bus passed them — delivery trucks were done for the day. Driving in the open car at night made Kate feel like a tourist in her own neighborhood. She'd never realized how many shops there were. Some flew Irish flags. Some had windows painted with leprechauns and shamrocks. They were all Irish, in a postcard sort of way. They were not like the great, dark sea of her youth, or the smoky peat air after a winter's rain, or her father, with his wide, red face and booming laugh.

Patrick kissed her hand. "Marry me," he said.

He said it so simply, it took Kate a moment to understand. When Patrick asked for Kate's hand in marriage, he wasn't even looking at her. He was driving, focused on the road. He patted Rose's dashboard, maybe for luck, and then continued on. "I should have asked you years ago. Mam said you were the girl for me — not those fast girls, but a loyal girl, a real Irish girl."

Looking back, Mrs. Harris's Sunday offerings of cake and song were a bit of a soft sell, but Kate had never imagined that Peg had thought so highly of her. For a mammy to turn over her dear son to a girl of any sort was a high honor, and it took at least forty years for the handoff to be complete. Still, Kate missed those Sundays, with Peg singing like the girl she once was and Patrick sitting in his chair with his sleeves rolled up, playing his guitar with his eyes closed, lost in the rhythms of the ages. It was lovely, really, but sometimes it made Kate even more profoundly lonely. Just the three of them like that seemed very sad. Sundays at home with all the distant cousins were more to Kate's liking.

In lush times, back in Cobh, if there wasn't a wake, the old coffin table would be carried outside and covered with food. There'd be a rump of lamb from one of the farms on the other side of the island, and bowls of roasted turnips and carrots, mashed potatoes and wild ramps. And, of course, a sticky toffee or a sweet summer pudding covered in a tart mash of crushed blackberries and strawberries that had been gathered in the forest on the way home from the convent church. Whatever wild mushrooms they had found would be browned in pork fat until crisp. There would be warm brown bread with sweet cream butter served with all manner of cheese and smoked wild salmon; and, because it was Cobh, whatever the Old Man and Kate had caught that morning in the harbor aboard the *Bébhinn,* that tiny boat of his, would fill out the feast. It was usually pollock but sometimes bream or skate—whatever could be caught, skinned, and poached would fill the ticket. Even eel would not be thrown back but smoked and served cold. And there would be music. And dancing.

If there was a wake, however, the body would be on the table, and the food would be lined up on assorted blankets strewn upon the thick, green grass.

Patrick stopped at a red light. Rose's engine idled. "You don't have to answer right away," he said.

"That girl the other night at the pub—"

"Just a girl, I told you."

"The poem you left, the Yeats—"

"I meant it."

Kate had seen the way other women looked at him at the shop, but before she could say another word, Patrick stopped her. "The truth is, I could drive all night with you, Kate. I can't say that about many."

That was as close to a confession of love as Kate had ever expected from him or from anyone. She spent her days imagining other people's lives, stitch by stitch. The ivory silk of romance was not for a woman such as Kate.

"I don't know if I'll be good at marriage," she said.

"I don't know anyone who is."

The Wife, Kate thought, and picked the last bit of pink whorl from her skirt and let it fly out the window and into the cold night.

Maggie Quinn and Big Mike might have seen Patrick park the car in front of the building and put the top up. They might have seen him walk up the stairway with Kate—but they didn't come out of their apartment. They might have even heard when Patrick, out of nervousness, dropped Kate's keys in the hallway, and then the jingle that they made when he unlocked her door. It didn't matter. At that moment, the entire world seemed asleep except for Patrick and Kate.

"Don't turn on the lights," she said, and so he didn't.

Kate took Patrick's hand and walked him past the Chanel toile, folded neatly on her cutting table and now gathering dust, past the slight kitchen, packed with Maggie's boxes, all those little coffins filled with the shadows of the First Lady, arranged in alphabetical order, and into her bedroom. Kate's single bed was pushed up against the bank of windows. Her bathrobe was a puddle on the floor. The moon was indifferent. Instead of stars, streetlights huddled around each window. Incandescent voyeurs, they shone through the lace curtains that had taken Kate nearly the summer to make.

Her coat.

Her hat.

One shoe.

Then the next.

Another rule broken, Kate thought as she undid the buttons of her dress and let it slip to the ground. Patrick brushed his hand against her cheek, as if by accident. His eyes were the kind of blue that sailors fear—a blue so calm that the possibility of danger is forgotten. They were the kind of blue that invites recklessness. With his lips against hers—there was heat. Again. It surprised her.

One stocking was unrolled, and then the next.

Each kiss was a question that they lingered on, until finally Patrick said, "Kate, are you sure you want to do this?"

The answer was no. She wasn't sure at all. But he knew that. Patrick picked up her bathrobe from the floor and wrapped it around her as if he'd done it all his life. "Sit," he said, although his voice cracked a bit. He slipped her feet into the pair of thick cotton socks that she'd laid on top of her dresser.

"You need some sleep."

"I'm sorry."

"Nothing to be sorry for."

He pulled back the blankets, and she slid between them. She was tired. She hadn't noticed before. Patrick appeared not to listen as she said her evening prayer, but when she finished, Patrick said, "Amen." He had prayed too.

"I should go," he said.

"No."

Kate moved over slightly. The bed was so narrow, there wasn't much room.

"Can you just hold me?" she asked.

"I can."

Patrick lay down on top of the blanket: afraid to crush her, afraid to breathe. Kate closed her eyes. He slipped his arm around her as if he were a giant who had hoped that the story would end with the words *ever after*—or maybe never end at all. He kissed her hands gently, as if they were made of china. After she fell asleep and was safely deep in dreams, he left quietly, quickly. He was careful not to wake her. When Patrick closed the door behind him, he made sure the lock caught.

CHAPTER TWELVE

"If you adore her, you must adorn her. There lies
the essence of a happy marriage."
—Anne Fogarty, *The Art of Being a Well-
Dressed Wife*

*O*n Monday morning, Mr. Charles was waiting for Kate in the
workroom, wearing his best suit, the black pinstripe with the dove-
gray vest, and the soft Italian loafers he only wore for important
clients. The silver of his hair looked newly minted. There'd been a
change in plans. He now had a backer for his shop. He was going to
make the announcement that day. Mr. Charles needed an answer.
Kate needed to work.

"Just hear me out," he said, and sat down in Kate's chair in what
Maeve called his "Rat Pack pose," with a cigarette in one hand and
a coffee cup in the other, talking at her, not to her. Kate leaned
across the large layout table and began to carefully pin the delicate
navy lining to the pink bouclé so that she could quilt the two pieces
together. She was tired of steaming the fabric, tired of trying to
block it. Clearly, it did not intend to stop shedding. So she decided
that she would just quilt and try to tame the bouclé that way. Kate

was trying to concentrate, while Mr. Charles was trying to make a point.

"You have to say yes, Kitty," he said. "Not just for me, but yourself. You were born to it. Like Vreeland was born to it."

Kate understood. A desire for perfection had led Mrs. Vreeland to open her own lingerie shop in Mayfair, and that began her career all those years ago, and that desire was just like Kate's. Mr. Charles did have a point.

"She had her nightgowns fitted at least three times. Did I tell you this?"

He had. Twice. Mr. Charles was getting as bad as the Ladies.

"Her kippers were cloistered nuns," he said. "Their finishing work was so beautiful, customers would weep."

Kate had to wonder what the nuns embroidered on negligees that would make grown women cry, or why the sisters even agreed to do that sort of work. Handkerchiefs were usually the only accessories within their purview. There had to be some sort of commandment that forbade nuns from embellishing knickers, although Kate couldn't think of one. *God leaves too many loopholes,* she thought, and made a note to speak with Father John about that at a later date.

By now, the other girls had arrived for the day and were working around them. The mice of Ready-to-Wear were laughing, gossiping, and zipping through seams at their usual breakneck pace. Maeve was basting the marks she'd made on a white Dior gown that had to be let out because some nameless debutante had had too much French pastry, pâté, and cheese on a recent sojourn. "Kate, are you listening to me?" Mr. Charles said.

"Shouldn't you keep your voice down?"

"No one cares," he said, but he began to whisper anyway. "The point I am trying to make is that when Wallis Simpson bought three nightgowns prior to her weekend with the Duke of Windsor, it was quite clear that Mrs. Vreeland's tiny shop had work brilliant enough to bring down an empire. That made it famous. That's what we'll do. That's what we can do together, if you trust me. We could make the clothes that change the world."

Kate grimaced. The American divorcée and the duke—everyone knew that story. But the idea of Mrs. Simpson buying naughty knickers for their tryst seemed to make the fairy-tale romance disappointingly tawdry.

Mr. Charles took a long sip of coffee and a drag from his cigarette. He was planning to announce the new venture at closing time. "Right before everyone goes home, so there's no time for extended, tearful good-byes."

Maybe this was a good idea—exciting, even—but Kate couldn't leave Chez Ninon now.

"What about this suit?"

"Are you in, Kate?"

Mr. Charles seemed to avoid looking at her. He was looking at his manicure instead. It was disconcerting. He clearly didn't understand what was at stake. This was the first line-by-line Chanel that the Ladies had ever done. And it was certainly a first for Kate, and maybe the last.

"I have to finish it."

Mr. Charles fingered a corner of the bouclé until it began to unravel again. "Kitty, it's just day wear. Unimportant. The Ladies will find someone else. The Wife will soon be coming to us directly."

The idea seemed impossible for Kate to believe unless this new mystery backer was Mrs. Vreeland herself. The editor had, after all, helped with the design of the inauguration gown, and quite a few other things, too. She was very close to the Wife.

"Kitty. Trust me. This suit is insignificant," he said. "It's not like the India dress."

"It's a Chanel."

"No, it's not. It's a Kitty," Mr. Charles said as he walked away, trailing blue smoke behind him. "See you at six."

Kate looked at the Wife's drawing again. The wrap-over skirt, the unfitted jacket, the gold buttons—all offset by that brilliant chameleon-like pink. She imagined the First Lady in it, waving and smiling. Tilting her extraordinary head just so as she announced how sad she was that Camp David was not suitable for her children, because her children were remarkable, and you do not send the children of destiny to a backwater camp with bears and mud—or whatever she'd say. *No matter what she says, it won't matter. The entire time that the Wife will be speaking, the perfect pink bouclé will catch the light in so many ways and give her skin such a sweet, childlike glow that no one will remember exactly what she says. Cotton candy, climbing roses, the blush of brides—that is what will be remembered. Not the excuse.*

"I can't leave the suit," Kate said, but Mr. Charles was gone.

Twist your thread, wax your thread—Kate repeated this over and over again. The needle was so very small. The silk thread was slippery and too delicate to use. It was slow going. The bouclé needed to be quilted to the silk with the smallest of stitches, in tiny, straight rows, one inch apart, before anything could be cut or sewn together. And each stitch had to be perfect. The notes from Chanel demanded it.

The wax smoked and made Kate cough. The thin silk thread broke with alarming regularity. The eye of the needle seemed to grow smaller each time she had to thread it. This wasn't just any sort of lining for any sort of jacket—the quilting of lining to the bouclé was what made this jacket extraordinary. There was no way to explain it—it went against reason—but each minute stitch provided not only structure and support but an incredible softness.

Every now and then, Kate would pick the fabric up and rub it against her cheek quickly. She was careful not to stain it with the oil of her skin. She just wanted to commit the feeling of it to memory. How could something that looked so practical feel so luxurious? That quality, the "poverty de luxe," or "luxe cachet," as the Ladies called it, that "hidden luxury," was what made Chanel remarkable.

Twist. Wax. Twist. Lunch came and went without her. Kate's tea turned cold. Her hands became so cramped that she could barely rub them together to warm them. But she had to keep going. She needed to get as much work done as possible so she could leave early—preferably before Mr. Charles's announcement—and go to mass at St. Patrick's. And, after last weekend, to confession, too.

I have lost my mind, Kate thought, and yet she could not stop thinking about the scent of Patrick's skin, the rhythm of his breath, and of falling into a soft sleep in his arms. Of course, she was too embarrassed to tell any of this to Father John. At St. Patrick's, no one knew her. Or Patrick Harris. If Kate got off a few minutes early and ran all the way there, it would not be communion yet, and, technically, if you arrived before the Liturgy of the Eucharist, you'd have legally attended—at least, that was what Maeve always said. And she would know. Maeve made it a practice to slide into the Good Shepherd just before the host was raised, as if she were blocking a kick full bore between the crossbars.

"Maeve, could you cover for me tonight? Just ten minutes?" Kate said. Maeve grunted, which probably meant yes. She was still struggling with the white Dior. Its beaded bodice needed some sort of insert, which would ruin the dress completely.

"Can I count on you to clock me out at six, then?"

"Sure," Maeve said. She didn't even look up, which was odd. In fact, now that Kate thought about it, no one had actually looked at her directly all day long. Something was wrong. Kate went into the loo to look in the mirror. Her white cotton shirt needed ironing; the back of it looked like an accordion. And she'd forgotten to put on nylons and makeup. She'd been so busy worrying about Patrick Harris and her immortal soul that she'd come to work looking a sight.

Kate wished that someone would have said something earlier, but no one had. Maybe they didn't even notice. Maybe they never noticed her. Even Schwinn, who came to ask Kate about the schedule, never even met her eye.

Invisible, she thought.

Kate wondered how many days in the past six years she'd come to work and gone completely unnoticed. Even when Miss Sophie stopped by after lunch to examine the quilting, she said only, "Good job." Then walked away. Maybe Mr. Charles was right. Mrs. Vreeland was an exceedingly plain woman: horse faced, an ugly child even by her mother's own account. Yet she grew to be someone so unblinkingly brave that she lived in an apartment, which was entirely beet red, and instructed women to do and wear all manner of absolutely outrageous things: "Why don't you wash your blond child's hair in dead champagne, as they do in France? Or wear violet velvet mittens with everything? Or turn your old ermine coat into a bathrobe?" And who on earth wants to have huge spots of red on their ears? Mrs. Vreeland. And if she does, then everyone else does, too.

I could do that, Kate thought. *I really could.*

But the pink suit was still on Kate's table.

At five-thirty, Kate knew she had to leave before Mr. Charles got back from wherever he was. He'd been gone all day. She leaned in to Maeve and quietly said, "If I leave now, I can catch the reading of the Gospel. I always like the opening salvo. You still okay to cover for me?"

Maeve had torn the entire beaded bodice out of the white Dior gown and was piecing in an insert that would not match. "Right," she said.

That was a good-enough answer for Kate. She covered the quilted pink bouclé with a length of cotton and gently rolled it. She then tied it with a white satin ribbon. She placed it on her desk, out of the way. No one seemed to notice that she'd stopped working. *Of course not,* she thought, *because I'm invisible.*

When she put on her kid gloves, which were now at least a size too small, and also the somewhat wilted Lilly Daché hat, the din of the sewing machines and the gossip only seemed to grow louder.

"I'm leaving," Kate said again.

Maeve looked at her directly. "Another convertible ride at midnight? Maybe you should fix your hair first."

"What?"

Before Maeve could say more, Miss Sophie walked into the room. "Yes. Do fix your hair," she said. "You have a gentleman caller, and he's bearing meat."

In the blue sea of the Ladies' office, Patrick Harris had pulled up a side chair and was sitting at the nearly French desk, with the Ladies. They were radiant. It was as if it were Christmas morning: tape and shreds of butcher paper littered the faux Louis XIV table. Patrick Harris really had brought meat. That was probably why they'd let him in the front door.

The three of them were sitting around the delicate gilt desk, chatting away as if it were perfectly natural to be in a fashionable ladies' shop in Manhattan looking at raw pork. For Miss Sophie, Patrick had brought a huge slab of pork belly, skin on. It was ready for the roaster. For Miss Nona, there was a package of both white and black puddings, with the sausages wrapped together in a braid. Patrick was quite famous in Inwood for his sausages. He was very particular about what kind of pig the blood came from and how the oatmeal was cut.

Kate now knew what part of the pig Patrick Harris thought of the Ladies as—the cheap yet tasty bits. *Cheeky,* Kate thought.

"Good meat is one of life's sublime pleasures, Ladies," Patrick said in his charming butcher voice. The Ladies giggled like schoolgirls.

"Patrick, we should go. The Ladies are very busy," Kate said. It was getting very close to six p.m., and Mr. Charles would show up any minute. It didn't seem like such a good time for the two men to meet.

Miss Nona said, "We were just having a nice chat about the local cafés."

Miss Sophie leaned in to Miss Nona. "I told you that Kate and Mrs. Harris's boy were sweethearts."

"That's not true—I told you."

The Ladies went on bickering as if Kate and Patrick weren't even there. Kate looked at her watch. "We really should be going." She wondered where Mr. Charles was. Probably having a martini or two for courage. The thought of him leaning over a bar rail made her feel sad. Kate knew how nervous he could be about things. She'd seen his hands shake, but she'd always looked the other way. She didn't want to embarrass him. None of the girls did. At times like that, they wouldn't look at him at all.

It is as if he is invisible, Kate thought, and had to smile. If that was true, then maybe Kate wasn't invisible at all. Maybe back-room logic was kinder than she'd thought.

The Ladies stood. "You're a good boy," they said, as if Patrick were six years old. He blushed.

Miss Nona leaned in and kissed both his cheeks. "You know we miss our Peg. Your mother was invaluable to us. She ran the Ready-to-Wear Department with a kind but fiscally aware heart."

"Peg was like our daughter," Miss Sophie said, and kissed him too. Then the two women embraced him, overcome with emotion, crushing Patrick in their wobbly arms.

"She spoke of you both often," he said, and the Ladies kissed him again. Patrick's face was now smudged with their lipstick.

"You're a very sweet boy," Miss Nona said.

"He is," Miss Sophie said. "You really are."

The Ladies walked them both to the front door, going on about "our dear Peg." Kate looked at her watch. It was six p.m. She turned to see Mr. Charles walking into the showroom behind them, followed by the back-room girls and the grand Mrs. Molly Tackaberry McAdoo and her tiny black-and-white fluffy dog. They all hovered around him, all except for Maeve, who seemed confused. "What announcement? I'm working. Can't you see that?" She was waving the Dior bodice like a flag on the Fourth of July. The small dog began to jump on Mr. Charles's best trousers.

The Ladies looked at Kate and then at Mr. Charles. They knew. They knew exactly what this announcement was all about. They smiled at her, eyebrows raised.

"I hear our Patrick's planned a lovely dinner for the two of you," Miss Nona said.

It was a test. Patrick was an unwitting participant, but the Ladies were certainly testing her.

"Is that Mr. Charles?" Patrick asked.

"It is," Miss Sophie said.

"Let's just give it a quick hello, shall we?" Patrick said, and before Kate could stop him, he made his way across the elegant showroom with his hand outstretched for a shake or, perhaps, Kate thought, a duel.

"Pleasure to meet you. Patrick Harris, Kate's boyfriend."

Patrick was enjoying himself greatly. He slapped Mr. Charles on the back and pumped his hand back and forth as if priming for water. Mr. Charles smiled. He didn't look happy or angry, just abandoned. Even with his fine clothes and high-handed ways, he and Kate had been friends. Mr. Charles had shown her great kindness. He'd made her a beautiful suit, which she loved, and shown her how to sew in ways she'd never imagined. More important, he believed in her. She'd not understood that fully until this very moment. She could see that Mr. Charles's hands were unsteady.

"I should stay," Kate said to Patrick. "Just for the announcement."

Mr. Charles shook his head. "It's fine," he said quietly.

"But?"

"It's really fine, Kitty. Have a nice night."

Patrick placed a hand gently on the small of Kate's back and guided her toward the exit. He paused for a moment and looked back at Mr. Charles. "Nice to meet you, Chuck."

In the nondescript hallway outside the showroom, Patrick and Kate waited for the elevator.

"What on earth were you thinking?" she asked. "Did you come in the front door? You know the service door is in the back. And *Chuck?* You called him *Chuck?*"

"You call him *Chuck.*"

"Not in front of people."

"In front of me."

"You don't count."

"I'll take that as a good sign."

Kate could see through the showroom window that Mr. Charles seemed to be hesitating. The Ladies looked impatient.

"I'll apologize later," Patrick said. "Buy him a pint or two, although he doesn't seem like a pint kind of fella. He calls you Kitty? I'm surprised you haven't slapped old Chuck sideways for that."

"Your display was uncalled for."

"It was absolutely called for. That's what men do. We're like mad dogs spraying."

"I can't believe you called him *Chuck*."

"The mom-and-pop scheme for the shop was not a fifty-fifty deal, was it? You would not be equal partners, would you? I took one look at him and could see that. Am I wrong?"

He wasn't.

Kate could hear the cars on Park Avenue honking as they cut in and out of traffic. Life was swirling around them. She looked back into the showroom once more. Mr. Charles was explaining the details; Maeve would certainly fill her in tomorrow.

Kate hit the elevator call button over and over again.

"I'm sorry," Patrick said. For a moment Kate thought he was apologizing for the way he'd treated Mr. Charles, but then he said, "I'm sorry, but I spoke to Father John at confession today. I mentioned the other night. Thought I'd warn you."

Kate felt the words like a slap.

"You had no right."

"I had no choice."

"Patrick. Please. Not here. I work here."

She looked back into the showroom. The entire staff of Chez Ninon had encircled Mr. Charles, but Mr. Charles was looking at Kate.

"I'm taking the stairs," she said, and opened the exit door. Ran.

"Kate, please."

Patrick was bigger, quicker. He caught Kate before she reached the outside door. They were both breathing hard. He wiped the tears from her face with his handkerchief.

"Kate. Father John said it's not a big deal. He told us to knock it off, that's all. A few Hail Marys, an Our Father, a rosary—he loves the rosaries—and knock it off until we get married. He's a footballer, for Pete's sake. He understands."

The stairway was dim and damp, a purgatory between the Ladies' world and Kate's. She wished she had some Chanel No. 5 to take the stench out. Patrick put his arms around her.

"Father John was happy for us, Kate. He really was. If we're going to Hell, he's driving us there in Rose. He's quite fond of her Oldsmobility, too."

Patrick opened the service door. Rush hour on Park Avenue was not elegant, just loud. He closed the door again quickly. "Here's the problem," he said. "I want to kiss you, but I made a promise to Father John, and I don't want to wait until we sit down at some stuffy café."

He pulled a box out of his jacket. It was black velvet and threadbare. "Peg bought this herself, when the butcher shop started doing better."

For all his bravado, at that moment Patrick Harris looked quite unsure of himself. It was barely a ring, a diamond chip in a thin gold band. The metal was nearly worn through.

"Patrick, I said I would think about it."

"I know. But why don't you think about it while you're wearing the ring? Get used to it. See how it feels. Take it for a test-drive. I test-drove Rose."

Patrick slipped the worn ring on Kate's finger. Her hands were swollen. It was tight. "I think you'll make a grand butcher's wife. Peg loved the shop, she really did."

A mom-and-pop shop, Kate thought.

For a moment, she wanted to run again. But then he kissed her.

CHAPTER THIRTEEN

"Give them what they didn't know they wanted."
—Diana Vreeland

$\mathcal{B}$efore the election, the unions had repeatedly scolded the Wife. The International Ladies' Garment Workers' Union raised more than three hundred thousand dollars for her husband's campaign and made sure that ILGWU members were at every rally possible, and yet not only did she wear French clothes, she very rarely wore a hat. Within their ranks, the powerful milliners' union, which was angry enough at the President's unwillingness to wear a hat, seemed permanently incensed with Her Elegance. Angry letters flooded the campaign office. After the election there could be no more excuses.

The first official hat was a Christian Dior. It was black velvet, with a narrow front. French, not American, but at least it was a hat. It was chosen quite by accident. The Wife had contacted the custom shop at Bergdorf's and asked for a private showing of their stock. Marita O'Connor brought the very best in millinery to a suite at the Waldorf. None of it worked. The Wife's aversion to hats was not just a personal preference. It was a matter of mathematics. She had a head as big as a balloon, and towering hair. In order to fit her, a hat would have to be a 7¾, an XXL—at the very least, twenty-four inches. In desperation, Mrs. O'Connor put the Dior on the Wife backward, and a reluctant history was made.

The only way she could wear the Dior was backward; it wouldn't fit otherwise.

"Can't be surprised," Schwinn explained. "The girl wears ten-A shoes."

It was six-thirty a.m. Kate thought that no one would be at Chez Ninon at that hour. She'd skipped church again to work on the suit. But instead of peace and quiet, Kate got Schwinn. He'd come in to steam dozens of pillbox hats that he had made for Orbach's runway show. It was his first real order for a department store as a milliner. "You can't tell anyone, Cookie. The Ladies will be miffed."

"Miffed? They'll be raging if they see you've used their workroom for Orbach's runway show."

Everywhere Kate looked, there were hats. And they were all pink.

"You told them about the Chanel suit, didn't you?"

"The Ladies may have sworn you to secrecy about the suit, but not me. Orbach's is now, categorically, over the moon for pink—but you didn't hear it here."

"The Ladies will blame me."

"No. They'll blame Cassini. They love to blame Cassini. His first show for Saks was all pearls, pillbox, and faux Givenchy—it looked like he took an armful from the Wife's closet and ran."

"But Orbach's? How could you?"

"How could I resist? No one can resist Orbach's."

It was true. Even Maison Blanche bought there. Kate often

stopped by the department-store windows for a look herself. Or-bach's had ads in every magazine: "Who Needs Wholesale?" "Be-cause Your Eyes Are Bigger Than Your Purse!" They advertised their clothes as "French couture originals," but they were not French or couture, and they were certainly not original. They were won-derfully cheap and surprisingly well made. Their clothes were so much better than Macy's couture copies. Kate had even thought about buying one or two herself. They were pirating whatever they could, like the Ladies—but on a grand scale. Instead of a handful of copies, they made hundreds.

Orbach's was not Chez Ninon, of course. There was no cham-pagne. No country-club manners. No dressers or fitters who spoke only when spoken to. For Orbach's customers, it was cash and carry only. Unlike the Ladies, Orbach's did not allow returns, alterations, fittings, or deliveries. Yet, every season fifteen hundred women or more stood in line for hours, waiting for the doors to open and for the fashion show to begin.

Orbach's always had two models walk down the runway at the same time; one would be wearing the original and the other the Or-bach's copy. It was nearly impossible to tell the two apart. Like Chez Ninon, Orbach's had "private friends," movie stars such as Lauren Bacall who were guaranteed a seat and ushered in through the back door. Many of the Ladies' clients attended as well. The Ladies hated Orbach's.

"I could be fired," Kate said.

"Cookie, you worry too much."

Pink hats were all over the back room—on the layout table, in her work area. Schwinn apparently had worked through the night.

"Try one," he said. "How about this?"

It was a raspberry pink. There were other shades of pink, too—hot pink, bubblegum, rose, and blush.

"Apparently, everybody who shops at Orbach's asks for her hat. They're magic. And today, that's what they will get. Magic," Schwinn said. As with the Wife's pillbox hats, these all had plastic tortoiseshell combs sewn into each side of the grosgrain ribbon to hold them firmly in place. Schwinn placed the hat on Kate's head, with the wide band in front, and pushed it slightly so that it sat on the back of her head, just as Mrs. O'Connor had done for the Wife.

"This way, when you're photographed, the hat won't get in the way of your face and block your beautiful features."

"That's clever."

"That's Hollywood, and that's why Cassini gets to be the secretary of style. A costume designer from Paramount Pictures was exactly what Maison Blanche needed." Schwinn removed the pillbox and began teasing Kate's hair into a makeshift updo. "There is not an original idea in that man's head, but he can whip up the kind of beauty that the public wants to see. Nothing too extreme, just pretty. And American."

Kate had really never thought of it that way, but it must be true. He dressed his wife, Gene Tierney, and then Grace Kelly, his girlfriend, and they were both all-American beauties.

"It's quite a trick, if you think about it," Schwinn said. "He's a Russian, born in Paris, but he's sharp enough to understand how Americans see ourselves and what our dreams are."

Schwinn sprayed Kate's hair in place with the White Rain that one of the Ready-to-Wear girls had left behind. The hair spray made Kate sneeze. He then put the hat back on her head. Arranged it. Secured it. He held a hand mirror up so she could take a look. Kate looked like someone else. Someone she didn't know.

"You look sharp, Cookie," he said. "Nice neck."

The pillbox was not as vibrant as the raspberry tweed of the suit; nor was it as complicated. It didn't catch the light in the same way. It was a dull replica. But there was something about it that was remarkable nonetheless.

"Very nice," she said.

"Nice? It's the accessory of the moment—maybe even of the millennium. Old women. Young women. They put a pillbox on their head and imagine what it's like to be her."

Looking in the mirror, Kate could imagine it too. She tilted her head to the right, as the Wife often did in photographs, and wondered if she could ever whisper something clever to Patrick in a coy, cultured way. She'd stopped by the butcher shop that morning on the way to work. It was so early that the pig men were there, and she and Patrick had had a rather extended conversation about the beauty of the Tamworth pig. He was quite enthused.

"This is the Irish Grazer. If you were a pig, Kate, that's what you'd be. Red hair. Loves apples. Sweet eyes, like you. Makes excellent ham."

It was a bit disturbing to think that the man she was considering marrying thought of her as a lovely pig—one he was delighted to slaughter. Kate was still trying to figure out what to make of that, especially since Peg's ring was now jammed tight on her finger. No amount of butter, ice, or shampoo could slip it off.

"Even from beyond the grave, our Peg is not a subtle woman," Patrick had said.

Coy and cultured conversations did not seem to be part of Kate's future plans.

"Keep the hat," Schwinn said. "Suits you. My gift."

"I don't need it."

"Since when is fashion ever a question of need, kiddo?" Schwinn added a large hat pin to the back. "Just in case there's a tornado."

"Are you sure?"

"Positive. Made a few extra. It will be your inspiration for the day."

And it was. With her pink pillbox hat tilted to the back in a jaunty style, and her red hair piled high on her head as if she were on her way to the Metropolitan Opera—ungodly noise, that was—Kate put on her white cotton gloves, rolled up her shirtsleeves, and began.

Chanel's construction was designed with an eye toward freedom of movement. There were three sections for each sleeve so that the arm could move without restriction. Kate cut, steamed, and stitched. Then she added the front panels, which needed to be matched ever so carefully, and then the back panels. Cut and stitch. Over and over again. Cut and stitch. Then, ever so gently, she steamed the seams into place.

When Maeve and the rest of the back-room girls arrived, they worked around Kate. "You look like you're ready for lunch with the queen," Maeve said. "Pink hat? That suit's made you half-daft already."

At noon, Miss Sophie was standing over her, holding another envelope from The Carlyle. "This is the second in a month," she said. "Is there something I should know?" Kate had forgotten about The Carlyle completely. Miss Sophie didn't wait for a response; she just turned and left. She was clearly upset with Kate. She didn't even mention the pink hat. The envelope made Kate's hands shake, and that wouldn't do. She needed a walk, needed to calm down. She knew she couldn't sew perfect stitches with a shake. Kate took off her white cotton gloves and slipped the envelope into the pocket of her heather tweed skirt. She didn't take her suit jacket or her coat. She was too upset to think that far. She even left her purse behind.

"I'm going to lunch," she said, to no one in particular.

The world outside Chez Ninon was warm enough, bright enough. Park Avenue was filled with shoppers; some had their drivers holding their packages. Some were harried mothers ferrying children across the busy streets. There were executives with cigars hailing cabs to make luncheons. And there were the drones—the office workers and girl Fridays—pushing their way toward the hot dog carts and empty park benches.

Kate had no idea where she was going until she ended up on Seventh Avenue, Fashion Avenue. It reeked of onions and old fish. The wide street was lined with men in cheap suits and yarmulkes. They huddled together, talking, their heads bobbing in nicotine clouds. These were the cutters—Kate knew that; their rutted faces were edged in dust and chalk. All day long, they cut fabric. That was all they did.

At Chez Ninon, the cutters were part of the Ready-to-Wear team. They were consulted with in meetings and spoke freely about the problems or benefits of one fabric over another. On Seventh Avenue, no one cared what the cutters thought about fabric, line, or color. They were mostly men, mostly Jews; they just cut and cut quickly, without complaint.

An unmarked door swung open as Kate passed. "Lunch is over," a foreman shouted. "Kikes," he said under his breath.

"How ugly," she said.

Kate couldn't believe that she said it out loud. But she wasn't sorry. It was ugly—although she wasn't sure if she meant the man, that horrible word, or that world in general—but she clearly meant it. *This type of behavior just has to stop,* she thought. The foreman gave her a nasty look. He spat on the sidewalk, not on her but close enough. Kate thought of seeing the good pastor on the subway train, with his beautiful blue tie and his remarkable courage.

Hate is such sorrowful business, she thought, and kept on walking. Lunch was over, but Kate couldn't go back yet. She wasn't ready to tell the Ladies about The Carlyle. She would probably be fired, and Maeve, with all her tricks and shortcuts, would likely finish the suit for Maison Blanche—and that would not do at all.

As Kate walked down Seventh, trucks jumped the curb and parked on the sidewalk; vans cut in and out of the skittish traffic. All around her, men were running with racks of dresses on hangers or pushing handcarts overflowing with fabric or trim or both. The windows on the second floors of the buildings were flung open, and the furious music of sewing machines mixed with the melodies of gossip from those mice, those back-room girls, the sweatshop girls. Polish, Russian, Lithuanian, and German, they worked for a better wage than they could make at home, but it was still not a good wage. At least now they were organized. They were union, and thirty-five hours a week meant thirty-five hours, no matter what names their bosses called them. In the suburbs, Kate heard things were very different indeed.

When she reached West Thirty-Fourth, Kate turned off the avenue. Between Fifth and Sixth she found herself standing outside

Orbach's. Above her in gold letters were the words OPEN TODAY UNTIL NINE. There were crowds gathered on the street, studying the windows. The display of the moment was clearly designed to sell "the Look," as Schwinn had called it. Window after window, everywhere Kate looked, she saw the Wife. There were dozens of mannequins, all fashioned in the likeness of the First Lady—with billowing hair and wide-set eyes—and dressed in the department store's versions of Her Elegance's clothes.

Copies, replicas, knockoffs—you could call them what you wanted, but they were amazing and totally convincing. The Wife was there in her double-breasted red "good luck" campaign coat from Givenchy—Kate still couldn't believe that Maggie had given that back to her, too. The Wife was also in Cassini's beige crepe wool dress from the inauguration ceremony, and the stubborn red-wool bouclé day dress, the Christian Dior by way of Chez Ninon, which nearly drove Kate insane.

"That one's mine," Kate told the lady standing next to her.

"I've got the red coat," the woman said. "The double breasted."

Kate wanted to clarify but knew that the woman wouldn't believe her. Or if she did believe her, Kate would seem to be bragging, and she'd done enough of that sort of thing recently.

There were groups of all sorts of women standing in front of these windows, dreaming. Some had packages. Some had children. Some were just milling around. Some were Midtown shoppers, with their smart clothes and small budgets. Some were tourists with flat shoes and cameras. There were three generations of Japanese women, pointing and giggling. It was just as Schwinn said—they were all under the Wife's spell.

"Nice hat," one of them said to Kate. "Orbach's?"

The woman had a Spanish accent. Her hair and skin were the color of chestnuts. Kate had forgotten that she still had the pink pillbox on. "Yes. Orbach's," she said, and the woman went inside to find it. A few others followed.

Kate looked at herself in the reflection of the window. It was, indeed, a very nice hat. It didn't quite match the violet heather of her skirt, but it didn't look that bad either. Behind her, across the street, Kate could see that tourists were lining up in front of the Empire State Building for the two p.m. tour. It was time to go back to the shop. Lunch was clearly over.

Kate still had no idea how she would explain her behavior to the Ladies, but there was one more window at Orbach's to see. Quite a crowd had gathered in front of it. It was formal wear. The star of any wardrobe, as Mr. Charles would have said. Kate moved through the crowd to get closer. The mannequin of the Wife was dressed in a delicate pink silk gown embroidered with sequins. It was the color of seashells, semifitted, not tight, with a demure bow at the waist. T-shirt formal, as the Wife called the style, a style that she had created and made famous by merely wearing it. It was as casual as a T-shirt, but with an elegant impact. The dress was a Dior knock-off by Mr. Cassini, and here it was being knocked off by Orbach's. Still, even with all those revisioning hands, it did what it was it was supposed to do, what Cassini always did—it evoked Hollywood glamour and yet a simple beauty. It was undeniably American.

The mannequin was not alone. Slightly behind her, there was another mannequin, dressed in a fine wool tux. The dark hair, Irish features, and blinding smile—nothing more was needed. It was modeled after Him.

They looked so happy—and beautiful. *I want that,* Kate

thought, and found herself on the verge of tears. She could hear her father's voice in her head—*Eegit*. The word was not harsh—*Eegit*—but said in the tone he reserved for those who were not the full shilling, those who were born the fools of the world, not the self-made ones, like her. These were mannequins, after all. They were not beautiful and in love. They were painted plaster, with nylon hair, but they looked so real. The way the Wife held her gloved hands, that delicate angle. The smile that was pure and not so pure all at the same time.

One tear. And then another. *Eegit.* A group of teenagers standing next to Kate began to stare at her. Her mascara was running. She'd left her handkerchief back at the shop and so she blotted her face with her white cotton shirtsleeve, which made her feel even more ridiculous. Kate wasn't sure exactly why she was crying, but she suddenly longed for the sea, the great vast sea out of Cobh, and that particular salt air. She longed for home.

She closed her eyes just for a minute, and imagined it. The last thing one sees when leaving Cobh is the Holy Ground, that bit of the verdant basin that no one can forget. And as your ship leaves the harbor, there are the fishermen's cottages stacked along the cliffs near the mouth of the cove. The House of Cards, as they're called. They're painted robin's egg blue, butter yellow, and pink—yes, pink: rosebud pink and coral pink. They are all sorts of shades of pink, like the Wife's suit. *Maybe that's why I love it so,* Kate thought, but knew the real reason she could not stop crying was Patrick.

He deserved an answer, but a butcher's wife like Peg spends every free minute knee-deep in blood and meat and not silk and satin. If they married, Kate knew she might have to leave Chez Ninon and this beautiful, perfect world entirely.

And yet Kate loved Patrick Harris, with his brilliant, unwieldy heart.

Kate needed a handkerchief, but the only thing she had in her skirt pocket was the envelope from The Carlyle. She opened it. *Might as well,* she thought. *I'm homesick, probably fired, and certifiably weepy—things can't get any worse.*

It was indeed another bill, but this time it was marked PAID.

Mr. Charles's business card was also enclosed.

Things can, indeed, get worse, she thought.

CHAPTER FOURTEEN

"A respectable appearance is sufficient to make people more interested in your soul."

—Karl Lagerfeld

𝓜iss Arlene Francis: "Has your name been in the paper in the last month?"

"Possibly."

Miss Francis: "Would any of us know you personally?"

"It is entirely possible."

Miss Francis: "You're not Salvador Dalí?"

He was not Salvador Dalí.

On the television show *What's My Line?* he'd looked pale and forgettable. Kate didn't know what to expect in person. The Minister of Style arrived in the showroom unannounced. Maeve had been right. Even though the pink suit was not his, he wanted to see how it was coming along. Professional curiosity, he said. While the intrusion was annoying, it was also Kate's salvation, because no one noticed her slip in the back door. A two-hour lunch for a back-room girl was not done. Maeve had clocked Kate back in after thirty minutes. "I know you'd do the same for me," she said, and helped Kate take off the pink pillbox hat.

"We don't want him stealing Schwinn's design now, do we?" Maeve said.

So much for secrecy, Kate thought.

The Carlyle was forgotten for the moment. The Ladies were thrilled that the Minister of Style had decided to pay a visit. They were chirping.

"So very handsome he is," Miss Nona said. "Dashing."

"He was in line to become Tsar of Russia," Miss Sophie said. She asked Kate to bring the jacket in herself—but to wait until the champagne was popped. "We want to make a grand entrance of it. Lipstick first, though," she said.

Miss Sophie took the last bottle of Moët & Chandon from the refrigerator and three cut-crystal glasses from the shelf.

"Just three glasses," Maeve said. "Apparently no champs for you, sister." Maeve handed Kate the tube of pink-violet lipstick that she'd liberated from the Ladies' powder room earlier that morning and held up a hand mirror for her. "The man's a gypsy. Watch your purse," she said, and then rubbed a little lipstick on Kate's cheeks, too.

"And, whatever you do, don't let him kiss you," Maeve warned. "He's Italian that way. You'll smell like garlic for a week."

Kate tried not to stare at the man as she laid muslin across the small gilded table and then gently placed the pink jacket on top of it. The shy peach color of the showroom walls made his Palm Beach tan radiant.

Playboy. Buffoon. Jet-setter. It was difficult to tell who this man really was, but his black suit was clearly Savile Row, probably Gieves and Hawkes. It seemed like one of their ready-to-wear endeavors that they'd once sold in shame through the back door. The fit was "semi made-to-measure," as they called it. The finishing was partly hand done; the rest was run off on a machine.

The suit was expensive enough but was not bespoke tailoring, not custom made. And yet, he wore it as if it were made for him and him alone, and perhaps that was all that mattered. But Kate could tell the difference. It was soulless.

The Ladies poured three glasses of champagne. He opened his briefcase and took out a long silver box that was the size of a cigar case and had khaki leather trim. Kate had never seen anything like it. He popped it open—inside was a camera. Miss Nona laughed with delight, as if the designer had just done a magic trick.

"Where did you get such a thing!"

"'Land,' they are called. Instant. Polaroid."

"Picture, please," Miss Nona said, and wrapped her frail arm around Miss Sophie. Each held a champagne glass and smiled broadly. They looked like two dowagers embarking on a transatlantic voyage aboard the *Titanic*. First class, of course. Their dresses were beaded shifts, reminiscent of the flapper style, and made of ninon, that fragile silk that the Ladies wore in their youth and still favored. It was Chez Ninon, after all. All they needed were rolled-up stockings and cloche hats, and it could be the Roaring Twenties.

Time may have begun to turn their bodies into shadows, but they still had that F. Scott Fitzgerald air about them.

The Minister of Style seemed bemused by it all. The flashbulb went off with a snap. He turned a knob and then opened the back of the camera and cut the paper away. "This is the photograph we have made," he said, but there was no picture on the paper.

The Ladies looked crushed. "Where are we?" Miss Nona asked.

"One minute. It must rest. Then we take the negative from positive."

Kate noticed that his accent sometimes seemed Russian, sometimes Italian, and sometimes French. It was very Mr. Charles of him. The Minister of Style shook the photo hard and placed it on the gilded table to rest. Then he turned to Kate.

"The jacket. Put it on."

He was surprisingly brusque. Kate hesitated. It was too large for her. It wouldn't show well. He'd hate it.

Miss Sophie patted her on the shoulder. "Go ahead, Kate. It's fine."

"Be our model," Miss Nona said.

Kate took off her smock and eased into the pink jacket. The sleeves were too long; they nearly covered her hands. The shoulders crept down her back. The first row of pockets landed just at her hips. The jacket overwhelmed her. And yet Kate wished there were a mirror so she could see herself, even for a second. It was so soft, so beautiful. It was like having a peony bloom around her.

Such funny flowers, so dependent on other things for their fleeting beauty, she thought. Ants, small and industrious, push the petals back until the flower is fully in bloom and fragrant. She'd learned that at school so many years ago and now Kate felt like the ant, taming this bouclé. The Wife was the sun, shining and indifferent to it all.

Kate closed her eyes and imagined the jacket was hers, and it felt as if anything were possible.

"You look like the runway girls do," Miss Nona whispered, and poked absentmindedly at Kate's updo with her long, clawlike fingernails. Kate wondered what her hair really did look like. Schwinn had apparently cemented it on the top of her head, and now Miss Nona seemed to be having a difficult time even moving it.

The Minister of Style did not look pleased. "Don't worry about that rat's nest," he told Nona. "I cut off her head when I shoot."

And now Kate knew exactly what her hair looked like.

A flashbulb popped.

"Turn," he said. She did. "Turn." She did again.

Each time Kate turned, he took a photo.

"Back to me, now," he said. "We must see the shoulders clearly."

She turned again.

"Good. Fine. Excellent. *Finis.*"

He was done with Kate. And, apparently, the jacket, too. The floor was littered with flashbulbs; some of them had burned small holes into the carpet, and some had seared the muslin he'd tossed aside.

"Clean this up," he said to Kate. "I don't want to step on them and ruin my shoes. Get a broom."

Kate wasn't sure she'd heard him correctly.

"Take off the jacket first. You shouldn't even be wearing it."

Apparently, Kate had heard him correctly. She carefully took off the jacket but did not get a broom or a vacuum cleaner. She held it in her gloved hands gently, with the lining side out, to show him her work. It was not the work of a woman who cleans a floor. The quilting was beautiful. Maybe if he saw it, he'd apologize to Kate. The silk had been sewn to the bouclé just as Chanel required; every stitch was nearly invisible and exactly one inch apart. The gold chain had been sewn into the hem to ensure that the jacket would hang properly. It was perfect. Kate had come in early to finish it, on her own time. Her hands ached horribly, but it was the finest work she had ever done. Kate had no intention of picking up a broom.

The Ladies could see that Kate was hurt. They were fluttering around her, trying to make the Minister of Style see that he should not insult their Kate.

"Kate's finish work is quite impressive," Miss Nona said.

"She's our very best," said Miss Sophie. "The stitching is so very amazing, isn't it?"

The Minister of Style ignored them. One by one, he shook each photograph and then peeled the backing away. He threw the negative paper, its chemicals still wet, onto the floor, with the spent flashbulbs and smoldering muslin. The chemicals would surely stain the carpet. When the paper hit a hot bulb, it sizzled and left an acrid smell in the air that mixed with the scent of soot.

The Ladies saw it all yet acted as if they didn't notice. They just spoke louder. Debris was piling up around the Minister of Style's elegant Italian shoes, but Kate would not get a broom. He laid each picture on the showroom table, arranging them as if they were cards in a game of chance that he, as high bidder, would certainly win. He scrutinized each one carefully. Finally he said, "The jacket is acceptable."

Miss Sophie looked as if she would pop. "The jacket is beautiful. How can you tell anything from these pictures? They're awful."

"The photographs are perfect," he said. "The suit is sufficient."

Sufficient? Kate couldn't believe it. The pictures were awful. The camera angles were odd. One shot looked as if it had been taken by a giant. The camera had been held so high overhead. Another picture was of the left side of the coat, but it was shot as if the photographer had fallen down and could only catch the image of the sleeve and collar. There were three pictures of her back.

"These photos hide the beauty of this jacket," Miss Nona said. "You can't see the shades of pink in the bouclé. These are all black-and-white." The photos made the jacket appear as if it had the texture of poured cement, like terrazzo floors, but the Minister of Style just shrugged. "This is the way your newspapers and television will see your handwork."

"But the pink—" Sophie said.

"Will not be seen. So no one cares about it. My concern is for a bad photographer or just a bad angle. That's what I am looking for. In order for the suit to become part of the White House collection, it must photograph perfectly, no matter what."

He chose one snapshot and threw the others on the carpet with the rest of the debris.

"You should take a picture of the quilting," Miss Nona said. "It is so refined. Very impressive."

"Your girl actually did the quilting?"

"Chanel required it."

"Maison Blanche did not need the quilting."

"But the agreement with Chanel—"

"Cannot be enforced. Chanel is no longer a member of the Chambre Syndicale. Did you not know that?"

Clearly they didn't. Miss Nona sat down, deflated. Miss Sophie poured herself another champagne.

Kate was furious, but she spoke quietly. "The quilting is what makes this jacket a Chanel."

The Minister of Style seemed surprised that Kate could speak at all. "Who cares about Chanel? Is it a Cassini? That is the most important question to Maison Blanche. If it is not a Cassini, it will not fit into the collection. It already appears to be too French, and that will be a problem. People will assume Chanel made it, and there will be more trouble, and that will not do."

"The White House demanded a line-by-line."

"And that is why I am alarmed. They were not thinking. I am creating the perfect state wardrobe for Madame la Présidente. It is a role she is playing. These clothes do not have to be well made. They only need to look well made when photographed. And they need to look American. This does not."

The Ladies began fluttering again.

"Then why did we pay Chanel?"

"It was so much money."

"Blame your President," Cassini said. "He was the one. He wanted her to have it. He demanded it be American. I did not even understand that this was happening until it was too late. It is your own fault. You should have contacted me immediately. Francois Zecca, he is the one who you should have been working with. The First Lady came to him about the suit first—did you know that? He is the one you have offended."

Kate felt awful; it was probably true. Francois Zecca was Cassini's own Mr. Charles. Beautiful manners, very Italian. So very handsome and elegant.

Miss Nona looked crushed. "We were not told we needed your approval. She's requested other clothes from us directly."

"No matter. You should have assumed and spoken to me as a professional courtesy. You brought all this upon yourselves. You accepted the order. You made it line by line, and that was foolish. Even a well-made copy is just a copy, after all. Not worth the trouble."

"But Kate spent so much time on it."

"Run the skirt off quickly on a machine. It will photograph well enough either way."

But it's a Chanel, Kate thought. *You can't do that to a Chanel.*

"We can do that," Miss Sophie said.

Kate couldn't believe what she was hearing. Miss Nona couldn't possibly agree, but she did. "If you want that, we will do that," she said.

The Minister of Style smiled. "Ladies, please," he said. "In the future, always consult with me when it comes to Maison Blanche. Even if they come to you directly. I am, after all, in charge."

Miss Nona and Miss Sophie promised they would.

"I hope we are forgiven," Miss Sophie said.

"Yes, I hope you can overlook this."

He smiled like the cat who'd had his fill of mice and was now quite pleased. "Shall we drink the champagne?" he said.

With spent flashbulbs, drying photos, wet chemicals, and smoldering trash piled at their feet, the Minister of Style and the Ladies sat down together to drink champagne and gossip. The Ladies looked frail compared with him, faded as old carpet. Kate couldn't believe what had just happened, and yet here they were—friends again.

"Kate, could you find someone with a broom?" Miss Sophie said.

There was no one with a broom. Miss Sophie knew that. It was the end of the day, and everyone had gone home. It was time for Kate to go home, too. She closed the showroom door gently behind her and took the pink jacket into the back room, where she wrapped it in clean muslin.

It was still a Chanel—at least to her.

She also wrapped the pieces of the skirt in muslin. Then placed the entire bundle in the Ready-to-Wear in-box, along with Chanel's instructions, even though they were no longer needed. Someone would just run the skirt off in the morning, maybe even one of the Ready-to-Wear girls. It would take less than an hour.

It was difficult for Kate to believe that the suit was suddenly no longer hers to make. It felt as if someone had died.

Miss Sophie had told Kate that when she was finished with the suit, she should wrap up all the remnants of pink and send them on to the White House. "Every last bit," she said. Kate was to put it all in a box and address it to Provy at Maison Blanche so that the diplomatic courier could pick it up.

Provy was the Wife's wardrobe mistress, her second-floor maid. Kate had never met her, but she had spoken to her on the telephone on several occasions, and she was very nice. It was Provy's job to replace buttons, adjust hems, and reweave fabric that suffered from cigarette burns. Since Maison Blanche gave clear orders that the Wife's clothes could not be replicated exactly, Chez Ninon always sent Provy all the usable remnants.

Kate measured out a quarter yard for Chez Ninon's files and put it in a plastic bag. Tagged it. She then folded up what was left of the bouclé and tried not to cry.

It was startling how much fabric remained. Kate knew she'd been very careful when she cut for the jacket, but there was clearly more than enough left for another suit. Perhaps even a pink suit done exactly as Chanel demanded.

Beauty must be honored, Kate thought. She cut a large swatch of the fabric and placed it in the box for Provy.

The rest of the pink Kate wrapped in more muslin and stuffed into an old Bergdorf Goodman bag that Maeve often used to "borrow" things from the Ladies, things that never seemed to make their way back to Chez Ninon. Kate took off her white cotton gloves and placed them on her desk. She punched her time card and pinned Schwinn's pink pillbox back on top of her towering red hair. Kate's hands were stiff as she buttoned up her coat. She picked up her purse and Maeve's bag and walked down the cement stairwell of Chez Ninon, into the cool night air. The door locked behind her.

October had finally arrived. It took Kate a block or so before she realized that she'd left her kidskin gloves behind, those poor leather gloves that had once been so beautiful had but never quite recovered from being caught in the rain. No matter. They no longer fit. *No sense trying to make something fit,* she thought. Kate stuffed her cold hands into her pockets; the bill from The Carlyle was still there, along with Mr. Charles's card.

Instead of making her way back to Columbus Circle to catch the train to Inwood, Kate started down Fifth Avenue, with bits of pink wool trailing behind her. Whorls of pink caught in the wind and stuck to her towering hair like wayward stars.

Mr. Charles laughed with pleasure when he opened his studio door and saw her standing there.

"Kitty," he said. "That color suits you."

"It's Kate," she said. "Thank you very much."

CHAPTER FIFTEEN

"Fashion is a language that creates itself in clothes
to interpret reality."

—Karl Lagerfeld

The Atelier, as Mr. Charles called his studio, had crystal chande-
liers and gold-painted walls. There was even a machine that sprayed
perfume into the air every ten minutes so that you would feel "intoxicated by lilacs," as Mr. Charles had said. Kate had stayed longer
than she'd planned to. Patrick wasn't angry, but he was clearly un-
settled by her visit with Mr. Charles. Perhaps a little jealous, and
that was just fine. Flattering, even.

"He made you an offer?"

"He did."

"He showed you his workshop?"

"It was lovely."

"My turn, then."

"Turn? He's not asked me to marry him, Patrick. It's not like
that."

"But he wants you to help build his business. And that's what I want too. You can't give your heart to both. He made his case. Let me make mine."

"Don't you want to know what I said?"

"I do. But even if you said no, you can't be a butcher's wife if you know nothing about what I do."

"That doesn't sound very romantic."

"There'll be a romantic moment later, trust me. Nothing's more romantic than dead meat." He was grinning, which made Kate laugh.

Patrick took off his topcoat and put on a fresh butcher's coat, long and white. He handed her a clean apron—"Hook it around your head"—and a twelve-inch steel knife. "And you'll need the gloves." They were not the thin cotton gloves Kate used to handle fabric, but roughly woven canvas. "Wrap your hair up so it doesn't get in the food," he said. Kate was suddenly glad that she'd washed all that hair spray out of her hair before she came.

"Do you need a hat? I can get you a hat."

Patrick always wore a white wool fedora behind the meat counter—very dashing and very old-fashioned—but he handed her a paper cap that looked like it belonged to a carhop.

"That's awful."

"Would you rather have a hairnet?"

"I'd rather eat supper."

"Soon," he said. He picked up a small silver saw. "Let's start with a special order."

"You're serious?"

He was. With a rather large thump, Patrick slapped the front quarter of a calf on the stainless steel table in front of Kate. The meat was soft and pink. "Veal," he said. "Your first cut needs to separate the brisket and the shank from the shoulder and then separate each of the prime ribs." He was pointing at where the cuts should be with a long skinning knife.

"You skin things, too?" she asked.

He laughed.

On the wall was a framed needlepoint, probably Peg's own handiwork. It was a poem from Robert Burns:

> *Some ha'e meat and canna eat,*
> *And some wad eat that want it;*
> *But we ha'e meat, and we can eat,*
> *Sae let the Lord be thankit.*

Kate hoped that there would not be a long tradition of meat poetry or too much skinning involved in their lives together.

Patrick patted the small front quarter with the flat of his hand. "See how tender?" he said. She couldn't look.

That morning, when Kate agreed to dinner, she expected dinner. She did not expect a class in Irish butchery. Kate put the knife down next to the joint. "It's a little late for this," she said gently.

Patrick indeed looked tired. "Right, then. We'll save the cutting-up part for another time." He picked up the quarter and balanced it on one shoulder, a trick she imagined that he'd practiced for the phone operators. It teetered there, making him look like a strong man in the sideshow. "In French," he said, "the word *entrecôte* means 'the good stuff.' The veal is the good stuff."

"You don't speak French."

"It's a butcher word."

He swung the joint around and slid it back in its place on the shelf, next to the rest of that poor baby cow. The shop was closed and cleaned. Tomorrow's special orders were lined up for early delivery. Patrick and Kate should have been on their way to the pub. He'd asked Mrs. Brown to make them a proper meat pie, with steak, Murphy's ale, and Patrick's own cured bacon. There'd also be a bit of mashed, because nothing goes better with any food than potatoes, butter, and cream. "A tad of parsley on top for the veg," he said. "A proper meal for courting."

But instead of having a proper meal for courting, or any sort of meal at all, Kate and Patrick were standing in the walk-in cooler, with raw meat stacked on the stainless shelves all around them. In the center of the small room, hanging between them, was a half of a cow, caught on a hook. It was split through its spine and hung upside down. A thick chain on a pulley held it steady. It reminded Kate of a nightmare she once had.

"This is good stuff, too?" she asked.

"Dry aged. Very rich. Brings in twice the price."

The carcass was enormous, bigger than Patrick. The skin was mottled, yellow and moldy. *Poor cow,* Kate thought.

"You'll get used to the smell of the blood," he said.

Poor me.

The lexicon of Irish butchery was apparently vast. *Rib eye, club steak, Scotch fillet, contre-filet*—which some called sirloin—and *strip loin,* which in a restaurant is actually called sirloin but in a butcher shop is usually *rump,* although it could also be *shell steak, Delmonico, Kansas City,* or *New York strip steak.*

"Patrick?"

"Cold?"

"It's slightly above freezing in here."

"With eighty-five percent humidity?"

"Absolutely."

At least she'd learned something.

Patrick took off his fedora and placed it on the hook. "Since we're not up to slicing tonight," he said. His hair was alarming in its independence, poking up here and there. With a skinning knife in one hand and a carcass in another, he looked slightly mad. *A man possessed by meat,* Kate thought, and, oddly enough, she wanted to kiss him. But he was too busy talking about the science of fat ratios.

The night was slipping away from them, and it was such a shame. Kate had taken such pains to choose the right lipstick, the right rouge. Her nylons were real French silk; the Ladies had given them to her last Christmas. The dress that she was wearing she'd never worn before. She'd been saving it for a special occasion. It was navy-blue crepe, with sweet cap sleeves and a flounce skirt, a lovely, feminine thing.

Kate hadn't planned on a night of raw meat. It didn't seem as if Patrick had. *Old Spice,* she thought. He'd shaved.

"The top side of beef is the one with a fat cap. Sometimes they call it *round* or *London broil.* It's used for pot roasting, cottage pies, or shepherd's pies.

"Tallow is trimmed fat. It has to be rendered before it's resold."

The language of bone and muscle seemed foreign to Kate. Was there any beauty in it?

Mr. Charles's atelier was so elegant, an amazing little jewel of a place, with carved chairs from India that were as ornate as thrones.

The rugs were hand-knotted Orientals. And there were cocktails. Kate had never had a martini before. It was very small and cold and strong. She coughed when she took the first sip. Mr. Charles had laughed.

"You have to be careful and sip slowly," he said. "Gin is designed to make one elegantly fluffy."

The gin had made Kate feel elegantly fluffy right up until the moment that Patrick began to explain the capricious nature of the walk-in meat cooler: The air conditioner is old and testy, the humidifier works but is covered in rust, and the fans overheat and must be watched carefully.

"Is everything in this room unreliable?" she asked.

"I hope not."

He meant her, of course. Patrick swung the cow slightly, like a child kicking a can. The chain creaked. He took off his butcher's gloves and ran a hand through his hair, and for a moment, he looked so profoundly tired. And lonely. And, perhaps, slightly afraid. "Peg loved this shop more than anything because it was hers," he said. "Nobody told her who she could speak to. She was the lady here. Don't you want that?"

"I do, but—"

"But it's a butcher shop?"

The side of beef swayed a bit. It was mottled like a bruise. The stench of it was overwhelming. The air conditioner cycled on and then off, and the humidifier hissed in the corner. "Patrick, the First Lady of the United States wears clothes I make—"

"And yet you're not good enough to speak to her."

"It's not that simple."

" 'Tis," he said. "You once said that the Wife is the 'best of us,' but that's wrongheaded. It's the other way round. She's not the best of you, Kate. You're just as lovely—more so, actually. And you're a real person. You sew until your hands go numb to help support your old man and Maggie Quinn, and for the pride of craft and country, both Ireland and America. She doesn't have your sense of justice or humbleness in front of a mighty God."

"Patrick—"

"Somebody needs to tell her to get off her exquisite bum and do something. Free Ireland. Get on the bus with the coloreds and Dr. King and his wonderful tie. Somebody needs to say to her, *Do something important because you can. If you're one of us, be us, then.*"

The rusted air conditioner rattled on again. Out of habit, Patrick leaned over and felt the air to see if it was still working.

"Patrick, in the neighborhood. What do they say about me?"

"Who?"

"People."

"Nothing."

"Maggie says—"

"Maggie's a little high-strung."

"But she's no liar. Tell me. Please?"

Patrick hesitated.

"Please?" she said again.

"It's just a joke, really. They call you Queen, but they don't mean anything by it."

"Queen?"

"The Queen of Inwood. It's just talk, though. It's like having a nail that sits up too high—you have to bang it down a little, or it will trip people up. You know what I'm saying?"

She did. *God save our glorious Queen*—Kate could still hear him singing that, the sadness in his voice. It was no joke to him. Maggie was right. Patrick was the only one who wasn't laughing.

"Kate, they just talk. It's just talk, nothing more."

She nodded but felt numb. Patrick took her hands, removed the gloves, and kissed her tenderly. "You can't pay people no mind, Kate. They say so many things they don't mean."

"And if we marry, what will they say about you?"

Patrick shrugged, but Kate could see that he'd thought about that, maybe even worried about it. Gossip can kill a business.

"You could walk away from the Ladies," he said, "if you're worried about what people are saying. You could work here at the shop and sew for people in the community—that would turn things around. There are thousands of girls in Inwood who need First Holy Communion dresses every year. Mrs. Brown from the pub makes a tidy business of it on the side. She can't keep up with the work, though. She'd asked Peg to take the overflow. You could do that. We could set up in Mam's room. Mrs. Brown likes you very much."

He'd obviously given this a good deal of thought.

As Patrick spoke, the geography of Kate's life grew smaller, until it fit into the palm of his hand. She wanted to say: *I told Mr. Charles no. I want to open my own couture shop. I know I can do this. Mrs. Vreeland did.*

Kate wanted to say all this to Patrick but couldn't. She was, after all, the Queen of Inwood. She was a nail to be pounded down.

"I love you," he said. "Always have."

"I know."

Patrick waited for a moment to hear her say the word *love,* but some words must be carefully considered. They complicate. They define. They own you. Kate wasn't sure she wanted to be owned, but she couldn't imagine her life without Patrick, either.

He looked hurt for a moment and then seemed to think better of it. He kissed her again. He was still searching for that word somewhere in Kate's eyes when he said, "Should we get some dinner? Shake all this off?"

"Please."

He took off his butcher's coat. He had on a tie, the Harris clan tartan—*How sweet of him*—and a freshly pressed shirt. It was supposed to be a proper date, after all. He was lovely, if men could be called lovely. He put on his overcoat and then stopped for a moment, as if he'd just remembered something. "I'm not saying you have to leave the Ladies."

"I know."

"Good." Patrick checked the air conditioner again, and the humidifier. "I think we're good."

"Are we?"

"We are. You know, I did have this little speech worked up for you. It was all about the unpredictability of dry-aged beef. How you can't rush it. Takes forever to do properly, but tenderness comes, always—but it comes on its own terms."

As promised, the poet butcher did have a big, romantic finish.

Kate said his name with such tenderness. "My dear Patrick Harris." Yes, tenderness. It surprised them both. She wondered, just for a moment, how many telephone operators he'd told his dry-aged meat story to—but then she kissed him for it.

It was not a chaste kiss, or a drunken kiss, although she still tasted of olives and gin. It was the kind of kiss that one remembers through both good times and bad.

"May we have our supper now?" he asked.

They could. And they did. But only after Mrs. Brown had a word or two with them about "punctuality being the road to heaven."

CHAPTER SIXTEEN

"Elegance is elimination."

—Cristóbal Balenciaga

*W*hen a garment was complete, the final step was to sew on the label. For ready-to-wear, it read *Chez Ninon. New York, Paris.* Couture garments, being completely handmade, were more complicated. Each label identified Chez Ninon, but it also bore the name of the owner, the date the garment was created, and the model number assigned to it, so that if its remnant was needed for repair work, or if the owner wished to have the piece cleaned and stored at the shop, it could be easily identified. It was a very efficient system.

The label for the pink suit was waiting on Kate's table when she arrived that next morning. There was a trunk show going on, but after it was over, the Wife was scheduled to come in for a fitting of the completed suit. It would be her first and final.

Everything was ready for her arrival, so Kate and Maeve snuck up front to see the show. It was Snob Dresses, the "It" dresses of the hour. Modest in design and outrageous in price, they were worn with the Wife's preference of a tiny, two-inch heel. They were "little nothings," more stylish than around-the-town dresses and more ornate than the yearly Little Black Dress that Chanel always showed with pearls. More important, at least for the Ladies, they were amazingly profitable if run off on the machines, with only a few hand finishes, just for show. The Ladies had written their regulars about a special trunk showing. *Straight from Paris, for Winter Cruise Season!*

Straight from Mr. Charles would have been more truthful. He'd designed every last one of them as his last act.

"Miss the old goat," Maeve said.

Mr. Charles and Maeve were about the same age, but Kate didn't want to mention that. She never even told Maeve about the Atelier or being "intoxicated by lilacs" or the gin martini. And, of course, the fact that Mr. Charles had paid her bill at The Carlyle would be a secret Kate would take to her grave. It was embarrassing enough to confess it to Father John.

The bright colors of the summer Snob had become passé, and so Mr. Charles had created an "Anti-Snob Snob" in somber tones. It was basically the same dress—a well-fitted sheath—with endless variations in black, brown, and gray. No prints. The necklines were bowed or slashed or cowled. There were pleats or buttons—but not both. There was a sleek gray silk Snob with an exaggerated Greek neckline that draped the collarbone, and a brown wool day Snob with a hem made of dozens of brown woolen roses. The black crepe cocktail Snob was low in the back and could be worn in reverse—and that was cheeky enough to garner a standing ovation.

"They've no clue they're snobs themselves, do they?" Maeve said.

The showroom was filled with about fifty people or more. They were all wearing pillbox hats and white gloves, drinking away the sorrows of bad haircuts and imprudent servants with Taittinger; the Ladies had sprung for better champagne this time because the profit margins for Snob Dresses were vast.

Mrs. Babe Paley was in attendance, sitting in her usual spot, facing the audience. She was not wearing white gloves or a pillbox hat. She was, as always, setting trends, not following them. Her long legs were casually crossed at the ankle; her dark hair was turning elegantly gray, as God had intended. Kate admired that about her.

Mrs. Paley had been the editor at *Vogue* years ago, then married the chairman of CBS, and then won some award for being well dressed. It wasn't so much that she was deadly beautiful, although she was—Kate could see that from across the room. It was as if she were sculpted from marble—the drape of her dress, the luminescent skin: there was a cool elegance to it all, as if she had remained untouched by human hands. The Ladies said she was not a trendsetter but a "fashion icon." An original. Kate knew what the Ladies were getting at. Every time Mrs. Paley made a note about a piece, nearly everyone in the showroom would place an order for the outfit and hand it to the runner. It was pandemonium. Everyone wanted to be an original too, and that made Kate laugh. She wondered if Mrs. Paley was just having a bit of fun with the crowd, making notes just to see how many people jumped at the sight. Babe Paley never ordered in public. Everybody at Chez Ninon knew that.

When the show finished, she would wait until everyone had left and then go back to her favorite dressing room, where the Ladies would have the models walk by her one more time. The rule was that while Mrs. Paley was making up her mind, everyone had to be perfectly silent. No talking. No machines. No loud noises. Even the Ladies were confined to their private offices. "She hates the distractions," Miss Sophie reminded the back-room girls.

And they call me the Queen, Kate thought.

She'd never gotten a good look at Babe Paley before, but now that she had, Kate felt nothing but pity. Whenever she looked up at the girls on the runway—with their pose-turn-pose-turn style—Kate could clearly see that her eyes were deeply sad. She seemed hopeless, somehow. Even with all that money and fame. Kate didn't know what to make of it.

Kate and Maeve were still watching the show when Schwinn sidled up next to them and whispered, "Maison Blanche." The Wife was waiting in the back room with the back-room girls.

It was really thrilling; even Maeve thought so. "How very 'just us girls' of her," she whispered.

Kate nearly ran down the long hallway to see her. She could hardly believe it. After all this time, and all these clothes, all these hours spent imagining her in one dress or another, Kate would finally get to see the Wife up close, maybe even have a word or two with her. To see her in that beautiful suit would be the most thrilling thing of all; she certainly would appreciate the perfectly quilted lining, no matter what Cassini had said. It would be impossible not to. *Just for a moment—maybe, just maybe—the Wife may even wonder if it is a real Chanel.* As long as she didn't look at the skirt too closely, it would be difficult to tell the difference.

There might even be tea. And if she had just a moment, if no one was talking to her, Kate could ask her about Cork. She could ask if she missed it, too. Maybe even ask after the Lees, because the Old Man would want Kate to do that. If there were still any Lees left in Cork, maybe she could get a telephone number for the Old Man to call, and they could all meet somewhere for a pint, if they fancied that, or just stroll through the English Market, looking at the wild geese, red currants, farmhouse cheese, and sweet butter.

At that moment, the world had become Kate's. *Queen of Inwood. Who cares what those people think?*

Schwinn opened the back-room door with a flourish. "Girls," he said, "meet the Wife."

Instead of the usual entourage of forgettable men in rumpled suits and Ray-Bans, and nervous assistants with wash-and-wear hair and practical shoes, there was just one single girl. She was a slight girl, actually. It was not the Wife at all but a girl wearing the Wife's pink suit.

Take that off, Kate thought as soon as she saw her.

"The new Wife," Schwinn said. "Maison Blanche has decided we're completely off-limits these days. No more sneaking around in tunnels for Her Elegance."

"Probably all the gawking the other day when she came round," Maeve said. She sounded disappointed but not surprised.

Kate, on the other hand, was shocked. She knew the other shops always used live mannequins for the Wife, but not Chez Ninon. *We're Blue Book,* she thought. *Miss Sophie, Miss Nona, and the grand Mrs. Molly Tackaberry McAdoo are Blue Book all the way. We're one of her own.*

"She's not coming back?"

"Sorry, kiddo."

At Chez Ninon they had dressed the mother and all the others in the clan of Lee for years, and then Her. But now the L&Ms and that air of Chanel No. 5 were gone forever. First Mr. Charles, now this. Kate had so many questions that they bled together and reduced themselves to just one: "Are we fired?"

"Nope."

Schwinn handed Kate the envelope from Maison Blanche. It was filled with drawings and a dozen or more orders. They certainly were not fired. They would still make her clothes; the trip to India alone would take a solid month of work.

He shrugged. "Looks like Maison Blanche has decided to set up a procedure for us because they are the government—and that's what governments do best. That, and memos."

Chez Ninon now had both. The memo even had bullet points:

• The live mannequin will now be used for all fittings. No exceptions.
• Photos will always be taken. If the outfit photographed meets the specifications stated, then the Chez Ninon label may be sewn in, and it will be eligible for inclusion in the White House collection. Once approved, all invoices will be handled in the usual manner.

Kate knew that meant Mrs. Tackaberry McAdoo would address the invoices as if they belonged to Mrs. Raymond A. Gallagher, the Wife's secretary, and then mail them to either the account at Riggs Bank or to the Father-in-Law, in Hyannis Port, depending on the "damages," as Maeve would say.

Neither Kate nor Schwinn could figure out whose desk the memo had come from. The paper was high quality, but plain and without a watermark.

"Very CIA," Schwinn said. "Untraceable and thereby deniable."

"I think the Minister of Style had it sent."

"Doesn't matter. She's gone."

It was difficult to imagine.

Schwinn took out his camera. It was an old Brownie, not a Polaroid, like the Minister of Style had. The pictures would have to be taken to the developer.

"Back to work for the mere mortals," he said. The mannequin, whose name was Suze, was still wearing the beautiful suit. "Give us a pose," he told her. "Something very Maison Blanche."

The girl's pose was arrogant and sullen, and that made Kate angry. She wanted to shout—*She's not like that, she's not a snob*—but didn't. Kate really didn't know what the First Lady was like, and now she would never know.

"No. No," Schwinn said to the girl. "We're looking for an I Hate Camp David but That's No Reason to Hate Me look. I need a look that's cheerful but pained."

The girl laughed. "Got it," she said, and tilted her head the exact way that the Wife did, her hips jutting out at an angle. She smiled winningly, but it wasn't the same smile at all. It didn't have that same playful spark. Maeve checked the fit. It was perfect except that the shoulder was slightly off.

"That's because of her swayback," Kate said.

"Right. The gammy bit. Nearly forgot."

Schwinn was clearly enjoying his role as White House photographer. He was thorough and sharp eyed. "Looks good, Cookie."

"Not *Cookie*—Suze."

"Suze."

Schwinn didn't even try to explain that every female he knew was either "cookie" or "kiddo." He was a names-optional sort of fellow. Unlike Cassini, Schwinn photographed the entire girl, including her head. Of course, the girl was younger than Kate, and the suit fit as it should. The skirt looked better than Kate thought it would, but she didn't want to look too closely at it. It still hurt that she didn't get to complete the job properly. In the end, the suit was beautiful and that's all that really mattered. Still, the vibrant pink bouclé overshadowed the girl. The navy silk blouse seemed dull against her skin. It was as if the model were just a child playing dress-up in her mother's clothes.

"What is it that makes one outfit look so different from person to person?" Kate asked.

"Karma," Schwinn said. "You're not born into the perfect dress; you're reborn into it."

CHAPTER SEVENTEEN

"To be well dressed is a little like being in love."
—Oleg Cassini

$\mathcal{T}$he next day, when the letter from Kate's father arrived, she didn't have time to read it. She usually made a ritual of opening it with a proper cup of tea and her feet in a warm bath of soaking salts, but she and Patrick were on their way to the rectory to talk to Father John about marriage.

"Can't he just give us a few Hail Marys and a rosary or two and send us on our way?"

"He wants to know if we're ready to announce the banns."

"And if we're not?" Kate asked.

"He wants to talk about that, too."

Misery. She put her father's letter in her purse for later.

Kate and Patrick walked hand in hand down Broadway. The sun was setting, but it was not dark yet. Impatient stars appeared, dim as shadows, but they still could be seen. The last remnants of Indian summer took the chill off the moment, making it warm enough to walk down the high street in just a smart hat, without gloves. Winter seemed impossible. They were nearly at the Good Shepherd Church when someone in a black Buick honked and waved.

"Customer," Patrick said, and so they both waved back.

"People will talk," she said.

"That they will."

Father John answered the door to the rectory himself. He was in a white shirt with the sleeves rolled up, black pants, and a black wool cardigan that one of the women from the Ladies Auxiliary had knit for him. He could have been any man. He didn't really look like a priest. He smelled of Ivory soap. His pale hair needed combing. Kate almost didn't recognize him without his collar. He was younger, softer looking, and a little too round around the middle. Cork's greatest footballer still had the air of an athlete — the mantle of the red and white, the Blood and Bandages, still hung about him, but now he was soft and pleased with his life.

"We can come back another time," Patrick said.

"You're not getting out of it that easily," he said, laughing. "Come in. Won't be that long."

Father John led Kate and Patrick down the dark, paneled hallway. There was a light on in the dining room and a mumble of voices.

"I'd rather be playing poker, but we're discussing the Harvest Dinner Dance and Car Raffle. We're still looking for some chaperones for the young ones, in case you two are interested. Are you interested?"

Kate had never noticed how tall Father John was before. How long his arms were, how large his hands. The good father certainly had been a spark on the field; he was the finest player she'd ever seen. He'd throw his body into a block so fearlessly that it was stunning to watch.

"Kate?"

"I'm sorry. What were you saying?"

He was towering over her, clearly amused. "I'm going to need to put on my collar, aren't I? I can see it in your face. You're in one of those dreamy moods of yours."

She was. That morning, the grand Mrs. Tackaberry McAdoo and her tiny black-and-white fluffy dog boarded a Pan Am flight to Washington to deliver the photographs of the pink suit. Kate hoped that the Wife would request to have the skirt redone. This time properly, by hand.

Unfortunately, if the Wife didn't like the pink suit at all, the Ladies would not get paid. The memo was quite clear. It was all Kate could think about; it was all anyone at Chez Ninon could think about. Every time the telephone rang, the workroom went quiet. Miss Sophie told the back-room girls that the stewardesses always let Mrs. Tackaberry McAdoo fly with Fred the dog on her lap. She was just that sort of lady. If anyone could talk the Wife into accepting the suit, it would be Miss Nona's niece. Kate hoped she was right.

Father John opened the door to his office and turned on the light. The room felt cold. It was just like being called into Mother Superior's office at the convent school. The priest put his huge hands in the pockets of his cardigan, which pulled the wool out of shape. He stood at the door, looking more like a student than a priest.

"I have to warn you both, I enjoy the sheer look of terror on your faces. I'm not going to allow either of you to leave tonight without a date set for the wedding."

"Lovely," Kate said.

"Fair warning, that's all," he said.

As soon as he closed the door, Patrick took out his reading glasses and picked up the newspaper. "Would you like some?"

Outside the office, a floorboard creaked. Kate wondered if Father John was standing behind the closed door, listening. Plotting his strategy. He was always a fine strategist on the field; it was not such a stretch of the imagination to think that he'd be eavesdropping. *After all, there's no commandment against that,* Kate thought.

"Would you like the women's section?" Patrick asked.

"I'm fine," she said.

He leaned over and kissed her cheek, shyly. Somewhere between the sky and the sea—that was the color of his eyes at that moment. He clearly wanted an answer from Kate, too. But he wouldn't push.

"If you want, we can sneak out before he gets back," he said.

"That would add another rosary to the penance pile."

"True."

Patrick became engrossed in the sports section, and so Kate took out her father's letter. The envelope was from the Commodore Hotel in Cobh. The hotel had been majestic in its day. The last passengers to board the *Titanic* slept there before their voyage. Maybe the Lees, the Wife's people, slept there, too. Her father had nicked the envelope. He was always stealing stationery from fancy hotels. An open door was all the invitation he needed. *Still incorrigible,* Kate thought, and opened the envelope. There was a letter, yes. But something else, too.

"Rose petals." Kate had forgotten about them completely.

Patrick looked up from the newspaper. She took a few from the envelope to show him. Brown and withered, from her father's garden, they'd obviously been pressed into a book the day she'd left. They crumbled in her hands.

I've heard about your pending change of status and have put your baby Jesus in the churchyard, he wrote. *Let me know when He can come in again. He's looking bedraggled.*

Jesus of Prague. It had been so long since Kate had even thought of that statue. If a girl was lucky enough to have one of her very own, it sat on the windowsill, as Kate's did. She loved making satin gowns to dress it up on holy days. It had a paste jewel crown and held a tiny ceramic world in one hand. It was quite regal, and good luck, too. If you dressed it up and prayed to it, you'd eventually find a suitable husband. Then you could pass the statue on to your own little girl. That was the way it was done in Cobh. The Prague child was put outside on the morning of your wedding to ensure a sunny day and a sunny life.

Apparently, Kate's own baby Jesus was now a lawn ornament until her father heard otherwise. *Word travels fast,* she thought.

"Everything all right with the Old Man?" Patrick asked. His reading glasses made him look quite scholarly.

"He knows."

"Maggie?"

"Who else?"

"And his verdict? Am I to be skinned alive or the son he never had?"

Kate scanned the letter. *It's somewhat acceptable that the boy is an Over-the-Bridger,* her father wrote, *only because he's Peg's boy, and your mam would have liked that. But he didn't even write me and ask for your hand, and that's rude. Those who live over the bridge are a different breed. It'll be a trial for you.*

"You'll be a trial," she said.

"That's a given. Anything else?"

Kate read ahead quickly. *P.S.,* her father wrote, *I did, indeed, nick the stationery as a commemorative gesture for your upcoming nuptials. Marriage is a lot like being on the Titanic—it's all fancy dress and good eats until you drown.*

"You don't want to know," Kate said.

She put the letter back in her pocketbook. The only thing she knew for sure was that her Prague child would catch his death in the churchyard, waiting.

"Should we call him?" Patrick asked.

"It's two a.m. there."

"Right."

"Right."

After half an hour and no sign of Father John, Patrick began reading the sports section aloud to Kate: Yankees, again. Home-field advantage against the Baltimore Orioles.

Roger Maris versus Mantle to break Ruth's record of sixty home runs in a season.

Maris hit his sixty. Mantle won't make it. Maybe his last game ever. He's an old man.

Patrick looked up from the paper. "You know, Ruth was once a minor leaguer for the Baltimore Orioles." Patrick had told her the story about Ruth slamming the ball out of the Dyckman Oval. He was always telling her interesting things.

"Do you really want to marry me?" Kate asked.

Patrick put the newspaper down. The poet butcher who named his car in honor of the President's mother, who played guitar for the prize of a fine-crumbed cake on any given Sunday after mass, this man who was usually so buoyant that he was unafraid to be sentimental or joyous or sing if there was a song that needed to be sung—this man seemed suddenly fragile.

"Will you have me?"

The door opened.

"Ready?" Father John asked.

Another very good question, indeed.

"Not yet," Kate said.

This time, Patrick and Kate turned on every light in her tiny apartment. Maggie's coffins were still stacked waist high in chronological order on Kate's kitchen floor. The zippers and rickrack and buttons and lace were bright as fireflies caught in a jar. Bolts of silk in twenty shades of moonlight stood upright like ghosts.

"This looks like the remnant room at Chez Ninon," Patrick said.

"Nearly."

"Is that why we're here?"

"If I must understand the fine art of Irish butchering to be your wife, then you can't be a back-room girl's husband with knowing why she loves it so."

"But Mam—"

"Didn't love it."

"She enjoyed it."

"That's different."

It was. Patrick had never realized that before; he had never understood that Kate was not like his Peg. "I'm sorry," he said, in a way that told her that he meant no harm. He was just a boy who loved a girl.

"Forgotten already."

The pink bouclé that she had liberated from Chez Ninon was still wrapped in muslin. Kate brought the lamp from her bedside table and plugged it in, turned it on, and shone it on the fabric. She put on her white cotton gloves and unwrapped the pink gently and held it out for Patrick.

"It's not just wool or sheep's hair—as you said. It has life," Kate said, and began to turn the bouclé to catch the light, as if it were a prism. "Every fabric has a voice. When you rub your hand quickly along it, you can hear its music. But it's not just the threads that sing; it's the life behind them. It's the song of those who tend the sheep and those who shear them, of those who dream in shades of cherry blossoms and shooting stars, and through alchemy and mathematics weave grace. It's the song of those who warp and weave and darn; it's the song of their lives, too. Because part of their lives, part of all their lives, was spent making something of such audacious beauty that it can nearly make the heart stop."

Kate was on the verge of tears.

"If pink could be thunder," Patrick said, "it would look like this."

"Exactly."

When the grand Mrs. Tackaberry McAdoo and her tiny black-and-white fluffy dog Fred arrived at Chez Ninon the next afternoon, there was champagne. The Chanel had been accepted by Maison Blanche. "The pink suit was beloved!" Mrs. Tackaberry McAdoo told the Ladies. And when Miss Sophie repeated this to Kate, she squealed to replicate the exact sound that Mrs. Tackaberry McAdoo had made. The noise sounded like someone had accidentally sat on Fred the dog, but since Kate had never actually spoken to Mrs. Tackaberry McAdoo, she could neither confirm nor deny the veracity of the impersonation. She had to take Miss Sophie's word for it.

"Did the Wife want the skirt redone?" Kate asked.

"Of course not! Perfect as is!"

But it isn't right, Kate thought. "Didn't she notice it was run off on the machines? Mr. Cassini said we needed to—"

Miss Sophie threw her head back and laughed. "Mr. Cassini says a great many things that no one listens to, Kate. I sent the skirt over to Jack at Oscar de la Renta. He's a little quicker than you are and a little cheaper, too."

Jack was Chez Ninon's "Overflow Man," as Mr. Charles had often called him. Jankiel Horowicz was old-fashioned and serious—Kate liked that about him. He'd been a tailor for the Polish army before the war, before the concentration camp, before his world fell apart. A quiet man, he did beautiful work. He didn't talk about his past, but Kate knew the stories and could see the sorrow in his eyes. She was glad that he was the finisher. He was a good man, and there was comfort in that.

So many hands and so many hearts, she thought. *Just to make one simple suit.*

Two weeks later, the story made headlines all over America: GALS WILL RULE ON CAMP DAVID. It was exactly as the Ladies had said. If the Wife and the daughter liked the mountain camp, then the family would abandon their leased country estate, Glen Ora, in Virginia. If not, Camp David would gather dust. Much to Kate's relief, the Wife was radiant in the pink suit. Even though the photos were in black-and-white, the suit still seemed incandescent. The Wife did seem reborn in it, as Schwinn would have said. No hat. No pearls. Gloves, though. The First Lady seemed to be wearing a different blouse with the suit, not one of the ones that Kate had designed. But it was difficult to tell for sure. She and the President were coming out of St. Stephen's Catholic Church on their way to Camp David, and it was windy. They looked happy.

Two days later, on November 14, the Wife wore the suit again. This time it was during what the newspapers called a "Korean gift ceremony," held at Maison Blanche, in the yellow Oval Room. The photo made Kate laugh out loud. On the far left, General Chung Hee Pak looked like a G-man. He was wearing dark tinted glasses, a shiny suit, and an ironic smile. On the far right, the Wife, who had just been presented with a chest of handmade clothes sent by female students in Korea, had a look of stoic horror.

Even in black-and-white, the chest of clothes looked absolutely dreadful. Kate couldn't even imagine what color they were, but they were shiny, with thick stripes and fat polka dots, and were to be paired with a hideous striped beret, which, although exotic, would probably never even be worn by someone as eccentric as Mrs. Vreeland. Standing next to the Wife was the President, smirking. He had a look on his face that made Kate think he might just announce that Her Elegance was going to duck into the loo to try everything on. Maybe even give a little fashion show. He looked like a man on the verge of a practical joke, and Kate liked that. She showed the newspaper clippings to Maggie Quinn at supper that night.

"It's a nice suit. It's okay," she said. Maggie seemed more interested in the articles themselves. "Did you notice that their little girl is Little Mike's age?"

Kate had not.

"And this is funny. The Wife is about your age. I wonder how you'd look in a pink suit like this."

Kate didn't even hesitate. "Reborn," she said, and that was when she knew that she would make this pink suit for herself.

CHAPTER EIGHTEEN

"Over the years I have learned that what is important in a dress is the woman who is wearing it."
—Yves Saint Laurent

$\mathcal{T}$he Chez Ninon telephone never stopped ringing. The questions from the press were endless. "Will the First Lady continue to buy from Norman Norell? Or are you copying his designs, too?"

"Favored colors are Gauguin pink, black, turquoise, gray, and white. Deny or confirm?"

With Mr. Charles gone, it was left to Miss Sophie to release Chez Ninon's most recent corporate position on whether or not there had been a shopping spree at the shop or if a new evening gown was one of theirs or had indeed been bought in Paris and flown back on Air Force One. Dealing with the press was not a task she particularly enjoyed.

That day, the reporters were even more insistent than usual. Chez Ninon appeared on the list of the designers for India, and by the time the Associated Press arrived at their door with a mimeographed questionnaire about the wardrobe, including cut, color, style, and "inspiration"—which was a polite way of asking the Ladies whose design they'd stolen—Miss Sophie had decided to delegate and handed the form to Kate.

"Fill in your part," she said. Underneath the heading *Travel Clothes,* someone had typed in *Pink Suit, Chez Ninon.* Kate nearly cheered. The Wife planned to wear the suit to India. It was amazing news. Maybe she and Patrick would celebrate. Maybe even have champagne. They'd planned dinner that night: it would be the first time since mid-October that they would have a chance to spend some time together. Thanksgiving was the next week. The back room was mad with dresses and suits for assorted family gatherings.

Patrick was deluged with orders, too. Without his father and mother to help, he spent nearly every waking hour brining and smoking and grinding and seasoning. He smelled like a rasher of bacon. It was not just turkeys that everyone wanted. Some wanted pork crowns, just to be contrary. And everyone needed both white and black puddings for a proper Irish fry-up for the holiday-morning breakfast. And there was nearly a trawler's worth of fish that had to be smoked to keep families happy before the turkey was brought, brown and glorious, to the table. There were so many orders for sausage that Patrick had been seasoning, grinding, and freezing for weeks.

"I can't even imagine what Christmas will be like," he said.

Awful, Kate thought, but was quietly glad that Patrick was so busy, because it gave her time to work on her pink suit without interruption. She wanted to finish it for Christmas to surprise him. She was going to wear it to church that morning, just to see that wonderful look of pride on his face.

They'd agreed to meet at 8:30 p.m. at the pub that night, although Patrick had warned her that he would reek of pork fat and probably be a little late. "Mrs. Brown knows you're coming, so she'll watch over you until I arrive."

Kate was so looking forward to their date. After work, she ran down to Bergdorf Goodman's to finally buy the Chanel No. 5 she'd had her eye on. She took the express train home. She had a hot bath and fixed her hair. She picked out a simple black dress, an LBD of her own design, which she knew went well with her skin color and set off the red in her hair.

If pink could be thunder. It was such a lovely thing that Patrick had said. It still took her breath away. She wanted the night to be special.

Unfortunately, Kate lost track of time.

She was not intoxicated by lilacs, as Mr. Charles and his clients were. But it did begin with the Chanel No. 5. Two dabs behind each ear, and a little in the crook of each arm, made her think of the Wife, India, and the suit. Their pink suit—although Kate's was still lying half-finished on her workroom table.

When she pulled her slip over her head, there was a rush of heat and sandalwood, and in that moment she decided that that horrible girdle and those nylons could wait. She put on her bathrobe instead. Out on the street, she could hear the laughter of couples going somewhere on a Friday night, but she still had time. She just wanted to take a minute to adjust a seam before she went. She'd been thinking about it all day. Then she'd finish dressing and run down to meet Patrick. Kate knew if she didn't fix the seam, she'd be thinking about it all night. And that would ruin everything.

Kate was clearly obsessed with the pink suit—and she knew it. Chanel's improbable architectural demands were addictive, like one puzzle after another, meant for Kate to solve. Adjusting the toile to fit her wasn't as difficult as Kate had thought. Quilting the silk to the wool was painstaking but not impossible. Even though she did sew it by hand, the skirt came together fairly quickly. Deep in its hem, Kate had placed a scapular of St. Jude, the Patron Saint of Hopeless Causes, just as her mother always had done with her best skirts, the ones she reserved for special occasions. "A little bit of the rebel county," she would say. It was a way to be proudly Catholic, no matter what. It was also convenient. If you need to beseech St. Jude to intervene for you in one hopeless cause or another, this was a better solution than taking an ad out in the newspaper or burying his statue in Isham Park. It would be comforting to have him hovering about.

The real challenge for Kate had been the jacket. Piecing the front to the back was a serious conundrum because some of the tweed was slightly irregular, too loosely woven, which gave it that beautiful look of being handmade, but also made it difficult to work with. And it would not stop shedding. That night, it took several tries, but Kate was finally able to fix the seam so that it matched and lay flat.

Unfortunately, she'd completely lost track of time until a knock at the door startled her. It was Patrick. And it was midnight.

"I'm mortified," she said.

It was obvious that Patrick had planned to be quite upset with her. He'd probably crafted a poetic and yet furious speech while he waited for Kate at the pub. Probably had one pint and then another and then whiskey for courage. But as soon as Kate opened the door, he'd forgotten it. She was standing there in her slip and bathrobe, covered in tufts of pink wool. There was the scent of sandalwood in the air. She was so pale and beautiful, even without moonlight, that he kissed her. Then kissed her again.

He kissed her neck, and she turned off the lights. He slipped his hand along the edge of her robe. She let it fall onto the floor. When he kissed the length of her arms, he was on his knees before her, as if in worship. She took off his coat, slowly. And then his tie.

One by one they shed the things of their lives until there was nothing left except that moment, not faith or country or history. They were adrift in a sea of pink.

After—their entire lives would now be measured by that word.

After they made love—slowly, painfully, but deliberately—Kate was surprised. It was not what she'd expected. It was like being caught in a swift current with storm clouds in your heart.

After, he lay with her in her small bed and kissed the salt from her forehead, until just before dawn. "I need to meet the delivery soon," he said. Kate, of course, had work.

She knew she would miss him that day.

"After mass, on Sunday," she said. "I'll give you a hand at the shop, if you like."

After.

Patrick was surprised but pleased. "Will you wear the suit to church?"

"It won't be done for a quite a while."

"Good. Save it for our wedding, then. We have to save something for the wedding, don't you think? Father John is going to be blessedly angry at us."

"Should I wear the hat, though? Just for fun?"

Patrick pulled her back into his arms again. Apparently, she should.

The raspberry-pink hat looked slightly odd with her navy-blue polka-dot dress, but Kate did wear it to church on Sunday anyway. It made Patrick laugh when he saw it. "That looks like an exclamation point on your head."

It did. She didn't care. Just wearing the hat made her incredibly happy.

The Sunday nine a.m. was not their usual mass. Nine a.m. felt like lunchtime to Kate, but they were taking Little Mike with them. "He keeps asking where his auntie Kate is," Maggie said. Organizing a small child into proper clothing took more time than Kate and Patrick ever imagined. When they finally wrestled him into his blue tweed suit with the tiny bow tie that never seemed to clip on straight, the three of them walked hand in hand down Broadway, to church. The air was crisp and not too cold yet. Christmas was still a month away. Little Mike had an endless stream of questions about Santa Claus and his reindeer.

"Does the baby Jesus ride in the sleigh, too?"

"No amount of Yeats can prepare you for the theological musing of a four-year-old," Patrick said.

The boy dawdled; Kate and Patrick did too. When they finally arrived at the Good Shepherd, Father John was making a pre-mass announcement. It was all about Rome: what Rome wanted, what Rome hoped for. *Who cares about Rome? This is Inwood*, Kate thought. *Just swing a little incense about and get on with it.*

The Good Father was wearing his gold brocade and white silk vestments. The embroidery on the back was so Schiaparelli, so intricate with bejeweled lilies, that Kate found it all, even the announcements, uplifting. But she couldn't eat it.

Fasting was difficult enough, and the longer Father John talked, the longer it would be before they had their promised breakfast of pancakes at the Capitol Restaurant. Little Mike was a bit whingey. Soon, the boy would be bouncing off the ceiling. Kate picked him up and stood him on the pew, between herself and Patrick. It was rude, of course, but it calmed the boy.

"Who looks smart?" Kate whispered in Little Mike's ear. "Who is the most stylish?"

He pointed at Father John. The boy had a good eye.

Kate could hear Patrick's stomach growling. Little Mike was sucking his tiny fist, but Father John went on talking about various ideas to "modernize" the Church.

"Tambourines, perhaps. They're very popular."

"He's going to turn us all into Protestants," Patrick whispered.

After mass, at breakfast, Kate and Patrick sat at the counter of the Capitol instead of in a booth so that Little Mike could spin around on a stool. They ate their fill of pancakes until they smelled like maple syrup, and drank glasses of milk with paper straws. Patrick showed Little Mike how to balance a spoon on the tip of his nose. And then they all did it—all three of them—smiling at the waitress, who was not amused. They left the diner laughing, each holding one of Little Mike's hands. They slowly walked him home, stopping at shopwindows along Broadway to show the child things like steel snow shovels and tins of fruitcakes stacked in the shape of a pyramid—any excuse to hold his small hand in theirs for just a little while longer.

When Patrick and Kate arrived at Harris Meats after dropping Little Mike at home, the butcher shop was stone-cold. The heat had been off all day. Patrick tasted like maple syrup when he kissed her. But it was just one kiss. "You need to change your clothes," he said. "Pork has a stench to it, and you'll never get the smell out. After, you'll have to bathe, too. Rinse your hair with lemon juice."

Kate could only hope that her pink pillbox hat would be saved from the stench. She took it off and, along with her good wool coat, laid it on Peg's chair, upstairs in the apartment, just to keep it safe.

Patrick put on his white coat and opened the walk-in refrigerator. "Once you change, you can do the sausage. I'll do the black pudding, unless you don't mind the sight of blood; then you can do the pudding."

Kate did, indeed, mind the sight of blood. She must have turned pale. "It does take some getting used to," he said.

As soon as Kate changed into Peg's "butcher's uniform," as Patrick called it, she knew it was a mistake to offer to help. The dress was cheap nylon and two sizes too large. Kate tied a length of butcher's twine around her waist. None of it fit her—not the dress or the stench of pig or the buckets of blood. It didn't feel like a world that Kate could ever get used to.

The walk-in was even colder than the shop. It was dimly lit by the red exit sign over the door, which made it look like a sideshow barker's vision of hell. The earthy smell of blood and rot made Kate feel ill. She pulled the cord above her head and turned on the light for Patrick with a click. "How can you see without light?"

"I know where I put things. There's light enough with the sign. No need to waste electricity."

The bare bulb swung. It was too bright, and it blinded her for a moment. When her eyes adjusted, Kate saw the poor half cow was still strung up on a hook. The long metal shelves were filled neatly with dozens of pale plucked turkeys, headless, two rows deep, and organized according to size. Patrick handed her a bucket. "This is back fat. You'll need that," he said. The fat was ground like hamburger and pure white. "It's cold enough to work in the shop, so we'll work there." He turned off the light. "It's brighter, too. No need for lamps."

Kate looked out the front window of the shop. It was just half past two, but Broadway was deserted. Telephone operators worked on Sundays, but perhaps they were between shifts. There was no one around at all. The massive building looked like an abandoned hive.

"Ready?" Patrick asked.

She was not. Everything in the butcher shop had a place except for Kate. She didn't even know where to stand.

"Wash your hands first, then put your gloves on," Patrick said. "Very hot water and then very cold. If your hands are warm, they will taint the meat."

Kate had no idea that making sausage was such an intricate process. On the long table, Patrick placed gallon buckets of pork cubes, back fat, and several small bowls of spices. Kate recognized the sage, but that was all. The rest was a mystery.

"It's all about balance," Patrick said. "Too much fat, and it's greasy. Too lean, and it's tough. It must be both salty and savory. You need to learn to balance things. No high notes. Just the same thing over and over again."

Kate wasn't sure if Patrick was talking about a butcher's life or the sausage, but she knew she'd never liked sausage all that much. After four hours of making it, she liked it even less.

By half past seven, they were exhausted. It took Kate a twenty-minute hot soak to get the scent of pork off her skin, and she still reeked of it. Very barnyard.

"It should wear off in a couple of hours," he said, and found her an old blue flannel shirt of his to wear until she was "less piglike in aroma." Patrick rolled the sleeves up twice, but the shirt still came to her knees.

While Kate had been in the bath, Patrick had showered downstairs in the shop with a hose. "I don't mind cold water," he told her. He warmed a can of tomato soup for them both, poured it into coffee mugs, and served it with saltines. "I'd fry up a few chops, but after all that sausage, it takes a while for me to be hungry again."

Kate understood. She couldn't even bear to hear the word *sausage*.

It was very cold in the apartment. "I've been in the States for twelve years, and I'm still not much for paying for heat," Patrick said. He handed Kate his mother's sweater. "It was her favorite." It was quite old. The wool was pilled, and it smelled like bleach, but it was better than many of Peg's clothes, which held the odd scent of violet perfume and dust. There was an entire closet full of them, hanging just the way his mother had left them.

"What are you saving these for?"

"I'm really not sure," he said.

Patrick clearly missed her. So did Kate.

The tomato soup was not fit to eat. It was an off brand that Kate didn't know. It didn't taste like real tomatoes. Awful stuff. She finished it quickly and was still hungry—starving, really—but it would have been rude to ask if there was any other food in the house. And she couldn't just get up and root around. It wasn't her pantry. Even though Peg was gone, it would always be Peg's.

Patrick was exceedingly quiet, as was Kate. There are different kinds of silences. This one was filled with words that could not be said.

At least they had the television.

"Would you like a glass of water?" Patrick asked.

"Yes. Thank you."

It felt as if they were strangers again.

Modesty was in short supply. Dressed in Patrick's shirt and his mother's sweater, watching television alone like that, made Kate uncomfortable, although *My Three Sons* was very nice. He'd turned it on straightaway. The widower had such sweet boys, all different ages, although they looked very Scottish, and with a name like Fred MacMurray, you had to wonder.

"Lovely hair, though."

As soon as Kate said that, she took off Peg's sweater. She was starting to sound like her, yammering on and on. "Lovely hair"—Kate couldn't even believe that had come out of her mouth.

Although it was true—MacMurray's hair had quite a roguish swoop to it—but still.

Patrick was lost in thought, not watching the telly, just sitting with the blue light tinting his face, and his tired blue eyes.

Kate wasn't sure exactly when she drifted off to sleep, but when she awoke, it seemed very late. The station was signing off for the night.

"This is WCBS-TV in New York City, transmitting by authority of the Federal..."

The screen went dark, and there was a high-pitched tone, like the squeal of an electronic pig. Kate turned off the set. She'd had quite enough of pigs for a lifetime. Still sleepy, it took her a moment to realize where she was.

"Patrick?"

The apartment was dark. It was not the same sort of darkness that Kate was used to. Her apartment was quieter and faced the river. His was right on the busy end of Broadway. Once the television was off, Kate could hear how loud the apartment really was. Up and down the street, pubs were letting out. Even on Sunday, some kept back-door hours for those who worked overnight and needed a quick pint with an egg cracked into it, a "liquid breakfast," before dawn. At this hour, after midnight, most of the bleary eyed were drunk and weaving their way home—from sidewalk to street and back again. Some sang the old songs, some the new. Some shouted to each other. Some shouted to God. Not Kate's God, but a sullen God in a heaven that clearly had no time for fools. There were fire trucks and screaming patrol cars racing to one spot of trouble or another. There were telephone operators leaving their shifts or arriving. Wolf whistles, too. Patrick's apartment was on the second floor, right over the shop, so everything seemed closer and louder because it was.

Living here would mean a lifetime of closing times, Kate thought, and shuddered. She couldn't imagine how Peg dealt with all this noise.

"Patrick?"

Her neck hurt from sleeping in the chair. Patrick had covered her with a blanket and tucked in the edges, and that had woken her up briefly. But he hadn't said he was going out. He hadn't said anything. He had just tucked the blanket around her and kissed her forehead.

"Patrick?"

He wasn't there. Kate wanted to go home and sleep in her own small, white bed. She wanted to be where she knew all the creaks in the floorboards and the voices of the neighbors coming home. But she couldn't just leave; that wouldn't seem right. Kate felt her way along the wall, looking for a switch, but no luck.

"Patrick?"

He wasn't sleeping in his room. She knocked twice.

"Patrick?"

Nor was he in the bathroom. Kate finally found the light switch by the front door and flipped it on.

"Patrick?"

Kate opened the apartment door and went out onto the landing. The stairs down to the shop were badly lit. A couple of lightbulbs were out. Kate thought for a moment that she heard Patrick's voice on the street; she held her breath and listened closely. It wasn't him.

Kate was a little dizzy from lack of food; she walked down the stairs carefully. She didn't want to fall. Unlike at home, there'd be no one to find her here if she did. The front door was locked but not bolted. Patrick was out. Somewhere. The door to the shop was also open.

"Patrick?"

She was whispering now. His white wool fedora was hung on the rack next to a neatly starched butcher's coat, ready for the next day. Someone opened the front door. There was a jingling of keys.

"Patrick?"

"Kate?"

He seemed surprised to see her. He was locking the front door behind him. He must have noticed that the door to the shop was open.

"You've come down for a midnight snack, have you?" he said, but his cheer seemed false. He'd changed his clothes. He was wearing a black sweater under his dark coat and dark pants. His silver hair was combed, although it seemed disheveled somehow. He'd had a drink or two. He smelled of stout.

"I've got burgers," he said. "With onions for nightmares."

He was holding a greasy white sack in his right hand. He said he'd run down to the pub and Mrs. Brown had thrown a couple of patties on the griddle. "I woke up hungry." There was the overwhelming scent of seared beef and raw onion. Yellow mustard, too. But there was something else. Something he wasn't saying.

"It's so late for food," she said.

"Consider it breakfast." The hamburgers were wrapped in waxed paper and still warm. "They've very fine burgers, Kate."

Kate felt that Patrick was hiding something. Another woman? It was difficult to tell. He seemed quite sad as he led her up the stairs and into his room. They ate the hamburgers on his bed, which was as small as her own. The white bedspread, the white sheets—it all felt very familiar.

When they were finished, Patrick turned his back and took off his shirt. She kissed him on his neck and then realized that she'd never told him about the pink suit, her suit—their suit now—and that the Wife planned to wear it to India. She knew he'd be as proud as she was, but before Kate could say anything, Patrick slipped out of her arms.

"Kate," he said. "I was thinking about today. And you—"

Her heart nearly stopped.

"I'm sorry," she said, and she was. Kate was sorry she wasn't Peg or an old-fashioned girl. She was very sorry she wasn't the kind of girl Patrick thought she was. But Peg's ring was still firm on her finger, it wouldn't budge.

"Nothing to be sorry about. I just got to thinking. This life I offer you isn't grand."

"It's fine—"

"It's not the Chez."

"It doesn't have to be," she said. He kissed her so gently; Kate hoped that was true.

CHAPTER NINETEEN

"In order to be irreplaceable one must always be different."

—Coco Chanel

The problem with a pink pillbox hat is that everyone notices it. Especially if worn in December at four-thirty a.m. And if it had been worn to church the day before, as Kate had worn hers, a pink pillbox would be impossible to miss. In a small place like Inwood, one quick kiss outside the butcher shop is all it takes to get noticed.

A week later, Father John came to the shop to speak to Patrick in person.

"A few of the parish ladies are not fans of Kate and are raving about 'moral grounds.' They'll object if you try to announce banns and marry in church. They don't know Kate like we do."

As soon as the priest left, Patrick closed the shop and arrived unannounced at the back door of Chez Ninon. DELIVERIES ONLY, the sign read.

"We can talk later," Kate said.

"We can't."

It was the middle of the afternoon. There was no privacy at all. There was barely enough space to stand in. Tarnished tinsel hung from the fluorescent lights overhead. Perry Como crooned on the radio. Christmas was less than a month away, and nearly every mannequin had been pulled out of storage. The clients all needed something: smoking jackets and velvet dresses for family dinners, or formal gowns and full dress tails for New Year's Eve. All the back-room girls, even the mice of Ready-to-Wear, were pitching in.

"Did you hear what I said, Kate?"

They were standing in a sea of headless mannequins. Whispering. *"Let it snow,"* Perry sang. Outside the long banks of windows, Manhattan braced itself for sleet. Patrick was pale. Kate felt awful about that but was relieved that he'd taken a moment and put on a coat and tie and nicked his face with a quick shave and a splash of cologne. He was presentable. Unexpected and unwelcome—but presentable. "We need to apply for a license right away. We can marry at the courthouse. It'll stop the talk."

Although the mannequins were headless and deaf, the back-room girls were not. The hum of the sewing machines, the chatter of gossip: it slowly wound down around them until all Kate could hear was Maeve's raspy breathing; her cold had gone from bad to worse, and there was no hiding the sound of it, not even over Perry's insistent refrain. *"Let it snow. Let it snow. Let it snow."* Patrick stood so close to Kate that he could kiss her, but he didn't. "This kind of talk is bad for business," he said.

She was holding an evening gown that she'd been repairing for the Wife. The Ladies had made it, even though they knew that Mrs. Newhouse, the magazine publisher's wife, had her own version of it. She'd bought hers during the runway show at Lanvin. It was the same show that the Ladies had stolen the design from for the First Lady. The gowns were nearly identical. Same color. Same beadwork. Same fabric. If the two women ever found out, it would be a disaster.

Kate held the dress like a barrier between Patrick's world and hers. It was quite heavy: floor length, with an ivory satin skirt. The bodice and shawl were completely beaded in a pattern of red roses over ruby silk. The beadwork was always unraveling. It was unraveling at that very moment, too. Small ruby beads slowly spilled onto Patrick's polished shoes.

"Kate," he said, "these women are objecting to us on moral grounds. It's not good. Do you understand?"

She did.

The beadwork would not stop unraveling, no matter how many times Kate fixed it. The threads kept snapping, and so the Wife left a trail of iridescent beads behind her everywhere she went. The problem was too much for Provy to fix. It was too much for anyone. It was a design flaw. The silk thread required for such fine fabric would never hold up under repeated wear.

And now Patrick was demanding a wedding.

It was an impossible situation on both fronts.

"I'm working," Kate said.

Perry was still singing. *"When we finally kiss goodnight—"*

The blue of Patrick's eyes no longer seemed blue but a thin, dull gray.

"Do you understand what I'm saying, Kate? A lot of my business is the parish."

"Let it snow," Perry sang. Someone turned the radio off. The workroom went quiet.

The gown felt so heavy in Kate's arms.

The rain of red beads continued on.

"This is the Wife's," Kate said.

She held the gown out to Patrick, as if the silk's memory of Her were sacred. "It was designed originally for an embassy dinner with Prime Minister Nehru. He wears very severe jackets, but always with a red rose boutonniere. To honor him, the Ladies decided that I should bead the entire silk bodice in red roses—even though we could get in trouble, because that's the same exact way the original was made."

Kate took Patrick's callused hand and ran his finger along a single rose. The beads unraveled and stuck to his skin. The rose disappeared. All that remained was the outline, the series of tiny holes in the fabric where Kate's needle had once moved deftly.

"It's too fragile," she said. "It's just too fragile."

Kate bit her bottom lip hard. It was a trick Miss Sophie had taught her to keep from crying. The Ladies didn't like it when backroom girls cried. "Even if you try to fix it, it can never really be fixed. Nothing can be done."

Kate wasn't talking about the dress. Patrick rubbed his fingers, and the beads fell onto the floor. He watched as they rolled off his shoes and under a mannequin. He looked so helpless, standing there with his bad shave and crooked tie. There were so many things that could have been said at the moment, but neither of them said a word. Patrick gently took the dress out of her arms. He laid it on her table carefully. The silent mannequins were a forest around them. The back-room girls forgotten, Patrick held Kate in his arms until their racing hearts slowed a bit.

"I love you," she said, and was surprised how fiercely she meant it.

"I know," he whispered.

The radio went back on. The workroom began to hum again. Kate, embarrassed, looked at the tinsel hanging off the lights above their heads. It looked more like brass than silver. "I need to get back."

"Of course."

Patrick hesitated as if he hoped she'd change her mind, hoped she'd grab her coat and run through the snowy streets with him, all the way to the courthouse, because that was what her heart wanted—but she couldn't. It was nearly Christmas. There was still too much work to be done.

As soon as the door closed behind Patrick, Kate missed him.

At six o'clock, Miss Sophie caught her by the arm. Kate thought that the Ladies had heard about Patrick's visit and weren't pleased, but it wasn't that at all.

"Maison Blanche called," she said. "Provy used all the material that you'd sent. For the pink suit. Cigarette burns. Reweaving. They need another yard to fix it for the India trip. Two would be best."

Every last inch of the remaining pink bouclé was in Kate's suit. There was no fabric left. Miss Sophie put her arm around Kate and whispered, "I know some of the girls take bits with them."

Kate was too embarrassed to speak.

That night, in Kate's small apartment, amid the chaos of fabric piled everywhere—the bolts and swatches and rolls—she sat with her pink suit on her lap. In the kitchen, Maggie's copies of the Wife's clothes still remained stacked in chronological order. The boxes were gathering a thick layer of dust. Those clothes were beautiful and could be remade to fit Kate. But they were not the suit. The suit was a Chanel. And it was hers.

Kate desperately wanted to keep it.

She wore her white cotton gloves. Her seam ripper was too rough for such delicate material, and so she'd sharpened the thin Jowika fish knife that her father had given her. REPUBLIC OF IRELAND was stamped on its blade. It was amazingly sharp and always provided a clean cut. The Old Man made her fillet everything they caught for dinner with it. "It will keep you humble," he said.

The irony did not escape her now.

It was snowing outside. Patrick would be at the pub for dinner in a couple of hours. If Kate hurried, she could catch him there. She didn't want to go to sleep without seeing him again. Didn't think she could sleep at all, if things were left the way they were between them at Chez Ninon. But that meant she had to work quickly, and very carefully. Since the silk was quilted to the bouclé in hundreds of perfect stitches that were exactly one inch apart, to remove even one improperly could cause a run, and the yardage would be ruined, unusable.

At best, Kate knew that she could only provide Provy with a little over a yard of fabric. And it would have to come from the skirt. The jacket was not cut from a single piece of bouclé but from several pieces that had been sewn together, and so none of that could be saved. It would completely unravel if she undid the stitching.

The skirt would have to do.

The hem was the place to start. St. Jude's scapular, with its inscription, *Whosoever dies clothed in this scapular shall not suffer eternal fire,* was removed first. Kate put it around her neck. She wanted to pray for forgiveness but couldn't. She didn't even know where to start. She'd gone too far. She'd broken too many rules.

Kate carefully picked at the stitches with her father's blade and thought about the Island. Some still believed in Brehon's law, the laws of honor there. The regulations of proper behavior were quite clear. Of course, it's easy to be clear when your world is very simple: The sun rises. You fish. You work. You fish again. The sun sets.

The more she thought about home, the more Kate realized that the pink suit was not hers to have. It had nothing to do with her life. It wasn't a part of her. If it had come from the Island, the wool would have been dyed in variations of wild pink thyme and the deep rose of St. Dabeoc's heath and that particular geranium pink-magenta of the bloody cranesbill. And while the bouclé was spun and woven and blocked, the secrets and dreams and fears and laughter and cups of tea and sweet-cream cakes and blue jokes and awful puns and razzing and anger and songs and prayers and tears and love—yes, love—of those who were born on the Island would have brought it to life.

It would be of the Great Island and of Cobh, the port of County Cork. It would not be of Cumbria or New York. But home.

This is merely an unraveling of another person's life, not mine, Kate thought. And the work went much quicker for it.

After a couple of weeks, Patrick stopped asking Kate to marry him, but Peg's ring remained firmly on her finger. It was not because it was stuck there: she'd had it stretched so it fit properly now. Kate wore the ring because she could not imagine a day passing when she would not hear Patrick's voice. Every day, on the way in to Chez Ninon, she would stop by the apartment to make porridge for them both. He liked his with bitter fruit—unsweetened mashed strawberries were his very favorite. He made a very nice pot of tea, which was a skill that Kate had never quite mastered. She brought over her mother's Belleek teapot for them to use. And he brought out Peg's bone china cups.

Breakfast together was about the past and the present. The future was never mentioned. Patrick pushed the kitchen table to the front window. While they ate, he'd prod Kate into a running commentary on the fashion sense of the telephone operators as they went in and out of the building across the street.

"Thumbs up?"

"Her lipstick's too red—it betrays her intentions."

"Is that good or bad?"

"It depends on what her intentions are, doesn't it?"

It was certainly more entertaining than television.

Patrick had taken to packing Kate a lunch of banana-and-butter sandwiches on white batch bread, which he made himself. There was also a thermos filled with raspberry squash, *rasa,* as it was called, or orange juice when it wasn't too dear. For teatime, he sometimes included his own version of Marietta biscuits, which were dead plain digestives, just as they were on the Island, but lovely all the same.

They had both learned to cook, somewhat. Kate could assemble a breakfast with the best of them, and Patrick was gifted with Peg's ability to bake. That pleased them both. Baking helped Patrick forget how badly business had fallen off since all the talk began. "It's really quite therapeutic to bang around some dough," he told Kate. If it made him happy, it made her happy, too.

They were determined not to let the gossip get to them. Late suppers were still taken at the pub, always with a proper pot of tea during the week and a halfie on the weekends. Mrs. Brown served them kindly every night and tossed anyone out who gave them a second look. Sometimes they would come in for sessions night. Patrick would bring his guitar, and Kate would sing a chorus or two. If Mrs. Brown wasn't there, they came in anyway, because it felt like home, like Cork, and they weren't willing to give that up, no matter who made a snide remark about them or told a pointed joke or two.

They carved out a bit of happiness for themselves, but it was still difficult to know that Patrick spent his days standing behind the shop counter, in his starched butcher's coat with his white wool fedora angled just so, just looking out the window. Waiting. Only the telephone operators came in now, which wasn't quite enough to keep the place going. After a time, Patrick started talking about selling the beloved Rose and her Oldsmobility. But Kate hoped that was just talk.

After—there was that word again—after everything, they couldn't return to the Good Shepherd, despite Father John's reassurances that people would forget, especially if they married. It just didn't feel like their church anymore.

On Christmas morning, they took the A train into the city, to St. Patrick's. It was all gold and glory there, not like at the Good Shepherd, where God had a pulse and a heart, and it was Ireland's, not some high-and-mighty version of it. After the mass was finished, a plaster Jesus was laid in the crèche. His arms were outstretched toward them, but Patrick and Kate turned away.

After was a very difficult word, indeed.

In March, the Wife traveled to India, and Kate told Patrick that the pink suit had gone along, too. "It's like you're with her," he said. And so the ritual began. Every day, Patrick would gather newspapers and magazines with articles about the trip, and he and Kate would go to the pub, eat their dinner, and search for the suit.

"Why not?" he said. "Just for laughs."

The First Lady's trip began with a caravan of steamer trunks being loaded onto the Pan American jet, along with the Wife's entourage: the ambassador, the Wife's sister, the Secret Service detail, the assistants, the secretary, the hairdresser, and Provy—who Kate thought looked quite glamorous for a personal maid. The Wife was not wearing the pink suit.

"Maybe tomorrow," Patrick said, and he was kind enough not to mention that most of the articles went on at great length about the seemingly endless amount of trunks filled with "unworn gowns from the most expensive couture houses in the world, Lanvin, Oleg Cassini, and Chez Ninon" and how shameful it was to have all these fancy things made up for India, "a land of extreme poverty." When Kate read that, she was embarrassed enough for the both of them.

Every night after, the press covered the First Lady's trip in excruciating detail, from her elephant rides with her sister to her visits with children at a hospital. Her radiant smile and gentle charm seemed to make people happy, but the reporters also dwelled on the protests over her Somali leopard coat and smart mink sweater.

On St. Patrick's Day, a Saturday, the First Lady took a barge across a lake surrounded by stone tigers. The photograph was in color. It was daytime, but she was wearing a sleeveless apricot silk cocktail dress gathered at the waist with a bow. It was a Cassini, designed specifically to be photographed. The silk was sturdy. It dazzled in the sun. You couldn't take your eyes away from her. All the crowds who lined the shore knew it was the First Lady making her way to the Maharana of Udaipur's white marble palace to a lavish party in her honor. They cheered and threw marigolds and lotus blossoms in her wake, although many of them looked like they hadn't eaten for days.

"What's the point of that?" Kate asked.

"Beauty," Patrick said. "Isn't beauty its own reward?"

Kate had thought that all her life, but now she wasn't so sure. So many of the starving were children. Patrick leaned across the booth and kissed her.

The next night, Patrick did not bring the *Times* to the pub for dinner. Instead, he covered the table with old newspapers that he'd found in his basement. "Your girl may not be that much of a Holly," he said. The papers were peach from age and brittle. There was a picture on the front page of the Wife, back before everything, back when the President was just a senator. He was being wheeled on a gurney, to his second back surgery in seven months. He seemed to be dying. The look of fear on the Wife's face was thinly hidden.

"You have to look beyond the clothes," Patrick said. "She loves him quite clearly. You can't let the clothes get in the way. They're just things."

That day he'd taken all of Peg's belongings and boxed them up for charity.

"Things aren't people," he said. And Kate loved him all the more for it.

The pink suit was finally worn by the Wife on the way home from India. Much to Kate's delight, the press took color photographs. Although the pink was not as bright as she remembered it to be, not as bright as her own jacket, the women of India had never seen a color like it before, and a newswoman was quoted as saying, "I would love to have a sari like that."

The suit was worn with a single strand of pearls and pearl earrings, which made it seem plain to Kate. But there was finally a matching hat. Unlike Schwinn's version, this one had a thin line of blue trim, which made it stand out when photographed and drew the eye to her beautiful face. When Kate told that to Patrick, he laughed. "They really are a clever lot," he said. "It makes her look like a sweet, playful girl."

It did, but Kate was no longer sure that mattered. "She'd look better if she were doing something useful."

CHAPTER TWENTY

"We live in a dark and romantic and quite tragic world."

—Karl Lagerfeld

October 1962

*I*t had been more than a year since the pink suit was made. Chanel was no longer the latest thing. When the Ladies arrived back from the Paris shows that October, they were wearing Shetland-wool miniskirts. Everyone could see the Ladies' knees, which was a sight that seemed to make only the Ladies ecstatic.

"André Courrèges! The man is visionary!" Miss Sophie said.

The back-room girls were not so sure.

Miss Nona's knees were like two shriveled apricots; Miss Sophie's were like blushing grapefruits.

"Do they not have mirrors in France?" Maeve asked.

The trip was a great success. The Ladies had copied every single dress Courrèges had presented, and it was their intention to fill the racks of the showroom with skirts that looked like bath towels. It was a new year and a new collection.

"The First Lady, circa 1962," Miss Sophie announced.

After the meeting, Kate was called into their perfumed office. *Lilacs,* she thought. Apparently Mr. Charles had started a trend. Kate tried not to stare, but Miss Sophie and Miss Nona, in their tiny plaid skirts, were a remarkable sight—and not in a good way. They'd paired their skirts with frilly lace blouses that looked as if they had been stolen from the wax pirates at Madame Tussaud's museum. Ropes of gold chains and pearls wound round their necks.

"We'd like you to be in charge of fabrication at Chez Ninon," Miss Sophie said. "We'll mock up the designs. You can create the patterns."

Kate wasn't sure she'd heard that correctly. "You don't want me to do the finishing anymore?"

"In addition," Miss Nona said.

"Yes. In addition."

In addition? There weren't enough hours in the day already. The Ladies sat there smiling at Kate and waiting for an answer. They seemed so happy, Kate didn't know how to tell them no. Miss Sophie leaned over and patted Kate's hand, as a mother would. The gold bracelets on her arms rattled. "We'll need you to help train the new girls, too. They'll be two."

"And we have a present for you," Miss Nona said.

"Yes, we do."

Miss Sophie crossed the blue glass floor in slow, halting steps, which made the tiny skirt and the frilly lace of pirates seem all the more tragic. She opened the closet and took out a large white box with a red ribbon. Miss Nona watched with great concern as her partner, the "younger" one, made her way slowly back to the gilt desk that they shared. The package seemed bigger than the woman.

How much longer can they do this? Kate thought.

By the look on the old woman's face, she could see Miss Nona was wondering the same thing too. She turned to Kate and said, "Money. Did we mention the money?"

"I don't think we did!" Miss Sophie said as she sat, slightly winded, and placed the package in front of Kate.

"Well, Kate. It will be twenty dollars a week more for you. The two girls will do most of the finishing. You can take the Wife, Mrs. Paley, and Mrs. Astor for yourself."

"You'll remain in the back room for now, but you'll be, more or less, Mr. Charles."

"Is that agreeable? You'll get the present either way, so don't let that sway you." Miss Nona pushed the large package over to Kate, as if to tempt her.

"Thirty dollars a week extra. It's a supervisory position and a lot of work," Kate said.

"Twenty five," Miss Nona said.

Sharpen your pencils and recalculate, thought Kate. "Twenty-five dollars and one percent of the profit if the Wife buys the miniskirt and it catches on."

"Twenty-five dollars and half of one percent if the miniskirt trend still holds by October 1963."

It was a deal. Miss Sophie pushed a stack of *Vogue* magazines across the faux French desk. "Study up," she said. The model on the cover had her hair wrapped in a length of gold lamé.

Miss Nona tapped the photo with a crooked, tiny finger. "See, you could make a skirt out of that! Think of the profit! It's barely a yard of fabric!"

Miss Sophie pushed the gift-wrapped package closer to Kate. "Now open it."

The Ladies seemed as excited as children at Christmas.

The ribbon fell to the floor when Kate pulled it. She took the lid off the box. Even the tissue paper was pink. Kate was speechless.

Miss Nona said, "I saw the man from Linton at the Chanel show, and he had some samples left over from last year. It's not an exact match, but it's close enough."

It was the pink bouclé, about three yards of it, neatly folded and wrapped in tissue.

"I don't understand."

"I felt so badly when you unraveled it," Sophie said. "I hated to make you do that."

The Ladies looked so very pleased with themselves. "Thank you," Kate said, and bit her lip so she wouldn't cry.

Miss Nona stood. "The model will be here any minute."

Kate hugged both the Ladies, something she'd never done before. Miss Sophie tapped her watch. "Time is money," she said, but hugged her back.

The Wife's model, Suze, was late, detained by reporters again. The press made it a practice to follow her ever since she had gone to The Carlyle for a drink after work with friends. Reporters were in the bar, hoping to catch a glimpse of Her Elegance, and overheard Suze talking about the Wife. The poor girl's life had now become impossible.

An hour later, Suze called from a pharmacy somewhere in Midtown to check in. The photographers had been trailing her all morning. "I'm not sure how to get rid of them," she told Kate on the telephone. The girl was nearly hysterical.

"Stop crying and get on the bus," Kate said firmly. "No one who is going to see the Wife would ever take a bus."

And it was true. The model arrived ten minutes later, which made Kate quite proud. Being a Mr. Charles, even a More-or-Less Mr. Charles, was obviously her calling.

That day, the fitting did not go well.

"I miss the Wife," Miss Sophie said and sounded more forlorn than usual. Suze was a very sweet young woman, very good at modeling, and very pretty, in a First Lady sort of way, but she was such an exhausting and expensive complication. In the past, Mrs. Molly Tackaberry McAdoo and her dog Fred would simply meet with the Wife and show her the Ladies' sketches. They would have champagne and discuss all the options. It was very civilized. Now, because of Maison Blanche's memo, every season —including Pre-Winter and Cruise—when the Ladies came back from Paris with drawings for the Wife, they had to quickly knock off copies, often sewing them directly onto the model in large, loopy stitches. When done, a number was assigned, and the model would pose for photos.

"Think *Cole Porter!*" Schwinn would shout.

The girl would hold a cigarette in a long, sleek holder and tilt her chin in a bored but beautiful way.

"Think *Lunch at the Ritz!*"

She would hold a champagne glass as if to toast and tilt her chin in a bored but beautiful way.

"Think *I am so sick of Lady Bird going on endlessly about Texas!*"

The girl would just appear profoundly bored.

And then they'd do it all again for the next outfit. Hours upon hours, day after day, the model would stand motionless while the two old women cackled and stitched around her. When the piece was done, she'd be photographed, and then they'd start all over again. It was exhausting to watch.

Neither bothered to remember the model's name. She was either "darling girl" or "dear girl." It was an enormous amount of work for two women in their late seventies. The Ladies were quickly winded. *How much longer can Chez Ninon continue?* Kate often thought.

That morning, when the first miniskirt was snipped and basted and then photographed for the Wife, Miss Sophie handed Kate the drawings and said, "I need toiles for these in sizes eight to fourteen, which you will clearly mark as if they were sizes two to eight. Understand?"

She did.

"And be very careful," Miss Sophie said. "This is groundbreaking. True originals."

Originals that we copied from André Courrèges, Kate thought. The Ladies apparently still had some life left in them.

It was half past one when Kate finally sat down to lunch. It was another banana-and-butter sandwich, which she'd grown quite sick of, but since Patrick always cut off the crust, just as her mother had always done, she couldn't tell him to stop. That was the last moment of calm Kate would have in a very long time.

She looked up from her sandwich; Maeve was dressed to leave. She looked bloodless, and she was holding Kate's coat and hat out to her.

"There's been an explosion. The New York Telephone Company. A boiler in the lunchroom."

Maggie Quinn usually brought Big Mike lunch on Fridays so she could make sure his paycheck found its way to the bank instead of the pub.

"The entire street was destroyed."

Patrick.

⬦

Smoke had shut down the trains; the subway was closed until further notice. The buses weren't running either. No cabs. No phone service. Hundreds of cars were detoured, and some had been abandoned in the clogged streets. Kate and Maeve took a bus as far as it was willing to go and then ran all the way to Washington Heights. They couldn't get closer to home than 175th, and that was miles away. They hitched a ride on a milk truck and then ran up Broadway. It looked like a used-car lot.

Out of breath, cold, their feet aching, they kept on running, past the abandoned cars, past the others who were running too. The closer they got to the telephone company, the heavier the smoke got. Maeve gave up somewhere on Dyckman. "I can't go on," she said. Kate didn't hear her. She didn't notice her drop away.

When Kate finally arrived at Patrick's butcher shop, the intersection was overrun with police and firemen. They were covered in ash, darting in and out of the big building across the street, panicked as ants. "Everyone stay calm," a man on a loudspeaker said over and over again, but his voice was tinny, and it had rained glass and steel and concrete—the request was impossible.

Kate tried to make her way down to Patrick's shop, but she couldn't get through the crowds. She crawled on top of a car that someone had abandoned. The smoke was thick, but she thought she could see that the windows at Harris Meats were blown out. The hanging sign was gone. The shop was dark. It was difficult to see anything else.

"Get down," a police officer said. Kate pointed toward the shop. The car rocked back and forth in the crowd. He reached his massive hand up to her.

"It's not safe here."

It was true. Behind her, the telephone company was no longer a building but a huge, wounded beast, creaking and moaning. There was not just a fire, although the fire was still burning. There was not just an explosion, although the walls were still collapsing.

A group of women jumped out the windows, onto the street. Some were caught. Some were not.

Panic will not do, Kate told herself. She pointed toward Patrick's shop again. "I'm the butcher's wife," she said, and it felt true.

The policeman understood. He pushed his way through the crowd, with Kate following in his wake. *Don't panic,* she thought. But it was difficult not to. What was once the sidewalk outside Patrick's shop was now the edge of a crater filled with drifts of debris, spikes of glass and twisted steel. In front of his shop, in neat rows, there were bodies. Mostly of women. Some had blankets over them; some were covered only with coats or sweaters. Some looked as if they were sleeping. Some seemed to have stopped speaking midthought: their eyes were blank, and their mouths were slack.

"I'm sorry," the policeman said to Kate. "You'll have to stay back."

The streets of Inwood were no longer filled with music. Tears fell like sheets of rain. Kate wandered for hours through the crowd, searching. She overheard snips of stories from those who could still speak.

"Like an atomic bomb."

"Like ten thousand cars backfiring."

"It was as if two trains collided."

Five hundred people had been in that building; the hospitals were overflowing.

Kate asked everyone she met, "Do you know the Irish butcher? Have you seen Mike Quinn? Or his wife, Maggie? They have a little boy; he would have been with them." Most knew her family, but no one seemed to know where they were. Kate kept walking in circles until finally she found a man who said he knew Patrick.

"The butcher ran in," he said. He looked like an accountant, wearing a thin cotton shirt rolled up at the sleeves and a tie.

Kate wasn't sure she'd heard him correctly. "In?"

"Into the building after the explosion. He and some of the transit fellas—the uniform men, subway maintenance. Last I saw, they were pulling debris off people. Carrying them out."

"They ran in?"

"They did."

The man didn't remember seeing Patrick come back out again. "Walls were toppling over. Tough to see anything."

Kate's breath was irregular. *Fear is such a silent thing,* she thought. *It winds its way around you until it holds your heart in its hands.*

"You need to sit, before you go down," the man said.

"I need to know what happened."

"All I know is that most of the survivors are in the hospitals by now. But if you go to the triage area in the parking lot, my boss is making a list of the others."

"The others?"

"The ones that didn't make it."

The parking lot was next to the garage where Rose was kept. It looked like a war zone. Someone had written the words *triage* and *morgue*—with arrows pointing in different directions—and taped it over the EMPLOYEE PARKING ONLY sign. Men and women were lying across the hoods of cars, as if they were beds, talking to nurses who moved quickly from one to the next. Some were sitting in chairs, wide eyed and panting. Priests and ministers and rabbis were leaning over the dead and dying. Kate didn't see Father John, but she was afraid to look too closely.

In the midst of all this chaos, a man sat at a card table, calmly making notes. He seemed to be an executive. He was wearing a suit and looked unaccustomed to making lists of any kind. His jacket had been burned in several places. His face was dirty.

"Name?"

"Patrick Harris. The butcher."

The man looked at her oddly. "Harris Meats, across the street?"

"Yes. The Irish butcher."

"I'm sorry," he said.

The word made her go cold. "Sorry?"

"Next of kin only."

The man obviously knew the shop well enough to know that Patrick was unmarried. Kate's heart was pounding so fast, she felt dizzy.

"Then Mike Quinn? My brother-in-law."

The man checked. Then checked again, just to be sure. "No Quinn. You'll have to call all the hospitals. Have you tried their house?"

Kate ran all the way home.

For the rest of her life, Kate would remember the stench of burning oil—and running. The sun slipped into the river as if exhausted. Without electricity, the neighborhood was dark and smoky. Candles flickered in some of the windows that she passed. She kept on. She ran up the 120 steps of Step Street, straight up, and then down her street, to her building. Once inside, she took the stairs two at a time. She'd lost her shoes. Her feet were bloodied. Her bones felt as if they would break. The door to Maggie's was ajar. The apartment was dark, as was the rest of the neighborhood. Kate knocked.

"I hope that's room service."

Patrick Harris.

The thin moon shone through the living-room windows. Kate could make him out, but just barely. He was sitting on the floor, leaning against Maggie's ugly couch, wrapped in Big Mike's stadium blanket, which was a blue plaid of suspect origin—not the Quinn tartan. He turned on a flashlight.

"That blue suits you," she said.

Kate was afraid to touch him; she was afraid that if she did, he'd disappear.

Patrick was covered in soot. His face was burned. His hair was singed away in places. He had never looked more wonderful to Kate.

"You look like a building fell on you."

"They're heavy things."

"And Maggie?"

"She's excellent. Your sister was halfway to the bank when it happened. She and Little Mike stopped by the shop on the way, so I know they were unhurt. Thank God she's such a mercenary when it comes to Mike's pay. She swooped in early and avoided the show."

"Mike?"

Any hint of a smile disappeared from Patrick's face. "I don't know," he said. "Couldn't find him. Nobody was here when I got here, either."

"He wasn't on the list, though. I had them check. That's something."

For a moment, Patrick appeared confused, and then he understood what kind of list she was talking about. He looked relieved. "Good," he said. "That's a bit of good news."

Kate held out her hand to him to help him up. He wouldn't take it.

"I don't want to get the sofa dirty." He handed her the spare key that Maggie kept under the front mat instead. "Don't lose it."

She held out her hand to him again. "If you wreck her beige carpet, Maggie will be unforgiving."

"My leg's asleep."

Kate didn't believe him. She pulled back the blanket. Patrick's leg was bleeding. It was wrapped in someone's cotton shirt, which was soaked with blood.

"It's fine," he said. "Keep it clean, they told me." Patrick tried to get up, as if to prove that he was fine, but couldn't.

"It is not fine."

Patrick's leg was clearly not fine, but they both knew there wasn't anything either one of them could do about it. The hospitals were filled. There were no doctors to call. Kate was suddenly furious.

"You went in. After?" She was nearly shouting, speaking in fistfuls of words. "After it exploded? How could you?"

"How could I not?"

Patrick's eyes were rimmed in tears. He pulled Kate into his arms and held her for a very long time.

When the telephones were working again, Kate called the Old Man. She'd kept the number of Fogarty's Pub in Newtown, even though her father told her that she shouldn't phone unless she hit the National Lottery. The call was passed from a local to an overseas operator, there was ringing and then more ringing, until finally Mrs. Fogarty herself answered. It was half past five in the morning in Cobh. "Kate! Dear!" she shouted over the static. "Are you coming home?" The woman sounded so far away. Kate suddenly missed her so. She had a kind word for everyone, and that always meant a lot.

"I'm sorry if I woke you, Mrs. Fogarty."

"Woke me? Been up for hours. I'll send one of my boys to get the Old Man. He'll call you back."

"No. I'll hang on."

It was a small fortune for every minute, but Kate didn't care.

"Well, aren't you the great success, wasting money on telephone calls? Of course, I'm not surprised. It's hilarious the way the Old Man shows off your pictures. He's got them all hanging on his brag wall."

For a moment, Kate thought that the woman was confused. She'd never sent the Old Man any pictures of herself. "This is Kate, Mrs. Fogarty. Not Maggie—"

"I know that. I'm not daft. He's got the newspaper photos of all those frocks clipped up nice and hanging on the wall. Quite impressive. I hear you're quite tight with She Who Must Be Obeyed—the Wife. What's she really like?"

"I couldn't say—"

"Of course. Sworn to secrecy and all that."

In the background, Kate heard one of the Fogarty boys shout, "He's got one leg in his trousers. He'll be here in a flash."

Then Mrs. Fogarty said, "Just between us girls, the Old Man misses you something fierce. We all know you're doing well, but he stands out on the docks every morning and watches the ships come in. He's done it ever since you left. Are you coming home? Is that why you called? Because if that's why—"

The Old Man was winded when he took the phone away. "What happened?" He sounded as if he'd aged twenty years since Kate left, instead of just a handful.

Kate told him all she knew. The day was cold. The boiler was new but had not been inspected. "It smashed through the lunchroom like a rocket, bouncing off the ceiling and walls, maiming and killing everything in its path, one hundred and nineteen people in all—mostly phone operators and linesmen. Mike was hurt, but not that badly. He and some of the other linesmen helped the wounded out of the building. He's fine. Although Maggie was out of her mind with worry."

The line went quiet. Kate thought she heard a seagull's cry, but it was a cry of another sort. And so she told her father the other reason why she'd called—the reason that had become so very clear from the moment she opened the door to Maggie's and saw Patrick Harris slumped against the sofa. It was time for the poor, bedraggled Jesus of Prague to come in. "We're getting married."

All of the moral objections against Patrick and Kate were suddenly meaningless. The Irish butcher had run into the fire, and in a neighborhood like Inwood, that made him a hero.

The great Father John, the most famed of all the Blood and Bandages of Cork, wept at the altar when, for the benefit of church and state, Patrick and Kate finally said, "I do."

Even though Kate had taken the time to sew the matching pink bouclé skirt by hand, just as Chanel required, and did place the scapular back in its hem, she did not wear the pink suit for her wedding. She wore her mother's wedding dress, as Maggie had, instead.

CHAPTER TWENTY-ONE

"Adornment, what a science! Beauty, what a weapon! Modesty, what elegance!"

—Coco Chanel

May 1963

For the Blue Book set, maternity fashion began with Hermès. He'd designed the Kelly bag for Princess Grace of Monaco in 1955. The large, square purse was to be carried in the crook of the arm to hide pregnancy from photographers whose assignment was to "get one of the belly." If so inclined, the owner of the bag could also pop the "paparazzi" in the head with it, *La Dolce Vita*–style. The purse was quite durable, and the gold hardware could leave a fairly impressive gash.

For seven years, the Kelly bag was the only stylish thing about pregnancy. Then, in 1963, Her Elegance announced that there would be a third child, and it was suddenly fashionable to be pregnant, as long as you were wearing the "Young Arrogant Look," as some of the press called it, of Maison Blanche. A-line dresses—even if you weren't with child—were a "must-have." And the chemise, which could be cut wide at the hips, was once again adored. Lane Bryant, who specialized in larger sizes and maternity clothes, designed an entire line of "First Lady maternity wear" and advertised it in every major magazine.

Miss Nona and Miss Sophie could feel the money raining down on them both, a torrential flood of cash, but there was something about it all that made Kate uneasy. The Wife's first pregnancy had ended in a miscarriage, and then there was a stillborn baby. Her boy and girl both had to be delivered by cesarean section. *What if it goes wrong?* Kate thought. Although she seemed to be the only person worried. The Ladies were working up dozens of drawings for a maternity collection for the Wife. The back room was filled with bolts of fabric flown in especially from Milan. From velvet to silk, each bolt was a shade of the rich vermilion red of Renaissance painters—the kind of red that Mrs. Vreeland, who was now the editor in chief of *Vogue,* adored.

At the planning meeting, the back-room team sat around the table. Maeve had liberated a tin of Danish butter cookies and made tea. Some of the bolts were laid out across the worktable. Even with all her apprehensions, it was difficult for Kate not be excited.

"I've never seen reds this beautiful. We've even ordered some ermine for trim. We'll have Her Elegance on the cover of *Vogue* in all her maternal glory."

"If she's not too busy heaving," Maeve said.

True. But that serene face, set against the deepest reds of the Renaissance, on the cover of *Vogue*—Kate could clearly imagine it. A short waistcoat beaded in pearls, and maybe pearls wrapped around her hair, too.

Schwinn was also inspired. "Just a thin line of ermine around the neck. And one of her dogs at her feet. She has a spaniel, doesn't she? Titian, Botticelli—they all loved spaniels."

"But is it too Italian? She's always been so..."

"French fried?" Maeve said.

"Court of Versailles," said Schwinn. "French revolution with a modern evolution. Modern and simple."

"I'm not sure she'll go Italian," Kate said.

"She went Indian."

"Not really."

"The Italians practically trademarked *la bella figura,* the good impression, with their fine designs," Schwinn said. "The Wife will surely embrace the Renaissance for her last pregnancy. It's very noble."

"Her last pregnancy?" Kate said. "How do you know that?"

Everyone at the table began to laugh, even Schwinn. "Cookie, do you know how *old* she is?"

"My age," Kate said, which sounded more defensive than she wanted it to.

"Dream on," Maeve said. "She's had some practice. You—they'd put you in the Guinness World Records."

They had talked about having children—two or three, at least. But the problem was not Kate's age; it was Patrick. She'd become afraid to even touch him. It was as if he could shatter. His limp was profound. His skin was pale. He barely spoke. Hardly ate. In his dreams, the walls of the telephone company would come crashing down around him over and over again. Sometimes, he'd cry out. Sometimes she'd wake up in the middle of the night and find him looking out at the rubble of the building across the street.

What had happened was impossible to forget, even if you tried. Even now, months later, Patrick and Kate were still finding fragments from the blast in the neighborhood, such as purses and shoes that had ended up on rooftops. There was a small leather diary in the alley behind the shop that was still locked but had had most of its pages burned away. Everything was a constant reminder.

Kate had written her father, asking for advice. He was the only parent she and Patrick had left between them.

"The sea has a way of healing," the Old Man wrote her. "It's time to come home."

Home.

The deep calm of the harbor and the soft silence of the countryside—Kate still longed for it all. The Island, with all its mystical ways, made her feel part of something primal and grand—part of life, perhaps. And without the operators from the telephone company, the butcher shop was failing. Some from the parish had recently decided that they couldn't live any longer without black pudding and bacon that was not smoked but fish that was. It still wasn't enough. The shop would close within the year. Patrick and Kate both knew it.

After the meeting at Chez Ninon, and after all that talk about babies, that night, Kate told Patrick about the Old Man's letter. He said nothing for a long time; he was thinking. And then it was Yeats. Always Yeats.

And now we stare astonished at the sea.

"Home, then?"

"Home."

There was moonlight, yes, but it was unnecessary. The cadence of their heartbeats was enough. Each kiss was like their last. But then there was one more and one more and more, until gravity felt as if it had been shattered and they were falling through the dark sea themselves, naked—innocent and not—lost in the tangle of sheets, tasting of sorrow and salt. *Finally, healed,* Kate thought and hoped it was true. They were going home.

The next week, there was an announcement that the Wife was canceling all her engagements until after the birth of her third child. No press requests would be honored. No further statements would be made.

The press release was clearly a bad sign. In the past, the Wife never completely ignored reporters. During her previous pregnancy, even though she was confined to her bed, she put on a brave face, rolled out from underneath the covers, and hosted a debate-watching party in Hyannis Port, wearing a single strand of pearls and a coral silk maternity dress. Technically, she was still following the doctor's orders: with her feet up, she didn't stray from her bright-yellow couch all night.

She looked radiant.

It was a brilliant strategy. Despite the fact that her husband had won the debate against Nixon, and that Nixon's mother had called her son shortly after the televised event to ask if he was ill, because Nixon did look ill, the Wife's perfect health was all the press wanted to talk about.

That was why this press release was disturbing. Her Elegance, always the tactician, had never strayed from the limelight before. The Ladies agreed and put the maternity line on hold. The bolts of beautiful red fabric were shelved in the remnant room. Not even Maeve dared to liberate them.

"It's going to be fine," Maeve told everyone, and checked the stock daily to make sure no one had walked off with a bolt or two. No one even tried.

Kate understood how Maeve felt, and how everyone came to feel. The reams of vermilion fabric seemed sacred. Just the sight of them made her think that maybe, just maybe, having a baby when you were past the age of thirty wasn't as dangerous as everyone thought it was.

Maybe it was a very good idea, indeed.

In June, however, when word leaked out about the acquisition of a new maternity evening dress, Kate had an awful feeling. The "leak" seemed like a desperate measure on the part of Maison Blanche. The evening dress that everyone was talking about was too extravagant—a deep-turquoise silk Empire gown embroidered with gold flowers and a matching upper coat. It was summer. "Where would you wear such a thing in summer?" Kate asked Maeve. "She's living at the beach."

"Well, she's not sitting home watching the telly in that," Maeve said. She was clearly buoyed by the rumor, as was everyone else was.

Maybe that was the point, Kate thought. A ball gown is for dancing. Dancing is what healthy women do. The Maison Blanche crowd was a very clever lot.

But if the maternity evening gown was a sleight of hand, a distraction, a bit of smoke to cover the truth, the Ladies didn't see that. The next morning, the back room was filled with pillows of all sizes, for all stages of pregnancy. The Wife's model, Suze, spent the entire day with sofa cushions tied to her slender waist, and her arms in the air, while the Ladies spun around her, like fairy godmothers from a bedtime story, pinning, tucking, and cackling. They were relieved. There would be a third child. A baby. It gave everyone hope—and a potentially enormous source of revenue.

"God bless the Wife," Miss Nona said.

"God bless every beautiful inch of her," said Miss Sophie.

And, even though she was leery of it all, Kate, who had begun to pray again, put a good word in to God herself.

Within the week, Chez Ninon had a line of Maison Blanche maternity wear. The clothes, mostly dresses, were beautiful, and flexible enough to be modified for the non-pregnant. And red—they were every deep and vibrant shade of red.

"Red is the new pink," Miss Sophie said.

Miss Nona called Mrs. Vreeland at *Vogue* to tell her so.

The sheer number of orders was historic for the small shop. Hundreds of dresses had to be made by the end of summer to meet the demand. Kate quickly found herself knee-deep in elastic waistbands and expandable rubber panels.

She hadn't quite told the Ladies she was going home yet. She'd tried but couldn't say the words. It didn't quite seem true.

CHAPTER TWENTY-TWO

"The Public does not begrudge their goddesses their extravagances."

— Marylin Bender

The farewell tour was Patrick's idea. Before they left America, they would take a week and travel to California, Texas, Florida, and all parts in between. "See the whole place, all of the United States, do it up right," he said.

Kate thought that seeing the entire country would probably take a little longer than a week, but Patrick was so enthused, she hated to spoil it.

It was difficult to believe, but they really were going back to Ireland. It was amazing how quickly the idea became a plan—and a very good plan for all involved. Patrick's uncle still had a butcher shop in the English Market in Cork City. He had no sons, only daughters whose husbands did not care for the trade. Patrick could partner with him, build equity in the business, and within a couple of years the shop could be his.

They would live with the Old Man at first. Train into the city and back. Kate would try her hand at design, maybe take a few dresses to some of the posh shops in Cork City for consignment. And she could still work for the Ladies when they went to the Paris shows. It was their idea: they didn't want to let Kate go.

"You're one of us, my dear," Miss Sophie told her.

"We had such hopes," Miss Nona said.

It was crushing to leave them.

Every moment together, Patrick and Kate plotted, planned, and schemed for happiness. Nearly every sentence was qualified with the phrase "But it will be better once we get to the Island." Although neither Kate nor Patrick could quite believe that to be true, their lives had become about the promise of it all. Every Sunday, there would be a roast joint in the oven, crusty golden potatoes, peas with mint, and puddings topped with bitter fruit and rich yellow cream. And there'd be proper pots of tea with buttered oatcakes served on a lace tablecloth. And peat fires to ward off the winter's chill.

And, perhaps, a child. Or two.

When the end of July arrived, a For Sale sign was placed in the window of the butcher shop, and Father John telephoned and spoke to Kate. "I can't believe you're really leaving," he said.

"Not right away. It will take a while to sell the shop." And then she told him about Patrick's plan for a "farewell tour."

"You're going to drive across America in a week?" He sounded skeptical.

"Patrick has great faith in his Rose, with her V-eight engine and remarkable Oldsmobility."

She thought she heard the priest chuckle. "I'll see you both at the rectory at half past two," Father John said. It didn't sound as if they had a choice in the matter.

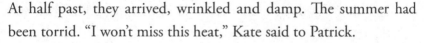

At half past, they arrived, wrinkled and damp. The summer had been torrid. "I won't miss this heat," Kate said to Patrick.

"Nor all this sun."

They sounded nearly wistful.

Father John was in the garden in short sleeves, his collar, and old cotton pants. He'd been pulling dandelions all afternoon. His face was deeply red, as were his arms. He poured them each a glass of grape Kool-Aid, chugged his down, caught his breath, and said, "Really? You're leaving? You know, they don't have sun in Ireland."

"It's not that we don't love America," Patrick said.

"We really love it," Kate said. She was surprised by how much she meant it. "But the business had fallen off—"

"A man has to work," Patrick said.

And that was true. Father John could not deny it. "Well, let's have a wee bit of a chat about your farewell tour, then."

The rectory office was dark and cool, a welcome relief. It was filled with the comfort of books. Father John turned on his desk lamp, went into his file cabinet, and took out three large manila envelopes filled with maps. He carefully laid the AAA TripTiks across the width of his desk.

"This is America," he said. "Been wanting to tour it myself. Do it up right, like in that television show *Route 66*, with the wind in my hair and the open road unfurling before me. Then I saw exactly how much unfurling would have to be done."

Just talking about the open road made Father John seem younger. But the open road was, indeed, daunting. His desk was quickly filled with maps and books.

"How long?" Patrick asked.

"If you drove straight through to Los Angeles using the freeways and not stopping to see any of the sights, and then turned around and drove back, it would take about ten days. If you didn't sleep and you had a lead foot, and ate sandwiches in the car, you could make it in a week. It's well over five thousand miles there and back."

Patrick picked up one of the maps. A thick yellow line with an arrow pointed downward on every page. "You'd need all of these?"

"You would. And more. To see the entire country, including the things you'd want to see, like the Grand Canyon, it would take weeks. Months, even."

Kate had suspected as much, and probably so had Patrick, but the thought of one last trip with Rose and her Oldsmobility had gotten them through so many dark moments. The idea of a farewell tour was so lovely. Kate would miss that car, silly as that sounded.

Patrick leaned over and held her hand. "Maybe we'll just drive for three days, down the coast and back," he said. "Just see what we can. Boston is nice, I hear."

"Or not. Either way," Kate said. "It's really fine."

"Or," Father John said, "you can see it all anyway." He opened his desk drawer and took out three tickets and held them like a fan. "Freedomland."

As soon as Kate saw the brightly colored tickets, the song from the ads ran through her head: *"Mommy and Daddy, take my hand. Take me out to Freedomland."* It was the largest amusement park in America—and just a few blocks away.

The priest handed the tickets to Patrick. "The park's promoters donated them to the Gaelic football team, and we have extras."

On the radio and on television, in magazines and newspapers—it was even featured on the *Ed Sullivan Show* and in *Life* magazine—the amusement park was advertised everywhere. "Just a half an hour on the subway from Times Square!" The park was shaped like America because it was the entire country in miniature. They even had a futuristic Satellite City, where you could ride a spaceship around Earth. Not the real Earth, but close enough.

"It's historical—and they have sea monsters," the priest said. "You could take Little Mike. I bet he would love to ride a Wild West stagecoach with his beloved auntie and uncle, or take a Chinese junk across San Francisco Bay. What child would not like that?"

Patrick, a Yeats man, was clearly not impressed. "It's not real, John."

"It's America; it doesn't need to be."

Patrick put the tickets back down on Father John's desk. "Thanks for the kind thought, but—"

"Little Mike will love it," Kate said, and picked them up again and put them in her purse.

In August, the First Lady went into early labor. The baby, a boy, died two days later. That night, Patrick and Kate were lying in bed, sleepless. Patrick was on his back, looking up at the ceiling fan, listening to the *tick, tick, tick* of it.

"I can't even imagine it," he said.

For Kate, the scenes on the television news were more eloquent than words could ever be. The President and the Wife were getting into their car to leave the hospital. The stunned look on their beautiful faces, and the way he shyly reached out to take her hand and then held it as if he would never let it go—it all said so much more than words could. *The wise heart is mute,* she thought.

Kate and Patrick lay in dark for a long time. When it seemed as if they had both finally drifted off to sleep, he said, "Did you know what the baby's name was?"

She did. It was Patrick.

"We should get some sleep," she said.

The next morning at breakfast, Kate announced that there'd been "enough sorrow." Patrick looked up from the newspaper. His reading glasses sat low on the tip of his nose. "We're going to Freedomland on Sunday," she said. "I'll do up my hair with the pillbox hat and wear the pink suit. I'll smile a good deal. It will remind everyone of happier times."

Patrick blew on his tea to cool it. Thinking. Then said, "It's a fine idea, Mrs. Harris. We'll give it a go."

They took Rose; they put the top down. Little Mike, in the backseat, was laughing. Patrick said the boy was basking in Rose's Oldsmobility. Although Kate was still not exactly sure what that meant, she laughed when Patrick said it.

As they drove, people they passed on Broadway waved at them. Kate waved back, as she'd seen the Wife do. It was the royal wave that the Queen herself did at her own coronation. It was just a slight twist at the wrist—a restrained move that oozed regality and did not suggest excitement. Kate mimicked it easily.

"It's probably the gloves," Patrick said. "White gloves lend themselves to poshness."

It was a dry, warm morning. Patrick took a very long way to the amusement park. In fact, he drove up and down Broadway a few times before they actually left the neighborhood. So many from the parish smiled and waved at them that it was difficult not to want to drive forever.

"Maybe we should wait until Thanksgiving to go back home," Patrick said. "Just in case business turns around."

"Once more around the neighborhood?" she said.

"Of course."

They both knew that the business would not turn around. At

least, not as much as they needed. In three months, they would be gone. Rose would be sold. But on that day in August, they were still Americans. They had the suit.

Freedomland U.S.A. was just three years old. It was owned and built by the same man who'd designed Disneyland, but it was bigger and better and had cost a staggering twenty-one million dollars to create. Kate couldn't remember the man's name, but she'd read in the *Post* that he was in trouble because he'd built the park without Mr. Walt's approval, using Disney's staff and designs and, perhaps, some of his money.

Freedomland was bigger than Disneyland even dreamed of being. There were eight miles of rivers, lakes, and streams. Its Great Lakes held 9.6 million gallons of water. There were also five hundred thousand yards of streets, six miles of railroad track, and fifty thousand trees. Nearly ten thousand cars could be parked in their lots. Over ninety thousand people could pass through the gates in one day. In an effort to help people grasp the sheer enormity of the undertaking, the official guide was eighteen pages long. It had a two-page color-coded map that alerted visitors to the restrooms, a fact that Kate greatly appreciated, and explained in great detail the seven regions of the four-hundred-acre park.

"Massive," was all Kate could say.

Even the traffic jam leading to the park was monumental, and they were soon stuck in it. After an hour of moving an inch at a time, Patrick Harris pulled the car off to the shoulder of the road just to take it all in for a moment.

"This is bigger than Ireland."

"That's because it's America," she said.

Parking was fifty cents, but the attendant waved them through. "No charge. Nice to see you, Mrs. K!"

Kate was surprised that the man was so kind and made sure that she waved that white-gloved wave directly at him. "Thank you so very much," she said, whispering, just as the Wife would have done. The man blushed.

"Well, wasn't that fun, Mrs. Harris?" Patrick said sweetly, and kissed her hand, but that was just the beginning of it.

On the streets of Old New York, in front of the miniature of Macy's department store, on the tugboats in the harbor, and at the suffragette rally that was interrupted by a gangland robbery of the Little Old New York Bank—even on the horse-drawn street-cars—there were so many people who wanted their picture taken with Kate that she started to smile, pose, and talk like the Wife.

"They must think I work here."

"Or they just like beautiful women."

When the parade marched down Main Street, the band nodded as they passed her. Kate waved. One of the policemen helped her onto a float of the White House, and she waved while Patrick and Little Mike ran behind, laughing.

Kate, in her pink suit and pillbox hat, waved her way through the Great Chicago Fire, where, miraculously, the flames did not frighten Little Mike at all. Nor did the tornado ride, where houses spun like ballroom dancers. Kate continued to wave for hours.

By the time they'd reached the Santa Fe Railroad, where they rode the Monson No. 3 all the way to 1906 San Francisco, Kate had become so tired of waving that she wanted to stop, but every-one still waved at her, and so Kate continued on.

In Chinatown, they ate shrimp chow mein with chopped celery, fried noodles, and the tiniest pink shrimps that Kate had ever seen. She waved between mouthfuls. On the Earthquake ride, where San Francisco shook apart and then came back together, she was still waving.

When they took the half-hour tour of the New England countryside in an old Model T, past vineyards and rippling streams, and then cruised the Great Lakes on the *Canadian,* a gigantic paddle-wheel boat, Kate posed for pictures at every possible juncture. Somewhere along the way, she began to sign autographs, too. She wrote in the same handwriting that she had seen on Her Elegance's drawings.

After nearly eight hours of being the Wife, Kate wanted to stop, but it was difficult. There were so many people who wanted the simplest of things—a photo, a word, and, sometimes, a hug. She could not deny them. At the seal pool, Patrick and Little Mike were hungry again and announced that they were in desperate need of root beer floats. Patrick remembered that they'd passed an A&W on their way somewhere but couldn't remember where it was, exactly.

"I'm not even sure I can find the car again," he said. Kate hoped he was joking.

The plan was to try to get to Satellite City just before the fireworks. The futuristic city featured the Blast-Off Bunker, an authentic reproduction of Cape Canaveral's control room. Little Mike wanted to watch a rocket launch. They all did, actually.

After the fireworks, Count Basie and his orchestra were scheduled to play at Satellite City's Moon Bowl, the outdoor amphitheater and dance floor. Kate had hoped they could listen for just a moment or two on their way out. Maybe have a quick dance under the stars. But they had to be careful not to run out of time. Freedomland was so large, and the day was nearly over.

"Let's map this out," Patrick said.

He and Little Mike sat down on the bench by the harbor, with the official guide on their laps. While they plotted their course, Kate took off her shoes and put her feet in the San Francisco Bay—at least that's what the sign said. It was just a big pond, really. *It's a knockoff,* she thought. And wondered what the Ladies would think of Freedomland—the greatest knockoff of them all.

Her nylons were ruined, but the water was soothing. The pillbox hat made her head itch, but she didn't want to take it off. Not yet, at least. Kate closed her eyes for just a minute; she couldn't remember the last time she was this tired. They'd seen less than half the park. *Next time,* she thought, and then caught herself. There would be no next time. It was now or never.

Kate yawned, and a man snapped one picture of her and then another. Her mouth was open. Yawning was not attractive. The Wife knew better than to be caught doing that, but Kate no longer cared. It was late. She was tired. She yawned again and hoped the annoying man would just go away, but he didn't. The man was moving around Kate as if to capture that particular quality that the Wife had. Kate was trying not to pay attention to him. He was like a spot on the edge of her vision.

Patrick and Little Mike were still looking over the map, trying to figure out the shortest point from here to there, when Kate noticed that there was a tear in her nylons. She wanted to slip them off—the garters would pop easily—but that man was still there, taking pictures. Kate refused to look at him.

She closed her eyes again and focused on everything else except the flash of the camera. There was the smell of popcorn, burnt sugar from cotton candy, and clouds of cigarette smoke. There was so much noise from the chugging railroad, the long drawl of the horn from the paddle wheeler, and a brass band in the distance—it was a lot like being in the city: the hum of it, life under the clouds. It was tiring, though. Everyone wanted something. Everyone thought you could be someone you weren't.

"Look this way," the man finally shouted. "You're making me waste film."

Kate looked at him. He was about her age, with sandpaper skin, wearing rolled-up blue jeans and scuffed boots. He was a roughneck. Behind him there was a thin young woman in a housedress; it was not the kind of thing meant to be worn outdoors, and certainly not to an amusement park. They were obviously together.

"Do you know how much film costs?"

"Sorry," Kate said, but she wasn't. She had a ticket, like everybody else.

The man pushed the young woman forward, next to Kate. "Go on, now," he said. "Stand next to her. Hurry up."

He must have been her boyfriend. Kate looked back to see that Patrick and Little Mike were still talking logistics on the bench. They didn't even notice the commotion.

"Would you like a photo with me?" Kate asked her.

The young woman nodded.

One more can't hurt, Kate thought, and hoped that the shot was from the waist up. When she stood and brushed herself off, the run in her nylons spread across her knee.

The young woman seemed apprehensive.

"It's fine," Kate said.

"Why are you dressed like that?"

That was the first time anyone had asked Kate that all day. It surprised her.

The man with the camera was growing impatient. "Just stand next to her. It's as close as you'll ever get to the real thing."

The young woman didn't move. "You don't really look like her," she said. "A little, but not much. The hair's totally wrong. From far away it's better."

"Viola, shut up and pose."

The thin woman in her threadbare dress tentatively stood next to Kate, as if she might run away at any minute. The vibrant pinks of the bouclé suit reflected off the woman's face and gave her a rosy glow. The man took the photo. Another flashbulb sizzled. She leaned in and whispered, "I lost my baby, too. Like the First Lady."

What was I thinking, wearing this suit? Kate thought. The young woman suddenly looked so pained. She seemed to be hoping for some words of advice, or comfort, but Kate had none. "I'm sorry" was the best she could do.

Viola shrugged, and then touched Kate's sleeve, the bouclé. She rubbed it between her fingers. "It's stronger than it looks."

"A lot of things are stronger than they look."

The young woman looked at Kate closely—not at the suit, but at Kate.

"Could be," she said.

This is how the story changes, Kate thought. The story of the pink suit was no longer about beauty or forgiveness. It was about strength.

Little Mike fell asleep in the car. It was amazing to Kate how big he'd grown in just a couple of years. He was nearly six years old now, and not a trace was left of the Gerber Baby smile he'd once had. The tour was a farewell to Little Mike, too. Kate hoped he would always remember it, and her. And Patrick. But she suspected that when they left, the next time she'd see Mike, he'd be all grown up. Maybe even married. His aunt Kate would be just a dim memory.

Kate kissed his salty forehead and wondered if the kiss would push its way through to his dreams.

Patrick carried the boy into Maggie's apartment and then drove home in silence. The night had turned humid. The pubs all along Broadway were closed for mourning. Some of the doors had black wreaths over them. Many of the signs were covered in black shrouds. After all, the President's baby was Inwood's own son.

The parking garage now held only Rose. The explosion had compromised its foundation. Rose and her Oldsmobility, her poetry of steel and thunder—Patrick and Kate would miss her so. They sat in the car holding hands until well past midnight. They didn't care that the garage was stifling hot and precariously tilting to the left. *Like the bats,* Kate thought, *always to the left, always toward home.*

"Our farewell tour," Patrick finally said, as if it were a summation of the day. The words were filled with wonder and regret. They made Kate feel a bit closer to heaven, but a bit closer to death, too.

That night their part of Broadway was quiet, as usual. The last bus came by, dotted with passengers. When Patrick went downstairs to take his shower in the shop, as he always did, Kate finally took off the pink suit. She was going to fold it, wrap it in tissue paper, and put it away—but didn't. She hung it in the shop window. It would be her gift to the neighborhood.

"It's like waving a flag," she told Patrick. "Patriotic." Then told him what the girl had said.

"Strength?" he said.

"Absolutely."

In November, the Wife wore the suit for the last time.

There'd been no orders for Thanksgiving at all. Kate and Patrick had taken the proceeds from the sale of Rose and bought two one-way airplane tickets—her Oldsmobility was apparently worth a good deal. The apartment was now filled with boxes. Some were to go to Maggie. Some were for Father John to distribute to the poor in the parish. Patrick would take only his butchering knives and a few clothes. "That's all I need," he said.

Tomorrow they would be gone.

Mrs. Brown had asked them to drop by for lunch before they left. "I'll miss you both like the devil," she said. Kate held her until they both stopped crying.

"Yes," was all Patrick could say. He'd recently discovered that he wasn't very good at good-byes.

Mrs. Brown had her rituals. Monday through Friday, between the hours of one o'clock and three p.m., she cleaned the pub. It was never open for lunch, and that was a perfect arrangement, because her "stories" were on television then. She was particularly fond of *As the World Turns,* although she kept the volume low unless it looked important—like an indecent proposal, or a marriage proposal, or both. She usually plugged the jukebox with change from the register. The music was loud and Irish.

"I like to have a good weep while I clean," she always said.

When Patrick and Kate opened the door to the pub, fiddles were whirling like dervishes; the accordion was breathless. A small black-and-white television was sitting on the bar, blaring. The place reeked of ammonia and Murphy's soap. Mrs. Brown was dressed for lunch but still had on her yellow rubber gloves. She was in a panic. On the television, the Wife was standing on a tarmac, holding a spray of roses. It didn't matter at all that the TV was black and white.

"That's your suit," Mrs. Brown said.

Patrick pushed the jukebox away from the wall. The needle scratched the record hard. He pulled the plug, but the music was still ringing in Kate's ears.

"After the shot hit," the reporter said, "his head fell into her lap."

Kate was speechless.

Into her lap—and the suit. The suit that Kate knew every stitch of, had lived every tuck and pleat of, had worried over, and cried over, and fell in love with Patrick over—this pink suit was the last thing the President ever saw. It was a particularly reckless pink, wild and vibrant, improbable in its beauty. And it had been made by so many hands, so many hearts. Those who were well known and those who were never known, and those whose names would be forgotten, not just Kate: it was part of them all.

After the shot hit, the President died with that vision of pink.

He died in all of their arms.

After, Kate thought. That word again. It was too much to bear.

That night, their very last in America, Kate and Patrick stood in the butcher shop, looking out through the window, into the deserted street. It was snowing, quietly. The snow was like an afterthought, like a task that had been forgotten in the chaos of the moment.

The pink suit was still hanging in the shopwindow.

"Shouldn't we take it down?" Patrick asked, but both knew they couldn't. The streetlight made it shine like a rose-colored moon.

Mrs. Brown from the pub was the first to arrive. She'd brought a dozen or more candles that she lined up outside on the windowsill, a store-bought constellation, which she arranged just so. And then came Mrs. O'Leary, thin as a ruler, whom Patrick had once thought of as "Sunday Morning Fatty Bacon." She'd brought more candles and some plastic flowers that she'd arranged in a glass vase. Father John and his altar boys soon joined them. The priest began to pray, "Our Father…" The snow fell harder.

One by one, people from the neighborhood gathered outside the butcher shop window to pay homage to the suit. Above them there were stars, but they were beyond the reach of those who gathered, and so they had brought their own. Their candles flickered, went out, and were lit again. They would not be denied the light.

When the crowd grew to the point that it spilled off the sidewalk and into Broadway, and then blocked it, Kate and Patrick could no longer see the profound brokenness that had surrounded them for all those months. The rubble of the telephone company had disappeared into the darkness. The only things they could see were the candlelit faces of the people they knew so very well.

They were beautiful in their sorrow.

After a while there was the sound of bagpipes. At first, the notes were confused and leaky, as if the players had tumbled out of the back of a truck, but then a song took hold in the crowd—"Amazing Grace."

Standing on the other side of the window, in the dark that was once their butcher shop, Patrick and Kate looked out onto a world that would not be theirs much longer. They could not sing along: the song, and the moment, and the loss—tomorrow they were no longer a part of it. Even though they still felt it in their bones.

More than anything, Kate wanted to reach out and touch the suit one last time, as the woman at the park had done, for comfort, for strength. But the suit was no longer hers.

She took Patrick's hand and kissed it gently and hoped that, in years to come, when people asked, "Whatever happened to that Irish butcher and his wife?" the bad things would not be remembered, nor the tragedy that had changed everything. All that would be remembered would be the suit.

It was a beautiful suit, after all.

ACKNOWLEDGMENTS

Of the real Aunt Kate, the real Little Mike once wrote: "Aunt Kate was a seamstress of note, [with] fine fingers like delicate pieces of spun glass..."

Mike Naughton, professionally known as "America's Best Dressed Ringmaster," grew up to run away with the circus and eventually bought one of his own. While there were three "backroom girls" from Inwood, his aunt Kate did the finish work for the pink suit, and so Mike granted me permission to use his aunt's real name as a way to honor her.

However, the Kate in this book is a product of my imagination. And while Mrs. Kennedy was, indeed, affectionately known as "the Wife" by many in the fashion industry, *The Pink Suit* is a novel. It is a work of historical fiction based on facts.

Writing *The Pink Suit* took me on a worldwide adventure that began at the Piper's Kilt in Inwood when I sat down at the bar and ordered a cheeseburger, and the man next to me told me that he grew up in the neighborhood. Even though the Yankees and Mets were battling on the televisions overhead, most in the bar soon added their story to his, and a vision of Inwood circa 1960 began to take shape.

Inwood is just that sort of neighborhood.

At the Capitol Restaurant, across the street, they showed me pictures of the old days, plied me with iced tea, and made a few calls to those who still could remember a Broadway lined with Irish flags. The staff of Good Shepherd School, including development director Joseph Smith, schooled me in the fine points of Gaelic football and gave me a tour of the grounds. Even at new places, like the Indian Road Café, I found photos and stories about how life once was. History is a point of great pride in Inwood.

In County Cork, with the help of Rachel Gaffney, who writes the blog *Real Ireland*, I met professors Claire Connolly and Jools Gilson from University College Cork, and the textile artist Sue Tector-Sands. They are wonderful women who graciously shared both meals and stories with me.

On the great island of Cobh, Peggy Sue Amison of Sirius Arts Centre befriended me and found me a lovely place to stay atop Gilbert's Restaurant. She also connected me with the force of nature that is Claire Cullinane, who drove me around for hours, telling me tales about the way of life on the island, and even coaxed some of the volunteers at the Fota House to give us a behind-the-scenes tour.

I'm still amazed that so many people helped me with this novel. The staff and management at The Carlyle hotel in New York City verified the accuracy of the scenes that were set there. Stephen

Plotkin from the John F. Kennedy Presidential Library and Museum answered my endless e-mails with professionalism and kindness. And when I found Mrs. Kennedy's live model from Chez Ninon, Susan Ullery Stewart, she was more than generous with her time and photos.

Susan gave me amazing insight into the Ladies' process of design—which really made me love them. I do want to make it clear that when they copied designers in the late 1950s and early 1960s, they were not alone in this process. While our fictional Kate is quite concerned over this practice, it must be remembered that she's really not a fashion insider. Many in the industry copied French designs and still do. It should also be noted that Chez Ninon often did get a license to copy some garments, especially in the later years, and designed originals, too. And after the pink suit, they copied several more pieces of Chanel, all licensed line-by-lines. However, they, like everyone else, were "inspired" by French fashions. Listening to Susan, and a few others who were familiar with the Ladies, I truly could imagine them at runway shows, sitting in the front and then sketching from memory at cafés and pinning their copies onto a young girl fresh out of modeling school while arguing about politics.

These women were something, that's for sure. Something wonderful. I hope I rendered their fictional memory with as much affection as I truly feel for them. They were trailblazers, and I thank them for that.

Many thanks also to fellow writers Tim Nolan, Sally Bedell Smith, and Jeff Kluger—they were all kind enough to encourage me in this daunting project, as did my longtime agent Lisa Bankoff of ICM.

Lisa is amazing, and I'm lucky to have her. In addition to her support, keen eye, and friendship, her knowledge of the NYC subway system and Inwood proved indispensable to the writing of this novel, as did the use of her guest bedroom. I could not love her more.

Jon Parrish Peede of the *Virginia Quarterly Review* saw an early draft of *The Pink Suit* and published sections of it, which gave me the courage to auction the book. My heartfelt appreciation also goes to publisher Reagan Arthur (Little, Brown), associate publisher Ursula Doyle (Virago Books), and editor Laura Tisdel (Little, Brown), who gave it life. I am also grateful for the support of my colleagues at Bath Spa University. Gerard Woodward and Dr. Tracy Brain provided keen insight and a guiding hand. Steve May, Maggie Gee, and Fay Weldon cheered me on in a rather elegant manner. I thank them all for their understanding and generosity of spirit.

Many thanks also to the unflappable Mr. H, my assistant on this project. I would have been lost without his fashion-industry experience, acumen, and Cole Porter wit.

And, finally, much love to my Steven E. As we all know, novelists are not easy to live with, and he loves me with such a kind heart.

ABOUT THE AUTHOR

Nicole Mary Kelby is the critically acclaimed author of *White Truffles in Winter, In the Company of Angels, Whale Season,* and the Florida Book Award winner *A Travel Guide for Reckless Hearts,* among other works. She divides her time between St. Paul, Minnesota, Bath, England, and the Great Island of Ireland.

READING GROUP GUIDE

THE

Pink Suit

A NOVEL
BY

NICOLE MARY KELBY

An online version of this reading group guide is available at
littlebrown.com.

A CONVERSATION WITH
NICOLE MARY KELBY

**A discussion of how the simple suit Jackie Kennedy wore on that
fateful day in Dallas came to represent so much more**

If clothes maketh the man, they positively invent the woman.
Clothes are a woman's stock-in-trade. They're how we present ourselves to the world, how we move through the world, and often how
we move up in the world.

Fashion's place in history is remarkable. If you want to call to
mind the whole history of Jackie Kennedy's persona, her history as
one half of a golden couple, of JFK's new political regime of hope,
and his tragic assassination, all you have to do is show a picture of
just one outfit—Jackie Kennedy's pink suit, the one she wore in Dallas on November 22, 1963. The one that ended up so shockingly
spattered and stained with her murdered husband's blood. The deli-

cate pink made the effect all the more startling. It's hard to imagine the shock being as great had Jackie been wearing a navy suit. The suit remains in the National Archives in Washington, and so great is the popular hysteria around this one event that it has been stipulated that it would not be safe for the suit to go on public display until at least 2103. Even now, fifty years on from the last time that suit was worn, it still looms large in the public imagination.

The history of a First Lady's outfit is always complex, but this suit has a history all its own, so much so that author Nicole Mary Kelby has written a novel charting the story of the suit, including the Cork seamstress who worked on it.

Jackie Kennedy was a big fan of Chanel, but she never wore the French designer's creations on state duty for fear it might be seen as unpatriotic. Jackie got around her sartorial problem by buying fabrics directly from Chanel in Paris and getting a New York City tailor, Chez Ninon, to make up the outfits copying the Chanel design.

In her book *The Pink Suit*, Kelby tells the story of Irish immigrant Kate as she works on Jackie's favorite suit in the back room of Chez Ninon. "I came across a website that had a little story in it by a man called Mike Naughton, who owns the Yankee Doodle Circus and said that his aunt Kate had finished the pink suit.

"Mike said she used to take the patterns and make those same garments for his mother, who lived in Inwood [in northern Manhattan], which at the time was an ethnic Irish enclave. They called her 'Little Jackie.' When Kate saw the suit after Dallas, she was never the same. She lost all of her joy in sewing. I started to think about what this suit really meant just to Kate, having it tied to a huge international tragedy."

Kelby was reluctant to go and see the suit (which she could have gained permission to do). "I didn't want to see it," she says.

The suit has become, as Jackie intended, a symbol of the great injustice that was committed that day in 1963. She refused to take the suit off for the whole day, covered though it was in her husband's blood, saying, "Let them see what they've done."

"This was also Jackie's favorite suit," says Kelby. "She had worn it several times. She had it created for her Camp David visit. She had three hundred pieces of clothing at the time of JFK's assassination. She didn't have to wear anything twice.

"When Mrs. Kennedy was a young woman, she entered a *Vogue* contest to write an essay to win the ability to work at *Vogue* in Paris as an intern. She won, but she didn't take it up. Her essay talked about being the art director of the twentieth century and how she would like to design her own clothes. What she did as first lady was she actually 'curated' how Americans saw themselves and how the world saw them. By her second year as First Lady, you started to see how other heads of states' wives dressed differently."

So what makes these outfits so iconic? Why did the pink suit become an icon when nobody can remember what Mrs. Lincoln wore when her husband was assassinated?

"The most fascinating thing about this story for me is that at Halloween, John Mayer went out with Katy Perry. She was wearing the pink suit and he was dressed as Kennedy, and Twitter went crazy. That pink suit is like a sacred thing now."

This interview was conducted by Edel Coffey. Originally published on March 30, 2014, in *The Independent* (Ireland).

QUESTIONS AND TOPICS FOR DISCUSSION

1. Kate takes pride in the couture dresses she makes while also feeling some scorn for the wasteful lifestyle choices of her clients. In some ways, she yearns for their glamorous lives yet also feels pulled toward the familiar and toward home. Despite this, her close-knit neighborhood views her as a bit of a snob. How does Kate struggle to balance the job she loves with loyalty to her community? Can a happy medium be found between these competing desires? Does she manage to bridge the gap between the two?

2. What tensions arise between Kate and her sister? Which of the women did you feel more sympathetic toward? In what ways are the sisters different—and how are they alike?

3. What do you make of the author's decision to refer to the character who we understand to be Jackie Kennedy simply as "the Wife"? Does this distance us from the character or instead give us permission to imagine her with less formality?

4. In a similar vein, how can fashion add or detract from a person's persona? Jackie Kennedy will forever be remembered for her iconic style, but has the public's interest in her wardrobe stopped them from getting to know the real woman? What difficulties do you think would ensue from having an exterior part of yourself—such as your fashion sense—become your defining characteristic in the eyes of the public?

5. *The Pink Suit* demonstrates how much influence fashion (and one's image) can have on the world of politics. Do you think that is still the case? In what ways does fashion continue to influence the political realm?

6. What is it in particular that made Jackie Kennedy a fashion icon? Has anyone made as strong an impact on fashion since Jackie Kennedy? Or is she incomparable?

7. What does the pink suit symbolize to you?

8. How does the rise of ready-made fashion change the world of the novel and the worldview of its characters?

9. *The Pink Suit* offers vibrant glimpses of Manhattan in the 1960s. What details do you remember best? Why did they make an impression on you?

10. Fashion allows us to create an image of ourselves, yet this image can confine as much as it defines. How does fashion relate to the American Dream, especially with regard to *The Pink Suit*?

11. Chapter 8 opens with the following quote from Diana Vreeland: "You gotta have style. It helps you get up in the morning. It's a way of life. Without it you're nobody." Do you agree with Vreeland's assertion? What do you think she means? How would you tie the quote in to some of the central themes of *The Pink Suit*?

12. Kate and Patrick eventually find a way to be together. Do they seem like a well-suited match? Why does Kate hesitate to take the plunge? How is Patrick's affection for his car thematically related to Kate's relationship with the pink suit?

13. Some of the final scenes in the book take place in Freedomland, a short-lived amusement park in the Bronx that focused on history. Kate wears the pink suit, and her presence has a significant effect on other park attendees. How does celebrating Mrs. Kennedy with others give Kate closure? Was she right to wear the suit?